Satin and Lace

Debbie McLouth

Published by Dynamite Romance Publishing, City, State
ISBN: 978-0-692-08608-7
Library of Congress Control Number
(Pending if applicable)
Satin and Lace / Debbie McLouth
Availabl.e formats: eBook | Paperback distribution
2018

Dedication

For my mom.

1

"How long do I have?" Evelyn asked with a quiet tone, almost like a child in trouble. Her deep brown eyes lifted up from her high cheeks that were rosy from the sudden heat, which deepened the natural tone in her complexion. She tried to remain calm despite the rampant pounding in her chest. She was about to lose her family home.

"Thirty days," Mr. Dawson, loan dept president of the Marine Midland Bank replied without batting his green eyes away from her tearful display. She watched his flaring nostrils, waiting for the smoke to billow out much like a bull moose. His thick-rimmed glasses rested safely upon that wide nose, giving him the appearance of an intelligent man. One that should be housed inside a science class or even college lecture because despite his nice appearance, he looked as if he could care less about her problems. He didn't want to know why she couldn't pay the bank what her father had not been able to. Didn't want to know how her father's untimely death had eaten up just about her entire life savings.

Her father had to take out a loan, using her mother's home to pay the hospital and nursing staff after her mother, Fran was been hit by a drunk driver and was a vegetable the last remaining days of her life. Her father, had done all he could to take care of the last member of the Habersham family. He in turn inherited her family stables but could do nothing with before, he himself ended up in the hospital sick with cancer.

The whole mess made Evelyn jump out of her seat and rush to the window with quivering lips. She tried to harness the tears that wanted to roll down her face, but couldn't.

"That's just a month." She argued with gumption. Normally she had the right kind of fighting abilities to eat men like Darryl Dawson up for lunch and have plenty of room for dessert. Normally she had a much bigger man standing in her corner when she knew she was fighting against something that was wrong. Losing her family Estate was very wrong and there was nothing she could do to help this situation. Nothing, but maybe pray, which was something she was very good at when times were really against her.

"You have had six months to get the amount due us, Ms Mitchell."

With glaring eyes and a chest heaving with pain she spun around.

"Do you have any idea how much it costs to bury someone?" She snapped. "I had to use my own money to put my father next to my mother. I had to have him transported from the cancer treatment center in Arizona! Do you know how much it cost to take him home?"

She took a huge step towards Mr. Dawson's desk but he did not move away. He barely flinched from her movement. "I couldn't pay you everything because I had to take him home. Can't you extend it for just a few more months?" Desperation was thick in her trembling voice. "I promise to get it in full, just give me a little more time."

"We gave you an extra month." He informed her with a short tone of his own and then added, "We have a buyer."

Evelyn stood still while her eyes looked at this stocky balding man in a gray wrinkled polyester blend suit. His jacket off and vest opened, revealing his light blue cotton shirt with a plain dark blue tie.

… Buyer she questioned silently.

"That's right," With a smug expression on his face and his thin lips curving into a weak smile he gave a nod. "A buyer wishes to purchase the farm in full, everything that is owed, plus the loan." He stood up exerting his authority to the fullest. "And the bank intends to sell if you can't get what is owed." His green gaze danced back and forth while he examined her teary eyes and then added standoffish, "I'm truly   sorry."

At first Evelyn's feet didn't know how to move. She remained right there by his desk just looking at the short despicable man with uncertainty in her eyes. What kind of mold did a person like him come from? A typical one, or did God create a special kind for a man such as the one in front of her. One with no care for the other person, or at all about what she was losing, only what he was gaining.

"You have thirty days Ms. Mitchell," His drone voice snapped her into attention. With a sudden jolt, she pivoted around and made a mad dash for the door.

Grimacing, she walked over his plush carpeting and out the fancy etched glass door of his office. Elegantly she descended the stairs, knowing or maybe sensing his gaze, as it cascaded down her backside, with his green reptilian eyes. She hoped he was enjoying her snug tailored pale pink skirt through the small glass cubicle he sat in at the top of the stairs. Wishing now, she'd worn anything else but the one skirt that came just to the top of her thigh, laying inches below her round firm buttocks and rode up her legs as she took each stair with care, trying not to catch her heel in the thick carpet as she stepped.

The moment her heels clicked onto the tan marble floor she picked up her pace, making an angry dash to the front door, which was on the other side of the building. Her stiletto shoes making a piercing trajectory into the marble with each step she took. Many of the tellers looked up with curiosity as she passed, which she ignored to the fullest degree. Her mind was miles away in thought of where she will find the money needed to keep her home, but as quickly as her mind thought and schemed, she came up short.

The afternoon sun cut into her eyes with a painful glare the moment she stood out into the haze of the day. Immediate sound came from every direction. People walking passed trying to get to their destinations without much interference. Horns blowing from impatient drivers, cabs mostly since the streets were covered with that same school bus yellow with checkered doors.

Evelyn stopped long enough to open her briefcase, slip in the portfolio with the bank papers and snag her sunglasses with her long thin fingers. Quickly she guided the frames onto her face with one hand as she closed up the case with the other. Then right after those brief seconds, her free hand went into the air to hail the first available cab.

"Taxi…!" She called out but a deeper tone overpowered hers. At first, she wondered if she had said anything at all, but then a tall shadow fell over her from the left side. Her eyes caught his frame as he reached out for the door of the cab at the same time she had…wham! They collided.

She turned her head to catch the tall stranger, meeting his face just inches away from hers. They were so close. Evelyn saw his deep set eyes, his tanned muscled jaw with a cleft chin, which was rugged with golden stubble.

Evelyn's eyes widened with appraisal of his handsome features and without warning, her heartbeat quickened beneath her chest cavity. Both reactions were uncharacteristically Evelyn's.

"Excuse me," His deep voice called out, his hand taking a firm grip over hers as their bodies continued to move despite their feet which; were firmly planted on the pavement. His quick reaction kept her from impaling the side of the taxi, instead her tall frame smashed into him. Quickly, she realized what was taking place, but couldn't stop what gravity had already started, when her body hit his, his free arm came around her small waist to help steady them both. He'd saved her from hitting into the steel door only to hit his hard frame. The jolt had almost knocked her glasses from her face.

"Are you alright?" He asked the instant they were steady and able to stand on their own accord. Evelyn nodded, pushing her glasses back onto her nose, taking note of the blue in his gaze.

Moments slipped by, as she stood there just staring at this handsome stranger. His blond hair was tight against his head and even though he'd stumbled, not a folic had moved out of place, making him just a tad bit more attractive. It was a rare thing for her to notice men as she was doing right then.

"Who's getting in?" The cabby yelled out in a deep Bronx accent.

The handsome stranger looked at her with those dazzling blue eyes and smiled delightfully in a crooked way. "Why don't you take this one?"

"...Share?" She found herself asking him. She watched as his eyes turned to the cab and then shrugged his big wide shoulders.

"If you don't mind, I am in a rush."

It was the least she could do. "I'm just going a few blocks." She exclaimed.

"Manhattan." He declared which was not as close.

9

"Who's ridin' today, huh?" The cabby asked once more.

"Put a sock in it!" The handsome man snapped as he opened the cab door.

"After you," He once more flashed her that smile and Evelyn almost fell into the cab when her heel caught on the curb. He snagged her arm, easing her onto the seat. He then was beside her. The cab immediately filled with his sweet cologne.

"Only one can ride." The cabby shook his head and raised his hand to wave one out.

"We're together." The man stated, taking Evelyn's hand in his and giving it a squeeze. "Drive." He then told the cab driver.

"Where are you heading?" The cabby's eyes and the stranger's both met with Evelyn's, but all she saw was the strangers deep blue ones, despite her glasses, and then felt the gentle squeeze he gave her hand. Despite the tightening of her throat, she gave the cabby the address.

"Thank you for sharing." The man whispered softly in her direction.

"I was going to be less then fashionably late."

"I'm glad I could help." She spoke softly. "Late is better than not at all, right?"

"Definitely better," He then cast a striking smile her way which brought on a sudden heat that tingled her while his eyes gave a lazy stroll down her frame. His features unrevealing whether or not he liked her attire, but the moment his blue gazes hit her knees and the exposed skin, she saw his eyes show much attraction and he didn't divert his eyes when she started to talk.

"I hope yours goes better than mine did just a few minutes ago."

"Here you go. Twenty five fifty." The cabby called out as

he pulled to the curb in front of her office building.

"Twenty five fifty?" Both she and the man beside her, repeated.

"Fare for you," the cabby smiled fiendishly as he looked at Evelyn and then gave a nod to the man next to her, "and fare for you. Out you go."

The stranger sighed deeply, but opened the cab door.

"Wait, what about your meeting?" Evelyn asked him.

"Watch this," The man whispered softly against her ear as she emerged from the cab with her case in her hand. She opened her case to deposit her glasses inside all the while her entire spine melted against his voice as it rippled all the way down her back. She shook as she turned to watch the man pull out his wallet, once more her fingers snapping the case closed without much thought.

"Wait." Evelyn snagged his hand to give him her share of the fare. She set her case down to retrieve her wallet from her purse.

"I got this." He winked at her as he handed the cabby forty dollars and awaited his change. The moment the money exchanged, he snatched up his case and slid into the cab. "Take me to Manhattan." The stranger's face was radiant with victory, closing the door as the next customer.

"Hey, that was a clever move." the cabby noted with a soft chuckle.

The stranger then turned his dazzling smile her way. "Thanks for the ride. I really appreciate it."

Evelyn didn't get to respond before the cab pulled out into traffic. She spun around on her heels to look up at the tall building in front of her. On the eleventh floor was her office/business.

Once in the elevator, she straightened up her appearance, pulling down her short skirt. She hardly wore such attire, but today was a fighting day. One she had lost every round. She sighed and closed her eyes to gain a little composure. She could not think about that right now. She had a business to run. If she wasn't careful, she will lose that as well.

The moment she shot through the door, Evelyn was greeted with Keli's curt tone. "Develand called. He can't make it tomorrow. Eileen is sick and can't make it this afternoon. And," Her secretary gave off a big sigh as she handed her the latest number sheet. "Sales are down."

Evelyn snatched up the sheet and kept walking into her office, without even a hello to Keli. She slammed the door shut and strutted to her desk, eyes on the numbers. Her fingers released the case by her desk as she sat heavily into her deep cushioned leather chair.

Gasping at the numbers in front of her, her eyes captured the ones that put a stop to her beating heart. Almost every one of her best sellers, were down. Only one survived the cut and she swallowed hard as she eyed that one particular item. The "Sheer Delights" was the only items to bring more than usual.

Evelyn took a deep breath, dropping the paper, turning her chair around and closed her eyes at the thought of what she will have to do tonight. She shivered, as the night's events will undoubtedly take place whether she liked the notion or not. In fact, she really wished that line of underwear would fall off the charts completely.

Turning the chair slightly, so she could look over her shoulder at the sheet again, she sighed more appreciatively. That line of wear was top of the line and one of the most expensive in the magazine. She should be happy they were selling as well as they were. The extra revenue will come in handy. She sighed again as she reached out for the phone.

"Yes?" Keli called back through the line. "Get me Steven

or Peter on the phone."

"Right away, is there anything else I can get you?" She asked sensing the undercurrent in her voice. Evelyn smiled with a shake of her head.

"No, thank you though."

Evelyn pulled the red marker from the tray at her left and started to circle the highest numbers on the sheet. She was almost halfway through the list when her phone rang. "Peter?" She called out.

"Steven. Peter is a little tied up at the moment." Steven chuckled softly over the phone.

"Sorry to interrupt." Evelyn purred through the line.

"Oh, no interruption, just a slight pause; one that only adds spice to the delight," The sexual overtones in Steven's voice made it quite clear of the adventures she'd put a temporary stop to by calling. "What can I do for you, Babe?" He asked her in the same tone with a slight higher pitch. "There is nothing better than to be tied to a bed post." He advised and then added, "A good spanking will do you just right."

Evelyn couldn't hold back her laughter. She had never had a romantic relationship where being tied up for any reason came into play. In fact, she has never been in a relationship where she trusted a man to tie her up for any reason, especially sexual ones. "Thanks, but I think I will pass."

"Are you sure?" He questioned and then added softly, "You really looked frustrated last week." He gasped through the phone. "Don't mind my asking but when was the last time?"

The phone on her end remained silent.

"You know." He urged forward. "How long has it been since you were tied to a bedpost?"

"What?" She gasped. "I am not answering that," *Never!*

"Oh your secret is safe with me," He coaxed a little further. "Come on, you can tell me."

"No I can, not!" She cried out. "...for Pete's sake! What kind of woman do you think I am?"

"A sensuous one...?" He questioned softly and then said, "Speaking of Pete, I do need to get back to him before he has a meltdown."

Ignoring his comment Evelyn lifted the sheet and sighed. "I need you guys tonight. Are you free to shoot some extras for next week's layout?"

"...Extras?" He asked.

"Yeah, the "Sheer Delights" line is our biggest sales items right now. I need some extra shots of them in the next few magazines."

"Of course they are!" Steven sang majestically. "The people know what they like and they really like sexy. Angie really has a mind for those designs. And the model, well she really knows how to wear it."

"Are you available later?" Evelyn asked, once again not acknowledging his statement.

"Yeah, sure we'll be there."

"Thank you." She gave off a deep sigh as she hung up the phone. Just as she cradled the handset back, her stomach let off an awful growl of protest. She had spent her lunch hour wasting time at the bank instead of eating. Lunch was usually her biggest meal of the day and she missed it. She pushed the call button to summon Keli.

"Yes?" She replied.

"Can you order me a sandwich from the corner deli down the street? Pastrami, on rye would be fantastic, with some Swiss cheese and a dab of spicy mustard."

"...Anything else?" She called back.

14

"Add a small bowl of salad with grilled chicken and vinaigrette for dinner tonight."

"Will do," Keli replied. "Shall I just bring it in when it arrives?"

"Please," Evelyn answered releasing the button a final time.

She got up and headed down to Angie's office to see if she had made any progress. If Evelyn had to put more of the "Delights" items in the layout, hopefully, Angie had more designs for her. Without knocking, she opened the door, trying not to look around at the floral displays Evelyn knew would be all around the room. Angie just loved flowers and sometimes went a little overboard with them.

"Oh hey, just the person I wanted to see." Angie held up a pair of thong panties for Evelyn to see. "What do you think about these?" The tan colored underwear dangled off Angie's first finger, waiting for her boss to take them. "Tell me what you think," She repeated with an eager shake of her head.

Today Angie's short pixie cut, was tight to her head, slicked back from a lot of mousse and it was the sharp color of red. Evelyn wasn't really sure what Angie's real hair color was because every month it was a different color. A year ago, it hung in long black waves down to her shoulders.

Evelyn slowly approached Angie's drawing desk where she was not so patiently waiting. Her big blue eyes twice their normal size.

Carefully Evelyn snagged the panties from Angie's finger, and upon first glance, they resembled an ordinary pair of thong underwear. They were tan, almost the color of sand on the beach with lace for the waistband and the strip that slipped between the butt cheeks of the wearer. The triangle that modestly covers the thatch between a woman's legs was almost non-existent.

Evelyn was about to ask what was so special about a pair of thong panties when her fingers touched the material and almost lost grasp of them they were so soft and satiny.

Curious, about its texture, she flipped the small piece of clothing over to examine it closer. She fingered the soft elegant lace and gave it a pull for dexterity. It moved easily and soundlessly. More curious, Evelyn brought it up for a better look. Her eyes scanned the material while she ran her thumb over the thatch and then over the lace, there was hardly any texture difference. Both were smooth and pliable to movement and touch.

Quickly her eyes snapped up to look at Angie, to find her genius smiling at her with her bottom lip tucked inside her mouth, waiting for her approval.

"Do you like?" Angie asked her in a soft whisper. "I have a bra to match," She exclaimed while raising her hand to reveal the matching top half of the set. "I think you should sell them separate." She advised as she handed the top to Evelyn.

Angie let the bra slip into her hands and giggled when Evelyn gasped in awe, her eyes showing the suspecting idea of the top to be half as soft and plush as the bottoms. Evelyn released the panties on Angie's desk so she could really examine the brazier.

The lacy cups were thin and very sheer. The clasps at the back of the waist were small and delicate. The bra was complete lace with no material. Flexing the soft cups Evelyn couldn't believe how smooth and completely soundless it was. Even the lace straps felt like spun satin. She kept running her fingers over the material, trying to come up with the right way to describe what she was feeling. It was softness and lacey, with flexibility, smooth as a baby's bottom; and yet, strong and very sexy as if it would be…

"I call it liquid silk," Angie broke into her thoughts…A second layer of skin.

**

"Here's the number's guide." Keli walked into Evelyn's office right at five on the dot. Evelyn had grabbed up her papers and the new garments that Angie had already made up. Her briefcase was lying on top of her desk waiting for her to fill so she can go home.

The number's guide was an outline of the next magazine to be printed. She had to proofread and check all photos before it went out. It was usually the last thing she saw before bed and the first thing she saw in the morning.

Grateful Evelyn took the book from Keli.

"Do you have your salad?" Keli asked her as she headed for the small fridge beneath the bar by the large bookcase. She smiled as Keli ushered Evelyn her meal without forethought.

"Thank you Keli. Going out tonight?" Evelyn asked taking note of the new dress she was wearing.

"A date, with Raymona's brother's, friend." Keli scrunched up her nose. "His name is Greg. We're going to the art museum and then out for a drink." She raised her eyes slightly. "I hate blind dates. I don't even know why I agreed to going." Keli sighed. "I'm hoping that he finds me dull and we call it a short night."

"Try having a good time. It sounds really nice." A kind of date Evelyn enjoyed. If things didn't go well after the museum, then drinks didn't even have to take place. Keli on the other hand, her kind of dates, were slightly more risqué with a high chance of an intimate ending.

"It sounds more like a trip to the dentist office." They both shared a laugh as Keli headed for the door. "Have a good evening yourself." Keli replied as she left the office, leaving the door open, snagging her sweater from her chair and got on the elevator.

Giving a final sigh of the hour, Evelyn snagged the pile to go inside the case. Her fingers toyed with the clasp on the latch, but found it not obeying her command of opening. She tightened her grip on the items in which she was going to put inside the case and tried the clasp once more, but with stronger effort, the latch refused to budge.

Exasperated to the extreme, she thrust the items to her desk beside the briefcase and snatched up the case to give it a thorough looking at. She hadn't locked it, she never locks the thing. It always caught and wouldn't release when the key was turned. To save time, instead of buying another that actually worked, she just didn't lock it.

She tried the latch again with two fingers pressing hard to slide the latch over but it still did not move, it didn't even give an impression of wanting to move. Quickly she reached into her jacket pocket and pulled out her keys. Maybe she had locked it and just didn't recall doing so. She found the small key and slipped it into the slot, and gave it a turn. Tried the latch once more but...it did not react.

2

Before the cab had stopped moving, Jackson had the money out of his wallet and slipped it through the Plexiglas partition, the door open and was stepping out despite the vehicle hadn't come to a complete stop.

"Hey." The cabby called out when Jackson closed the door to head towards the house.

"Keep it!" He snapped in anger. He then quickly took the long stairs leading up to the front door.

The moment he was inside Oliver his butler, took his case, and jacket before Jackson was out of the entrance way and heading towards the parlor.

"Afternoon, Mr. Slade. Can I get you any refreshments?" The butler asked remaining just outside the opened door to the parlor.

"No." Jackson replied in short.

"Yes sir." Oliver turned and walked away without anything more said. Jackson took long strides across the room to the bar, poured himself a whiskey and downed the much-needed shot. His lips curled and his throat constricted in displeasure as the liquid burned all the way down. He smacked his lips while he poured another and repeated the action twice before taking the crystal glass and hurling it into the nearest wall. He'd controlled his fury up to that point but could contain it no longer. His blue eyes bulging from their sockets as his brain throbbed painfully in his head. He hadn't been this angry in a long time.

He stalked to the sideboard of the bar and snatched up the

phone to call his father but then after a short thought, he furiously slammed it back into the cradle.

"Damn it!" He raged as he grabbed another glass and filled it up to the top before bringing it to his tense lips. He didn't drink all of the contents in the glass, before he spun away from the bar, spied the big tall wingback chair and rested his weary frame into the brown leather cushion with an exasperated sigh. His eyes danced around the dim lit room.

This side of the house was bright from the afternoon's sun that was peaking above the front part of the house, despite that fact this room always remained in a shadow. Cloaked and ready for many hours of down time. It was his favorite room. The only one he could sit comfortably and think without any kind of interruptions. Not even a bright sunny day. He couldn't use this room for his office. It was too dark making it hard to read even with a light on. The dark cherry walls and the deep brown Mahogany floors only aided to the room's somberness.

Strangely, he felt very comfortable in this room, as if it had been designed with him in mind when the house was built. Usually though, the room's mood was always slightly darker then Jackson's but today, today wasn't the case at all. Today, the room matched his mood to a tee.

Throwing his head back, leaning it against the high back of the chair, he placed the cool glass to his forehead and closed his eyes, *what to do... what to do?* Anger nipped once more at his brain while he thought. Just how was he supposed to get himself out of this new predicament? *Is there a way out of it?*

His fingers clutched the glass in fury but he refrained from throwing it as he did the first, even though he really wanted to.

Hours later, hardly eating any of the salmon delight in front of him Jackson angrily got up from the table and headed for the office with yet another glass of whiskey. He wasn't a hard liquor man normally, but today he needed something to take the edge off. If he didn't numb the anger and deaden the frustration, he was going to go to Elliott Slade, his father, and kill him.

The audacity of that man not informing him was appalling! Even just a hint of what was going to happen would have been nice. In fact, if Jackson had any idea, he would have done the rotten deed years ago just to be over it. All this time, he could have been secure in his inheritance but... *Nooo!*

Jackson fingered the etched crystal on the glass in his hand. Did Elliott know? He had to have. Of course he had, wasn't he at some point also in the same boat as himself? Of course, Elliott's older brother died which made him the next heir, but he knew just the same. He knew exactly what was coming.

Jackson mumbled as he passed the threshold to the office. "Why didn't you say something?" He asked to no one particular. His fingers danced over the phone in anticipation. He wanted to ask Elliott that very thing but felt his stomach churn at the thought.

Placing the whiskey on the desk beside his case, he slowly seated himself into the chair to work. Hoping that if he tried to work a little, the problem will solve itself. Hopeful, it will just go away altogether.

He fished into his front slacks pocket and hauled out his keys. He found the small key that would open the case and slid it home, but before he turned it, the latch sprung right open.

Immediately Jackson looked confusingly at the case with the latch hung open. His mind whirled in several different directions. He recalled closing the case at work, locking it, as he always did, but it was unlocked... *Curious*

He eyed the case as if it were going to explain itself. How did it become unlocked, he was the only one with a key. With his thumb, he pressed the latch back into place. Slowly he stood the briefcase on its end, turned it to examine it thoroughly and deduced it was not his, although, it was very close to being identical. Laying the case back down, he flipped the latch and again it popped open with ease. *Huh.*

He slowly opened the case and as he did so, he lifted his eyes to look around as if being watched and furthermore, was doing something wrong. When he realized what he was doing, he grumbled to himself and lifted the case completely open, to look inside.

A manila portfolio folder was right on top of a pile of items inside. He lifted it, sliding a pair of sunglasses to the side, about to examine it more closely when he spotted something very nice right below it. Laying the portfolio to the desk he grinned devilishly at the Satin & Lace magazine in front of him. His heartbeat picked up its pace.

Quickly his fingers snagged the magazine and brought it out for closer inspection. He leafed through its pages and just at a glance could tell it was last week's Issue.

His eyes eagerly devoured the articles of clothing on the cover and the way they were tousled on top of the small round side table with nothing, but the clothing on it. The dark cherry tabletop with its shiny unblemished surface made the white lace jump boldly off the page, catching your eye even if you weren't into sexy underwear. The elegant lace panties laid flat but not neatly on the mirrored image of the table. As if, they were dropped there, momentarily…

The bra… the *bra* was another matter entirely. It drooped precariously off the top, with a lacy cup prominently facing the camera, and its waistband hanging off, dangling. Caught in motion as if the garment had been tossed, willy-nilly, and that was where it landed.

It was a fabulous shot, it made him hard the moment he laid eyes on it, as it was doing now. It gave a world of thought to the boggled mind… were the garments carelessly thrown in a heated moment between strangers in a public place.

…Or maybe the panties came off first. In a delightful, teasing manner with a lot of kissing and touching. Which may have been why, it was almost too neat on the top of the small round surface. Only to have passion take over while fevers peaked and sensuality became omnipresent, the bra came off in a pent up lustful rage and flung away in a careless toss between husband and wife when the passion had built to unbearable measures and were no longer controlled.

Jackson reached out for the glass of whiskey, shifting slightly in the chair to adjust his body to accommodate his now aching flesh. He gulped down the last of the liquor in one swoop and he gasped at the harsh burn as it traveled down his throat.

His eyes scanned the magazine with approval. Whoever did the cover out did themselves they deserved a raise for crying out-loud! Because his first glimpse of that magazine was at the newsstand on the corner by the studio and he snatched it up despite knowing he had one sitting or would have one soon, sitting on his desk.

He'd bought the copy because he could not wait for his to be delivered by mail. The cover made him instantly think of that model, in the same pieces of underwear that was on the cover and he was not disappointed. She was on page twenty-four, laying on black satin sheets donning that same bra and panty, which disrupted his whole damn day with erotic thoughts of her with him when instead he should have been coming up with a sound way of getting said model, to join his agency. A hard task indeed, when the model was nameless, faceless and unreachable.

Moistening his lips, Jackson briefly eyed page twenty-four but the red circle caught his eye. The item number noted in red; and a number was beside it. Slowly he turned the pages until he found another red circle again with numbers beside it. Trying to figure out what they meant, he put the magazine on the desk so he could inspect the case again. Inside he found another copy of Satin & Lace but one he hadn't seen before.

He lifted it out and began to look through its pages. Nothing inside it was familiar except the model and what she was wearing, all of the poses were different then he'd already seen in previous magazines. He eyed the front with scrutiny and then suddenly dropped it, reaching to the left of his desk to the cabinet where Molly the maid would have placed today's mail.

In the bundle, was every fashion magazine being published in the world, with fast fingers and eyes, he scanned the stack dropping bills and magazines to the desk until he found what he was looking for. He smiled as he lifted the issue of Satin & Lace and eyed it for only a second before he snagged the same magazine that was in the case. Only, the one in the case had the red circles and some of the pages had been dogeared, for easy perusal.

Jackson browsed through both magazines to discover they were indeed the same. He looked generously at the beautiful model with almost nothing on. She had been the subject of many illicit dreams of his and many other men he was sure. Her smooth curvaceous hips holding thong panties tightly against that silky tan unblemished skin. She had a small beauty mark – the size of the tip of a ballpoint pen – a dot, just above the panty-line. Which shown in about every panty shot in the magazine.

Tentatively he ran his thumb over the black panties where the small triangle of silk that covered the little thatch of hair – color unknown – She shaved down there! Had to in order to wear so little and cover so much.

His eyes traveled upwards to another item. A bra and panty set. Rarely did you get to see the top and bottom of this model. Eagerly his eyes devoured the heavy cups in the bra. The firmness of each mound, covered with light brown cotton. In that set – her nipples were well covered, in others ... He quickly turned the page and with an enticing smile, he located her in a white satin & lace bra with satin straps, and side panels. Nothing but lace in the cups of which covered all of the underside of the breast, but revealed much of the tops, covering her delightful brown nipples, but did not hide them completely as the dark color filtered through and the budding peaks were clearly visible.

The magazine in his hand jerked spasmodically when his libido kicked in, instantly he was hard and aching again. This magazine – Satin & Lace – perfectly named with its perfect model was better than any penthouse or even real woman for that matter. Trouble was the model was only fantasy, a dream. He wanted her... more ways than one, and if he could get his hands on her. For the business: of course. She'd make him millions, which was why every agency around was looking for her, wanting to sign her on.

Jackson flipped to the back of the front cover and read the

name at the bottom of the page. Evelyn Mitchell. The address of the office was there, along with a phone number, but that number was only good for orders, he'd already tried it. Many, many times and got the same answer,

'I'm sorry we have so many models and a privacy clause, we don't give out personal information. Would you like to make a purchase?' Jackson leafed through the pages once more shaking his head as he did so.

"Many models, my ass," He mumbled to himself. He saw only one model page after page. No woman had the same hip line and curves as another. Some had a great bust and firm breasts, but only one had both the curvature and the sex appeal that this model had. No, only one woman posed in this magazine. Every panty shot had the beauty mark and the bras, filled with the same firm breasts that his mouth hungered to explore. There was only one model in their magazine. One perfectly beautiful model, that had every agency up in a dander.

Sighing, Jackson dropped the magazine to now study the briefcase he had thought was his. It was almost identical. Luckily, his was locked. His eyes lifted in wonder, *was this case Ms Mitchell's...* Could he be so lucky to have come across such a treasure and, *how* did he come by it? The only pocket that contained anything held just a plain ugly necklace. He lifted it curling his upper lip as he eyed the odd piece of jewelry.

The morbid looking thing had brown colored wooden rose buds and deep maroon beads, alternating all along the string, connecting at the base, turning into a solid string of maroon beads. At the end of the string was a brown cross with the maroon colorings carved into the bamboo styled wood. It didn't look appealing at all. He placed it back into the pocket and eyed the glasses staring at him.

He searched the entire case but came up empty with a name. He placed the magazines back inside and almost closed it down when he spotted the manila portfolio. He pushed the case aside sliding the folder closer he opened it up. Inside, he found bank documents. Foreclosure documents, past due bills, and last final statements. All of which had Evelyn Mitchell's name splashed all over them.

It seemed that Ms Mitchell was in a pickle of sorts and she had only thirty days to get herself out before she lost a big stud farm in Montana. She needed money... *A...lot of money...*

He has *a lot* of money...

He needed a wife...

...She would make a nice wife <u>and</u> she had something he wanted...

Jackson sat back in his chair, the portfolio slipping out of his fingers and down to the desk. Question was would she be willing to give him what he needed if he agreed to give her what she needed and if he were to get something else in the end as a bonus...

Lifting the golden bell on top of the desk and giving it a casual ring he sat back waiting for Oliver. His mind was deep in thought when the butler appeared in the doorway.

"Yes sir,"

"Have the car brought around. I feel like celebrating."

"Right away Mr. Slade,"

"Oh, and give Bonnie a call. I will pick her up around ten or so." Oliver nodded his reply before turning and leaving.

**

By the time Evelyn reached the phone, it was on its third ring. She had just finished up and was about to get in the tub for a long well deserved soak with some candles and a nice glass of wine. She almost let the phone ring but can't stand hearing an unanswered phone. It made her think of an unanswered prayer. Someone on the other end of the line was in search of something from her, not answering the call made her nervous and afraid for the soul on the other end. It was a foolish thought, but she could never shake the sensation an unanswered phone created. She answered on the last shrill, in a monotone voice.

"Hello. I am trying to reach Ms. Mitchell."

"That would be me," She replied softly.

"Good, good." The man answered. "I'm Jackson Slade, Uh," He paused and then said, "I think we shared a cab earlier today."

Immediately Evelyn stood up at attention, her robe falling open and her arm wrapping around her bare midriff with a certain amount of reproach. Trying to quickly conceal what he couldn't possibly see over the phone line. She even snatched the robe with her fingers, closing it around her practically naked frame.

Then she pictured him as she had seen him earlier. Tall, very robust, his shoulders were as wide as a football player's would be. She recalled how his jacket was snug in the shoulders and how his biceps stretched the material almost too tightly. The way his slacks also pulled to the limit while his thick leg muscles flexed tightly as he took the seat beside her in the cab, filling the small space between her and the door with his large frame.

She inhaled softly, closing her eyes as his cologne suddenly smacked her right in the face. It was an assault she hadn't expected and it made her sway and reach out for the sofa to prevent her from collapsing right there onto the floor. Subconsciously she grabbed the robe tighter around her

28

frame.

"I'm sorry to interrupt your evening, am I calling at a bad time?" He questioned respectfully. "I think we exchanged brief cases earlier and I was wondering, if it was possible to meet for lunch?" He continued to say over the phone.

"No you didn't interrupt anything," She fingered her robe once more. They'd just finished for the night and she was ready to settle in, getting a chance to eat her dinner.

"Why?"

"Why?" He repeated and then added, "Why lunch?"

"Yes."

"Well, I have a meeting first thing in the morning. Do you need the case before lunch? I was hoping to repay your kindness for sharing the cab and while I treated you to lunch, we could re-exchange our cases." He proffered with a tender charm she felt coming through the lines. Thankful that they were on the phone because saying no to those beautiful blue eyes while he spoke so sweetly would have been a definite problem.

She quickly shook her head in response and said, "Um, I don't think so."

"Do you need your case in the morning? I can have it delivered to you. I'd still like to meet for lunch though. I really would like to thank you for sharing your ride with me."

"No I don't need my case," She'd stopped off at the newsstand so she could work as planned.

"Splendid. It's settled then. Meet me at La Château say at one?"

Patiently Jackson waited for her answer of which he knew she couldn't refuse. No one refused La Château. You had to really know someone to get in that place or reserve well in advance. Years, sometimes, depending on the time of year you wished to dine there. Was he trying to impress the woman? *Yes...Of course!*

Evelyn ran her mind through tomorrow's agenda and couldn't recall if she was available at one. She knew she was free at two-thirty because she had to reschedule Develand's meeting, he couldn't make it in from LA. She smiled, knowing she had him in the lurch changing up the time, causing him to either dine alone, or with someone else... or, he would have to cancel and no one canceled La Château! *Not even you! What are you doing? Are you CRAZY...?*

She'd had the pleasure of dining there once and the food was incredibly delicious. French was her favorite. What was this man up to? Did he just guess or was he up to something? Quickly she ran his name through her mind but came up empty, aside from being very rich; everyone knew the Slade Enterprises. The television station and radio station owned by the Slade enterprises brought millions of dollars in each year.

"I'm afraid I'm not free then. In fact," She tried sounding remorseful. "I wouldn't be able to make it until two-thirty which is way too late,"

"Two-thirty sounds perfect," The man answered quickly.

"I wouldn't want you to have to cancel."

"I'll just call and change the time." He assured her.

"But you can't change the time; Not within the same day. No. Just have the case delivered to my office and I will do the same with yours."

"But I *can* change the time and I would really like to meet you rather than relying on others to make sure your belongings are returned safely."

Intrigued, she whispered softly through the line. "You can change the time?"

"Indeed I can. Two-thirty will be fine for me."

Evelyn moistened her lips at the thought of eating at La Château. The food will melt against her palate and her escort, she sighed... *oh my!* She just may melt with it.

3

Standing by the curb, she tried to hail a cab, which deemed daunting for such an easy task. Every cab drove right by her, seemingly not noticing her hand in the air and her meek voice yelling out. When one finally did stop, she wrenched the door open and slipped inside in haste. Her long flowing yellow skirt flipped up, getting caught in a gust of wind and nearly exposed her whole leg. The cabby whistled, raising his dark thick eyebrows in approval of what he saw.

"Take me to 2155 Lexington North." *Pervert!*

"Right away," He eyed the skirt she had raked back down her thighs and positioned herself sideways as she looked out the side window. Ignoring his lustful gazes, she glanced down at her jeweled watch to find she was running three minutes late. She fidgeted in her seat. She couldn't believe how eager she was to meet up with Mr. Slade.

She told herself it was where she was meeting him that piqued her interest and _not the man, but she couldn't calm her nerves all day even though she tried. Evelyn's mind kept going back to that cab ride and the way his hand felt when he held hers during the whole ride. It made her heart beat with excitement all over again and her palms; they were wet!

The cab pulled out front of the elegant restaurant fifteen minutes later. She gave the driver the fare and got out, tugging on her skirt and adjusting everything to look, *presentable?*

"Ms. Mitchell?"

The baritone voice that slipped down her spine like maple

syrup made her shiver as she erected herself to find Mr. Slade standing in front of her with his cockeyed smile that seemed to finish the job his sugary voice had started on her senses. Evelyn smiled back softly, discreetly wiping off her moist palm against her skirt before extending it out for him to shake.

Jackson spotted her the moment the taxi pulled up. He was going to meet it and open her door, but she had flung it open so quickly and then all he saw were legs. Long tanned legs that seemed endless as they slipped beneath her unruly skirt. Noting, this skirt was not nearly as short as the one yesterday, but much more revealing.

Remembering his manners he moved his gaze upwards, before she caught him ogling her silky fine legs, to catch her clean features. He saw she had little color on her face, but questioning the aggressive tight bun her hair was pulled into, he thought the color to be brown or maybe raven black, but he wasn't sure. He watched her smooth out the long skirt, about an inch or so below her knees when lying flat, before he moved forward to address her.

His chest heaved the moment she looked up at him, *hello...* Her brown gaze brought a stutter to his thoughts. Instantly he saw the same brown babies looking over her sunglasses that had become askew on her face when they'd collided the day before *...Bedroom eyes!* He was, immediately captured into her gaze and stymied for a brief moment.

"Hello. Mr. Slade." Evelyn took his hand and smiled even brighter. "Sorry I'm a little late." She stepped with him on her stiletto heels as they headed for the door.

"Oh no, you are right on time." His smile widened as he held the door for her.

At the reception desk, he gave his name and swiftly they were ushered into the dim lit restaurant. The tables they passed had crème colored cloths topped with blood red vases, with white lilies in each one. The water goblets were golden as were the tableware. The lighting throughout the place was minimal and very soft. Despite the sunny day, the atmosphere inside looked cozy with the hint of music in the background making it feel late in the evening.

Upon reaching the table, Mr. Slade pulled out Evelyn's chair for her and waited politely for her to sit down on the plush red velvet cushion. "Thank you," Evelyn expressed her gratitude as she watched him go around the table to take his seat. She found her eyes taking in his robust form without care of who was watching. The crème colored suit he wore was very handsome, tailored to his muscled tones, unlike the suit he wore the previous day. His red satin shirt added flare to the suit, and to complete the whole look was a thin crème tie of which he was tucking beneath the table as he positioned himself in the chair.

Upon further inspection of him, she noted his fresh clean face with a stern chin and the cleft that seemed to catch her attention the most. It was big enough to slip in her pinky. It was attractive and worked well for his broad face and pretty eyes. His blond hair, parted on the side dangled precariously down over his forehead hiding part of the light creases that appeared now and then when he smiled. She liked his smile, she decided.

"Your server will be right with you," The hostess briefly addressed Jackson. "Would you like something from the bar?"

"Whiskey," It came out without much thought. He needed something to settle his nerves. He then looked to the woman across from him. "What would you like?"

"Just a white wine," Evelyn answered.

"I'm glad you could make it. I really wanted to thank

you." Mr. Slade spoke to her the moment the hostess was gone.

Evelyn glanced around at the very elegant surroundings. "You really didn't have to go to this extreme."

The server arrived at that moment and began giving them the menu items being sure to mention all of the lunch specials of the day. Watching the man across from her make his selections after she had finished Evelyn realized of late, that he owed her nothing in return for the cab ride. He'd paid the fare...*Clever!*

Mr. Slade has asked her here for another reason and her mind was boggled with so many questions she didn't even hear what he'd ordered.

"In fact," She decided to call him out the moment they were alone. She cocked her head slightly. "You paid the fare for the cab, you owe me nothing. This will be Dutch." She informed him.

"I may have paid the fare, but you still allowed me the ride. Without your approval," He slyly smirked, knowing he had her once more but Evelyn was busy thinking of all of the things she most certainly approved of.

While assessing him once again, another server brought their drinks to the table. Evelyn took this opportunity to make the exchange. Slowly she pushed the case she had laid at her feet over the floor closer to him. The moment he did the same, she thought of his meeting and hoped he didn't need his case. She shot up in her seat.

"How did your meeting go?"

Jackson paused in thought trying to asses her question. He had no meeting; he just did not want to meet with her first thing in the morning. He was hoping that after their lunch she would have time to discuss things more thoroughly. He knew a morning exchange wouldn't be good timing. Did she know he had no meeting? Was this a trick to get him to confess?

He watched while her alluring brown gaze shifted in what looked like concern although she really tried hard to conceal it. His mind then flash-backed to the meeting she knew he had, yesterday. Immediate dislike filled him, he lifted the whiskey glass that was set near his hand and drank it down without a moment's hesitation.

He wondered why she was inquiring about *that* meeting. Did she know something? However, instantly found his worries nothing more than pure paranoia.

She had swiftly glanced down at the cases that now rested side by side. Evelyn's question was reared from the cases they'd just exchanged. She'd had his. Did his meeting go all right without his case? Asking, without really asking whether or not, she had delayed his meeting in some way because of it.

"It went just fine. In fact," He leaned closer, putting the glass down on the table. "I was hoping to discuss that with you; While, we eat." Her brown eyes danced in confusion. Why would he want to discuss private matters with her? "You need money," He stated nonchalantly. He didn't wait for her reply, if she had any. He continued with, "You need a... *lot* of money." He blinked a few times, batting those wonderful blue eyes at her.

Evelyn was stunned to say the least. Confused of what he was saying, trying to comprehend why he was speaking to her like this and trying to bite her tongue in anger. *How dare him!*

She was about to speak her mind, but the server came with their side salads and warm rolls preventing her from saying anything. Then to her horror, the moment the server left, Mr. Slade continued.

"Do you have it?" He asked her bluntly. "Because I do," She wanted to smack the smug expression right off his face, but then he went on to say indifferently. "Thirty days is not very long to come up with what the bank is asking for." Searing anger about brought her out of her chair.

"You read," She began but then checked her voice at the range she had it. Everyone was looking his or her way. She bit back her anger and glared at him.

"You read my things." Not a question because she knew he had. He was flaunting her shame right there in her face. *How DARE he!*

She about came off the chair again but was stopped when she realized his hand was over hers, holding it to the table. His fingers wrapped around her small delicate wrist tightly, but not painfully.

"How else could I know, who's, case I had?" He whispered in a calming tone to help sooth her. His eyes gleamed with understanding and compassion for the way she was feeling. "I had no choice but to read the documents to find a name."

Granted, Evelyn's name was all over those papers, Jackson didn't *have* to read each one to know who the case belonged to but that was a different issue and if she didn't bring it to the table, why bother with it.

Evelyn settled down just a few octaves and really studied the man in front of her. He'd gone through her papers only to find a name. It was logical, and she believed him, but he didn't have to bring her dirty laundry out into the open like that. That was *her* business, not his.

Without apologizing, Jackson never apologized for the things he's either done or said because he never said anything that wasn't true or did anything he should be shameful about. He released her hand, sensing she wasn't going to flee and said, "I can help you."

Silence enveloped around the table while her brown eyes stared into his blue ones, trying to figure out his meaning. Jackson then decided this conversation was taking a wrong turn. By thwarting off her sense of being duped, he lifted his fork and began eating his salad, allowing her to watch him and assess his words more thoroughly.

Evelyn wasn't sure how to respond to him, and his offer. She wasn't sure what exactly he was offering but, was certain there was an offer being played. Instead of asking, she took his lead and began to eat as well. Silence continued to linger about the table as they both leisurely picked at their food. It wasn't until the actual meal was served did he look at her and continue with his conversation.

"I think we can help each other, if you need helping out that is." His eyes searched her body language and found just how desperate she was. Her eyes swelled right up with un-yielded tears, but she controlled them and kept them all in check, not a one, rolled down her face.

He watched her carefully swap plates out and slowly begin to eat her lunch. Her eyes every now and then would come up to meet his gaze, he wasn't sure if she was trying not to look at him or if she was just incapable of keeping her stare where she wanted, which was right on him. Still trying to asses him, what he was trying to do. Definitely not trusting in what he was saying, but eagerly interested in what he may have to offer.

He fought the urge to laugh at her. She was split down the middle beside herself with what she wanted to do about him. Run as fast as she could or sit and listen to his plan. It was clear her need became her root and she remained where she sat, waiting for him to continue.

Not wanting to overpower her right away with what he

had planned out, he allowed their lunch to be consumed almost completely before he engaged in discussion once more.

"Do you have the money?" He questioned her, knowing what her answer would be. She wouldn't still be sitting there if she did. He watched as she slowly shook her head with a shallow expression on her face. She really wasn't happy about her position right now, he was though. She was in need of what he had and she definitely had what he sought. "Well I can help." He told her.

"You said that." She replied gruffly.

He nodded sternly and said, "Let me tell you a story," He leaned closer as his blue eyes seared into her gaze Evelyn shifted in her seat. She was uncomfortable being that close to him. The cleft in his chin called out to her in an odd way; she almost reached out to slip her finger into the crevice. Her eyes lowered to watch his lips move as he told her about his story.

**

The door to her penthouse closed with a silent click. Her fingers released her briefcase and her purse simultaneously, right there at the door as she slowly ventured inside. Her shoes came off next, stepping right out of them. "SSS." She gasped when her feet touched the cool floor.

However, she did not stop her movement towards her bedroom. Slowly she made it to her room, slipped her fingers into the waistband of her skirt then unbuttoned it, letting it open up and cascade down her legs. She shivered at the feel of it grazing her flesh. Next went the soft pale yellow blouse and then finally her undergarments. Almost lifeless she sauntered into the bathroom, turned on the shower and stepped inside the cold spray.

Her chest heaved silently as the tears finally came forth and she allowed them to flow. The remorse she was feeling had nothing to do with the tears she could finally shed … *Oh God!*

She shivered under the cold water but again, it wasn't from the water, it was from a deeper source and she couldn't stop herself when her knees buckled and she slowly descended to the floor of the shower and she sobbed.

Her apartment was silent and dark when the phone rang again. It had done so all afternoon but she wasn't answering it. For the first time in her life, she allowed the phone to ring off its hook. She remained curled up in a ball under her silk bedding, where she felt safe. Her mind was oblivious to the world around her. Every now and again, something will catch her, like the shrill of the phone but soon it went away and she could go back to her dilemma.

Nothing took president over what she was trying to achieve with her mind and soul. Because whether she liked it or not, her dilemma and world were about to collide and she needed to get a grip on what was needed to be done to accomplish this task.

Around midnight she called the office and left a voicemail on Keli's phone. She wasn't coming in. She needed a few days off. Please send the Numbers Guide to her house and she'll take care of the rest. Evelyn told her the guide will be ready and at the office first thing for the layout. If Keli had any questions call her and leave a message, she will check her machine during the day but will not be reachable herself. After that, she made all changes to the guide and packaged it to be on Keli's desk by the morning.

The rest of the time, she was busy packing up her personal things to go to Mr. Slade's home. His name was Jackson, but she couldn't bring herself to call him that. They were strangers for crying out-loud! *One she will be close to, soon!*

4

As promised, Mr. Slade's limo was out front waiting to pick her up bright and early that morning. The chauffeur helped her put her bags into the trunk and then settled in the back seat and watched as the scenery changed from city to rural in a matter of minutes. The leaves were just starting to change from the summer green to their fall colors that kept Evelyn's mind occupied for most of the ride.

She thought of Montana, what the seasons were like. Evelyn really loved the winters there. The whole countryside would be blanketed in white.

It will be Thanksgiving soon and the thought brought her immediate thoughts back to Jackson Slade, what he was giving her. Well, what they were giving each other. They both had a lot to be thankful for this year.

Evelyn turned to look at the massive house before the car stopped out in front. The long winding road they had traveled the past few miles hadn't been a road at all, it was the driveway. Now, the car was in front of a stone and white Tudor style house with etched led crystal glass in the windows and stained glass in the front door. The slate front sidewalk matched the front steps and porch. Big yellow long stemmed rose bushes lined both sides of the walkway and huge wisteria bushes sat on both sides of the front porch and a huge fountain centered in the front garden. It was a beautiful house with big topiary gardens on the side and front. She couldn't see the back but was certain the same would be back there as well.

Mr. Slade and another man stepped out onto the porch when she emerged from the car.

"Evie, darling," Jackson called out and when her eyes bulged from surprise he almost laughed despite himself. He met her half way down the walk. His hand without thought took her arm, gently gave it a caress and his mouth found her warm cheek. The action was complete and without a second thought of how this first meeting should go.

He then smiled both to her, and to himself. Things from here on out were going to be smoother then he first thought. She had accepted his greeting without question, even without wonder. She stood still, ready to receive him and he was certain she almost leaned in to him when his mouth touched her face.

Indeed, this was going much better than he had anticipated. Who knows what the next day may bring or even the next month. He was delighted with this new chain of events and it seemed as if his bride to-be was feeling much the same.

"This is Oliver, my butler."

"Madam," Oliver addressed her politely and very genuinely even though he did not smile.

"He will take your things up to your room," Jackson told her. "Why don't I show you around the grounds before we go inside? I can help you unpack later." He led her off the walk and around the corner out into the back, where a large garden with water fountains that matched the massive one out front.

"That went over nicely." He stated. Evelyn carefully pulled her arm away from his hand and gave him a perilous stare. "What?" He questioned.

"I told you this had to look as real as it can be."

Evelyn nodded. "In name only you told me."

43

He nodded assuredly. "Yes. For us, not for them," He pointed to the house. "They have to... They *must* think you and I, are in love and wish to marry." He eyed her brown bedroom stare. "I told you that. Everyone besides us, *must* see us happy and doing what lovers do before they marry and then after."

"I am not..."

"Shh." He snatched her arm and dragged her into the deepest part of the gardens. "Listen. I told you we aren't lovers, don't freak out." He gasped. "But we will be married. Legally and binding in every way possible. Except, the bed," He clarified for her. "Okay?" He eyed her for affirmation and when he didn't get it he repeated, *"OKAY?"* Evelyn sighed and then shook her head.

"I'm not much into touchy feely so you don't have to worry about me wanting to over step these rules." He shrugged softly. "Every now and then we have to keep up appearances, especially if family or the help is around." He eyed her cheek. "I kept it safe by kissing you on the cheek. I hope you don't mind but the next one will be an all out kiss."

Evelyn's mouth went dry at his words. She wondered if she was right for this part. Should she tell him about her past? He may not want to risk it with someone like her. She wasn't a touchy feely kind of girl either. What else was he going to pull while in public? Her mind asked all of these questions but never did she bring them out to the open. She needed this. She couldn't back out now, not with so much riding on it.

Mr. Slade took her all around the grounds. The further away from the house they got, the more space he put in between them. She was grateful for him being an honorable man, a man of his word.

"We have a few things I need to go over with you. Family issues, our issues. Why don't we meet in my office right after you settle in? Would you like for me to help you unpack?" He asked her as they approached the house ending their walk. Evelyn shook her head declining his generous offer. She really needed a little time to gather her wits. Slowly he led her into the back of the house and up the backstairs to her bedroom.

It took her longer than it should have to unpack the things she had brought. Her room was light blue in decor. A massive bed was in between the two windows where the morning sun was coming in and the huge walk in closet was on one of the adjacent walls.

There were two big cushioned chairs, one next to the closet door and the other over by another door, not the hall door. A settee was along the other wall beside the bed and on it, where two soft frilly pillows with the same styled material as the long drapes in the windows and the bed had a dark blue bedspread with lace trimmings on the edges. Fancy drapes hung off the roundabout curtain rod cut to the sides and attached to the posts on the bed. Quizzically she inspected the fancy drapes on the bedposts to find they unhooked and fell downward to close in the bed for added privacy.

As soon as all of her things were in a good place she decided it was time to head down to meet Mr. Slade. *Jackson.* She reminded herself, not that she didn't like his name. On the contrary, it was a handsome name it suited him well. She just didn't think she knew him well enough to call him by his first name.

She closed her door behind her and walked down the long hallway, looking at all of the photographs of very distinguished faces. One was a General, another, an Officer.

All were family of course. She studied a man that resembled Mr. Slade with captivating eyes, the same color and light colored hair but a thin mustache covered his upper lip. The picture was dated in 1909 a grandfather or great grandfather perhaps.

After her long scrutiny of the photos, slowly she made her way down the hall to find elegant tables and chairs along the way. A table with military medals caught her eye and she stopped to look it over. The Purple Heart and other prestigious medals placed about the tabletop in an artful display. She ran her fingers over the Purple Heart. She knew what that soldier had done to earn the medal. It was a sad way to be honored but honored nonetheless. It was a proud moment for family members as well as sad.

Slowly she made the sign of a cross with her right hand, with a silent prayer before gently kissing her fingers and tentatively touching the Purple Heart once more before leaving to head downstairs.

She passed several murals and fancy art pieces before she reached the end of the hall and descended downward. Along the walls of the staircase that was lit with fancy dome lights were more pictures with faces of men and women, more Slade family members; no doubt.

Again, she stalled out to look each over pausing at the last a bit longer then all the rest. It was a more recent picture of a tall man in his mid sixties. He had sandy blonde hair that was wavy and full. A mustache donned his upper lip and deep green eyes stared back with authority. He was strict. It showed in the depths of his un-creased face. He was hardened around the edges. So much so, he didn't even give a small grin as the picture was made. He didn't look at all happy with his life, or with anything in it. It appeared he'd been painted in the picture after it was made, he looked like a statue.

The woman sitting beside him in a high back chair looked much like him. Her auburn hair curled and touching her shoulders with perfect swirls. Her red cheeks glowed, but that was all that did. Her blue eyes, Mr. Slade's eyes, looked forlorn and so far away. Evelyn felt sorry for the woman.

It was obvious this was Mr. Slade's parents and she felt bad for the way they seemed so sad and distant. Even from each other. He wasn't holding her and, she wasn't leaning in to him. They appeared not to want to be near each other for the time it took to do the portrait. *How sad.*

With sadness, Evelyn continued down the stairs into the other parts of the house. Upstairs she met no one along her treks to the stairs, but the first door she came to on the main floor and to the left of the stairs she found a house cleaner in the room finishing up the dusting of the crystal chandelier above her head hanging on elegant ropes and wire.

"Oh. Excuse me," Evelyn smiled fretfully, entering the family room.

"Yes, madam,"

"I'm looking for Mr. Slade's office."

"Down the hall," The maid instructed. "Third door on the right, not the left, the library is on the left." She smiled at the overwhelming look Evelyn must have given her. The house cleaner stepped down off her ladder and walked her to the door.

"The hall is on the right, just past the main door to the dining room." She pointed to the large double doors and sure enough, there was a long hallway, veering off to the right or to the back of the house. The maid nodded. "Third door on the,"

"...Right." Evelyn replied.

The house cleaner nodded with a bigger smile. "Yes."

"Thank you so much."

"I'm Gladys, is there anything else I can do for you?" she asked politely.

"Can I trouble you for some tea?" Evelyn asked softly, not wanting to disrupt anything.

The maid shook her head uninterrupted. "...Is not a problem. Would you like hot or cold tea? I'll send Florence down in a minute."

"Cold please, thank you again."

Evelyn headed down the hall that differed from the one upstairs in many ways. This one was less cozy and more formal. More art pieces, sculptures, and paintings were in this hall, no personal items of any kind displayed here. She passed two doors on the right and only one on the left before coming to the two that were right across from each other. The left was the library, which she will have to remember that on the long nights she was sure to have a problem sleeping. On the right was Mr. Slade's office.

She knocked softly upon the dark wood door and then popped her head inside.

At the desk, she found him working at something laying on the shiny surface. At her arrival, he stood with a smile, which she returned freely without thought. "All settled in?" She nodded, stepped in and closed the door behind her.

"Sorry I took so long. I found the upstairs hall an amazing walk of history. I just had to stop and admire it all." She remained by the door just looking at the room not sure how far she desired to go. Her heart was thumping hard against her chest as if she had just run a mile in a dead heat. He remained at his desk apparently having the same dilemma.

Jackson tried to look indifferent about what he was looking at, standing at the door in a lacy white blouse and a deep blue denim skirt, that lightly kissed the top of her knees. Her face lightly colored about the cheeks and eyes. Her hair still pulled back in that ungodly tight bun and a pair of gold dot earrings spotted each ear lobe. She was nervous which was understandable, *so was he!* It wasn't every day he got himself engaged.

Despite her cold appearance, his eyes easily slid up and down her body with approval. Her full breasts filled her bra. She wasn't huge, but nicely endowed. Her waist, very thin and her hips swayed beautifully in time with her arms when she walked, her steps small to accommodate those high heeled shoes that made her buttocks push out and her legs look longer and sexy. He liked the way she handled herself in those shoes. It was a song all its own to watch her walking in a cat strut way. *Would she purr for him if he ran his tongue over those fine silky legs? Would she stretch out leisurely over his lap if he tickled them with his finger tips? And if he stroked her warmth would she...*Evelyn was almost against the door when a knock sounded on the other side and it started to come open. Florence, the service-maid, gasped in sorrow when Evelyn quickly sidestepped out of her way. "I'm sorry Miss," Florence apologized. "I didn't know you were right behind the door." Evelyn continued to move away from the door, but still keeping her distance from Jackson.

"I was told you wanted some tea?" Florence inquired as she set the tea over on the table closest to the desk, closer to Jackson. Evelyn watched as she set the glass of cool tea down and look over at Mr. Slade. "Would you care for anything Mr. Slade?"

I'd like this ache in my crotch to go away...

Jackson shook his head. Knowing the other woman in the room wasn't about to accommodate his needs in any way. Not while she was as nervous as a virgin in a whore-house. "Thank you Florence."

"Come on over here and have a seat." Jackson told Evelyn as he took the tea, placing it on the corner of the desk for her to take when she settled. He watched as Evelyn swallowed uncomfortably before stepping out towards the chair across from him.

Feeling like a spot on a white shirt, she took a deep breath before taking the seat. She snatched the tea, eagerly drank the refreshing liquid, cooling her dry throat. Jackson's deep tone filled the space between them as he began to laugh. She looked at him in wonder.

"You look as if I am about to snap you in two," He leaned forward, took her hand beneath his and sat down in his chair. He softly caressed her. "Relax." He took a deep breath, watched her do the same and then smiled. "Isn't that better?"

She snickered softly and he watched the right side of her mouth quirk up in a grin, which was not sensuous in any way, but made him quickly remove his hand before he snatched her forward and lay a big fat kiss upon those thick lips that seemed to jump out at him. *Man, what was going on here? Suddenly he couldn't control his hormones with a woman that resembled an old school Librarian. Maybe he just needed a quick lay before all of this kicked off.* Just a short quick encounter may do him right, settle him down before he really made matters worse. It was evident she could sense something was amiss about him and if he kept it up he was going to end up scaring her right on out the damn door.

"I'm sorry." She confessed in a whispered tone. "This kind of thing doesn't happen every day." She chuckled softly. "Not to me, anyway,"

"I'm sure." He agreed but then added, "Not that it shouldn't happen to you," When she looked sharply at him.

He smiled. "I have been drawing up a few papers for us.

50

Ideas we can bounce off each other." He slid the papers over the desk towards her. "I want to spend as much time with you as possible, which is why you're here."

He got up, trying to ease her tension that was building. She didn't like being in his home, he could feel her uneasiness. Jackson wanted to explain and tear down her fears and replace them with a whole bunch of other things to occupy her mind. "I want to get to know you." He admitted to her, which was true. If they were to marry, he must know something about her. "You should get to know me," He informed her. "Don't you think?"

Evelyn took another drink of the tea before she nodded, "Sounds reasonable."

"Of course it is, because if we find common ground between us, we will look more the part in public. I think we should spend a lot of time talking and learning about one another." He leaned his backside on the corner of the desk right beside her.

"Have you given the wedding some thought?" His deep blue eyes searched hers *Has she ever! All night long she thought about it.*

"I want this to look real, Evie." Evelyn felt her stomach twist inside from the odd warmth she felt at his tone. More so at the shortened name he'd used more than once. "I want to help you pick colors and invitations. It has to be big." He spread his arms out in demonstration. "Can you do big?"

"I think so," She replied in truth. The one thing she was sure about was that. She loved weddings and she didn't foresee herself ever having such a shindig and was actually looking forward to this part. She hadn't expected him to want to help but the idea wasn't half bad.

"Good. I want to help with the dress as well."

"Alright,"

She watched him go behind the desk and then looked down at the papers he'd slid over to her.

5

Hold hands whenever possible.
Kiss on occasion but not all the time.
Take the seat or chair closest to me when family is around.
Suggest a walk while in public if you need to ask me a question.
I buy Habersham Farm and release it to you after we are through.
You must attend most all social events my family invites us to.
No one is to know we are playing a game.
We will be married legally in the public eye including people at work and YOUR family.

Evelyn looked up at that point in his list. Her eyes scanned his features as he watched her read over his suggestions.

"…Something wrong?"

She started to shake her head, looked back down to the last statement she'd read, then looked back at him.

"Question," She sighed softly. "I have no family, this you know but my friends are very close to me. Very dear and I don't feel right lying to them."

He sat back in his chair. "In reality, you're not." He told her. "We are getting married. You don't have to tell them any more than that, if you choose." He could see her face lighten right up and her shoulders release the tension that

53

was building.

Jackson leapt out of the chair, quickly rounded the desk and placed his hands on her shoulders and proceeded to massage her tense muscles.

Oh! Heavens to mercy... she tried to hold in her shock, consumed by the onslaught of impeccable tingling that took over her whole body. Her tense muscles relaxed almost upon impact and she felt her insides quiver with uncontrolled tremors. *Please God, don't let him feel the way my body is reacting to these odd sensations!*

She'd never felt such strange twisting that was going on in her being. A touch of another's hands shouldn't bring forth such intriguing sensations. *He's not just a some...body; he is soon to be your husband! Aren't you supposed to feel these kinds of pleasures and want them, even hunger them?*

"As long as they see us as a loving couple when they do see us together, that is all I need."

"Mm," She shuttered silently when her moan filled the room. She'd heard him speaking, but was totally caught unguarded by the sweet touch of his fingers.

"Feel good?" He questioned right against her ear. Instant chills ran all down her back and goose bumps covered her entire body. She lurched forward when her nipples grew hard and started rubbing against the lace of her bra from the motion of his massage. A fantastic sensation she'd never experienced before.

"God yes," She answered in a husky tone.

"I bet this is *thee,* spot. Right there," His fingers stroked down her spine tenderly and then spread out, moving up her back and grip her shoulders in a firm grasp.

Jackson watched her as her whole body reacted to his swift ministrations to her shoulders. *I wonder...*

He slid his hands off her shoulders, taking his thumbs and

gliding them over the back of her neck massaging the smoothest part. Running his thumbs up and down, firmly pressing them into her flesh while his fingers carefully caressed the front of her neck. He'd been engrossed in what he was doing when suddenly *she purred...*

Really, another moan caught in her throat where his fingers played over her soft skin. The gentle throbbing he felt told him he wasn't imagining what he'd heard. The front of his slacks got tighter, but he suppressed the urge to do anything about. He didn't want to scare her off, but he could not resist the way her skin beckoned him, summoned him to taste her softness. Without hesitation, he leaned closer and grazed her neck with a tantalizing kiss.

At first, it was a light sweep of his mouth. A brush of his lips against her, but then it happened again. Deep in her throat, she purred telling him she liked what he was doing.

His hands grabbed her shoulders and squeezed them firmly. He closed his eyes as he deepened the kiss, pressing his mouth harder to her flesh. His throbbing erection aching, but he still ignored it, wanting only to taste her.

Growing bolder by the minute he slowly traveled to the side of her neck, taking much liberty with his mouth, kissing every inch of her delectable flesh. Sucking, and massaging her skin with his tongue, trying to pleasure her with every caress of his lips.

He lowered his mouth to her ear and softly breathed inside, taking his tongue and dancing it around her tender lobe. Her high intake of breath made him linger there longer then he had planned, giving her more satisfaction before he grew even bolder.

Moving his lips downward, caressing her chin, sucking in her flesh and again tasting her against his lips. Slowly turning her head to get a better shot of those beautiful lips he now hungered to taste, taking his leisure there on her chin, smoothing his lips under the ridge, giving her chills one final time before he trailed severe kisses all the way to his target. A moan filled the space between them. *Was it him? Damn, but she tasted so good and sweet!*

His thick hard on throbbed with desire to take even a bolder move, Jackson was still touching her neck, caressing her throat but it wasn't enough and gently glided his hand southbound, lightly grazing her firm breast.

Evelyn gasped inwardly the moment she felt strange tingling vibrations in her nipples that were very hard. Confusion stampeded her mind, but immediately she awoke when she felt a firm caress over her left breast and then to her horror, a very purposeful tweak of the sensitive peak.

All of a sudden, she was aware of what was happening. As if waking up from a nightmare she surged forward, breaking the ardent kissing their mouths had been doing. Her left hand came out, smacking him across that handsome face as she leapt from the chair, turning around to face him. The tea in her glass spilled over the sides and she felt the cool sides slide from her fingers, almost dropping it.

"No!" The single word shot out of her mouth the moment her other hand connected with his stern chin, gripping the glass firmly back in place.

His wide eyes were what she saw first, then the anger. She'd actually hit him...*Oh My!*

"I'm sorry." She gasped backing away from the chair, away from him if possible. She wasn't sure what he would do. *She hit him!*

Jackson had been struck, many times before but almost never had he been taken off guard like that. Usually he saw it coming, but this little minx had swept him up into a vortex where all he thought of was how sweet she tasted and how much he had to have more… *So much more!*

"W-what were you," She stammered putting her hand to her mouth. Her eyes glazed with confusion as to what took place and how it had gotten so out of hand. Her eyes met his and she trembled uncontrollably. Feeling the glass waver in her hand, she released it to the smooth surface on the desk before she actually dropped it. "What were you doing?" Her hand then moved to the breast he had been fondling and then turned in horror as she recalled what he had done.

"No." she shook her head ferociously. She then looked back at him with crazed eyes snatching up the papers from his desk. "You said public not private!" She scanned his eyes and then looked downward in shame. "Do you agree this will not happen again?"

He fought unlike he had ever fought before as he kept the humor of this whole matter at bay. She'd blow a gasket if he showed her disrespect right now. The humor he found in this was – *she* was a willing party and she liked what they had been doing, but he wasn't going to bring that to her attention. Instead, he shook his head in agreement – *for now.* He rubbed his jaw and said. "Agreed…"

Evelyn felt guilt and even pain as she looked up to find him relaxing the red mark on his face. Immediately she stepped forward. "I am so sorry." She watched his firm jaw as he moved. The cleft, a huge dimple in his face drew her full attention. How she wanted to slip her finger inside it, run it over his flesh, smooth out the crevice, toy with it if you will.

"Will you be alright?" She asked him still not looking away from his stern chin. "I don't know what happened." *…Understatement of the world! Had she really allowed him to kiss her that way? Oh, why was her breast still tingling as if his hand was still pressed against her nipple?*

57

She tried to shake off the last of her thoughts, looking away from him to avoid more confusion. Every time she looked at him, she felt his lips upon hers, his fingers touching her throat, her nipple, which undeniably wanted more.

Jackson finally took hold of the situation taking full blame. For now, that was the best course to take. "I got caught up in the moment." Evelyn eyed his blue gazes, but again couldn't hold the stare she looked away, shameful. "I'm sorry." *What?!? His first apology...? And for something he wasn't wrong in?*

...She kissed him back!

His heartbeat sounded hard against his chest, apparently trying to beat its way out. He humbly stepped away from her as his mind took everything in. Indeed, she kissed him. *MOREOVER, it was just a matter of time before he would taste those sweet lips again.*

He just had to bide his time and watch her for tells. She liked what had transpired between them and she will ask for more. Not by mouth, her body will do all the talking for her and he would be waiting to answer her.

Evelyn gave a nod and cleared her throat. "I um, I have a few things you haven't mentioned." She raised her eyes up to meet his.

"Sure, ok." He moved away from the chair, going back to his desk.

"What were they?"

"You um," She paused as she walked around the chair, not wanting to sit back down. "Didn't mention our finances," Jackson eyed her more cautiously, unsure exactly where she was heading with this. "I mean," She jumped forward to say, "I have a business, *YOU*," she surged on and then stopped, speaking more softly. "You have a very good business."

Jackson nodded. "And…?"

"What about a prenuptial agreement?" She inquired. Evelyn stood rigid while she watched him think. She wasn't going to back down on this. Even though this *marriage* was going to be real, it was going to be only for a little while as per the agreement. It only seemed right to have their assets aside from everything else.

"Prenuptial?" He questioned softly, his eyebrows narrowing down towards his nose.

Evelyn sighed as she approached his desk. "Granted, Mr. Slade we are going to be married, but for only a little while." She watched his eyes thin down to slits. "What would happen if something should happen to you?"

Jackson sat back in his chair eyeing the woman standing in front of him. She was out of the ordinary run of the mill type girl; for sure. Plain attire, plain features and yet, he found himself woven into her every essence. Hungry to taste those lips all over again, desiring to pull her to his desk and plunge into her warmth like a wild animal. It was a struggle, to remain indifferent while she talked, was that because of her or because she was speaking of things that really did not matter. He was not sure. *Would she purr again if he were to stroke between her silky thighs?* He wondered amicably.

"Well?" She asked and repeated her question. "What would happen?"

"Jackson." He answered.

Evelyn just looked at him in wonderment. "I am trying to be fair here. Doesn't this concern you?" she asked. "If we are married and you die, what happens to your inheritance that we are doing this for? Should it go to me, as it would in a normal marriage?"

She batted her brown eyes at him. Jackson fought with

what to say but then decided to just say what came to mind, as it was best that way.

He leaned forward as he spoke calmly. "It will be a normal marriage."

"You know what I mean."

He gave a nod and he meant what he said. Especially with all of the electricity that was floating around in this very room. She had magnetic pulls and he was a very large magnet, wanting to be dragged. He shifted in his seat, trying to ease the ache in his loins.

He was more than pleased that his marriage was going to be nothing like his parents. Separate vacations. Separate cars. Separate homes. Separate beds. At first, that was what he wanted. It would suit him fine, being one place and his so-called wife, in another. It worked for his parents and he was certain it would for him as well. Until, that is, he met Evelyn and he discovered a desire stronger then he had ever imagined.

...*Oh no! This marriage was going to be nothing like he expected.*

He smiled.

"What are you smiling at?" she asked getting leery of the way he was looking at her.

"Hum?" He blinked and then sighed. "Oh, sorry, I understand what you are saying. A prenuptial would be fine, but if something did happen to me, even if I signed such an agreement, my family wouldn't accept it."

Evelyn pondered over that piece of information. She hadn't thought about that. What about her piece of mind though? She *couldn't... wouldn't*, take anything of his if that were to happen. It wasn't right. Only on paper will she be his wife and she wouldn't feel right taking something that really belonged to his family.

"But Mr. Slade I just can't accept that answer. We must agree to sign something that releases me from your inheritance. Please." She begged him.

He could see that she wasn't going to budge on this matter and he didn't feel like arguing with her. "Jackson," He insisted and then said, "...If you wish."

She ignored the instruction to call him by name just as she did the first time. He was a stranger. She wouldn't feel right calling him by his first name. *Certainly felt right when his mouth kissed yours!* She chastised herself.

"Thank you."

"I'll have the papers drawn up by a different lawyer, not the family's, he will be obligated in telling my parents."

"You didn't mention separate rooms," She pointed out.

He hadn't? He leaned forward to look at his list. He then shook his head. He had meant to put that in there, it was going to be on the top but after today, it was no longer a necessity. Quickly he looked up at her with what he needed to say.

"The maids will not understand separate rooms," Which was so true but he did not add that his parents undoubtedly would. "They will gossip about it and eventually it will find its way to my parents." He tried to appear solemn and sincere to her wavering gazes as he spoke. He didn't wish to intimidate her but there was no way he was sleeping without her in his bed.

"For now, it will be fine but after we marry, we have no choice but to share the same quarters."

Evelyn slowly digested that and did not like it one bit. *It would be too tempting.* No! She scolded herself for thinking in that manner. She shut her heart and mind off from those sinful feelings. She couldn't share a room with him! A lady does not conduct herself like this! What would Father say to all of this? Lying and cheating to gain materialistic things that did not matter in the afterlife. Her soul and her salvation were the only things that mattered and it would do her well to remember that!

Despite what her mind was saying, she found herself nodding affirmation of what Mr. Slade was telling her. Her mother's farm was all she could see. For that was the reason for all of the lies and deceitfulness' that were going to come about. "Please, if you'll excuse me." Evelyn darted from the office and rushed out into the fall afternoon.

**

"What's...*this?*" Keli, Angie, Monica, Raymona and Jasmine all came bounding into her office. Keli dropped the newspaper she was holding onto the desk and looking straight up at Evelyn was her picture with Nicholas in the engagement section. He'd said he was going to put it in there, he had no choice.

She should have told her friends and colleagues about her upcoming wedding that was nearing at quite a fast pace. Evelyn glanced away from the paper with a sudden dry throat. She snatched the glass of water and as she drank some, her eyes caught Monica's hands grasping her narrow waist in a tight vice. Angie beside her was tapping her foot in anger. Evelyn suddenly felt her throat tighten right up making it hard to breathe, much less swallow.

She should have told them. They were more than just co-workers, *they* were her friends. Her closest friends and she should have said something about Nicholas, something about their wedding.

"*You,*_and Jackson Slade?" Raymona's eyes widened with shock.

"The man is *Hunk of the century!*" Monica added to the

dismay of the group of women standing before her.

"You, and *Jackson Slade?*" Keli repeated but this time, she emphasized his name with shock.

None of this really bothered Evelyn. These women knew her better then she knew herself sometimes. She was *not* the kind of woman to even look at someone like Jackson Slade, of whom she discovered was his middle name. Nicholas Jackson Slade was his full name and nothing remotely like the type of person she would date let alone marry.

He was too full of himself. He was cocky and very intimidating. He took charge and he did *not* back down from what he thought was right. He was a control freak. *He kissed like a freight train gone awry and his hands were velvety smooth and his fingers not too harsh when it came to caressing and rolling her taut nipple.*

Evelyn lurched forward in her chair. Why was it she could not forget that day in his office? She dreamed endlessly about the way his thumbs had smoothed out her neck, the way his wet mouth made her insides churn with feelings she wasn't capable to understand, *although she tried.* God knows she tried *all the time.*

The man was sensual in every way and nothing like the kind of man she would get involved. Men like that, were dangerous to a woman such as herself. She will end up hurt, standing with her heart in her hands, because that was the kind of man Nicholas Slade was. He was the devil and she was about to get very close to him. She had to be careful. This she knew and constantly reminded herself.

...But, it was so hard when her breasts tingled with anticipation of feeling his touch once again. Her lips quivered at the notion of his mouth taking hers in a carnal embrace. The way her body melted at the very thought of him...

"You want to explain?" Jasmine asked when the silence had gone on too long. Evelyn looked at her five friends that were as different to each other as peanut butter and jelly. One was short with red ringlets all about her head. One was tall with strawberry blond waves cascading down to her shoulders. Two ladies were medium height but one had black straight hair in the front that was just a few inches shy of touching her shoulders and the back was cropped off tight to her head. The other woman had hair flowing all the way to her knees in the sweet color of auburn, the red in her hair glistened like the red in a candy apple.

The last of the five was Angie and her obtuse hair that was now the color of fall. Some strands had a golden yellow hue, some were sharp red, some a light green and some brown and all of it was spiked straight up in the air with mousse, only two inches or three inches long and very festive. Only two wore the typical make up whereas the others choose the more modern tastes like green apple lipstick and fuchsia eyeshadow.

"We are not leaving until you spill the beans." Keli took the nearest chair and the others followed suit to any chair they could find.

Evelyn nodded as she eyed each of the women before her. "I'm sorry," And she was. "I meant to tell you." …And she did, truthfully did want to tell them, she just didn't know how. She sighed and smiled. "Things have been moving so quick."

"This is true then?" Keli asked her, lifting the corner of the paper. She eyed the picture then looked at Evelyn. Again, Evelyn nodded.

"Yeah," She looked at all of the girls with sadness deep in her heart. She did not want to lie to these women.

"When did you meet him?" Jasmine asked.

"…Where?" Monica asked right after her.

Again, her friends knew that Evelyn did not hang around his kind of *click* so how and where could they have met.

"We shared a cab." Evelyn found herself answering with the truth, which was the best anyway.

All five sets of eyes looked skeptically at Evelyn. Evelyn nodded.

"Yep, I shared my cab with him and then he asked me to lunch and the rest is what they say, history."

Keli thrust her body backwards into the chair as she looked at Evelyn. Her eyes, blinking, and her head moving from side to side. She was having trouble-believing Evelyn and then Angie asked, "You got lucky in a cab?" All five women nodded in unison.

"Wish I could have that kind of luck." Raymona stated admirably.

"And he asked you to marry him?" Keli asked and then added, "You said yes?"

Before Evelyn had the chance to respond Angie but in with, "Why wouldn't she?

He's a hunk…A *rich hunk* at that! Who *wouldn't* say yes to that face?"

"He has the deepest blue eyes ever!" Jasmine gave her assessment of Jackson.

"And those… muscles!" Raymona added. "Man, he can hold me any day." She shook her head and then giggled. "Is he a great kisser?"

Evelyn was grateful for the way her friends have taken over her answering of Keli's hard question. It was really a private question she really didn't want to answer. It would be a lie if she had. Then before she had the chance to coral her emotions, her body gave away her answer to Raymona's very private question. One she couldn't deny if her life depended on it.

Her hands trembled, her heartbeat doubled and she felt her face grow heated at the thought of Nicholas' mouth over hers. It was an impulsive reaction and the women all snickered in response to her unusual act of appetence.

...*Oh God* she prayed. *Help me to lose this wickedness and help me shed these impure thoughts before they take hold of all that is Godly.*

6

Dressed in her underwear and a robe Evelyn collapsed onto her big bed and closed her eyes. She needed strength to get through this evening. She had come right home from work and up to shower and pick out her clothes for the evening, but... She gasped loudly. What do you wear when you're meeting the parents of your fiancé?

She'd gone through her entire wardrobe and still came up with nothing. *This is nuts!* She told herself. She was fretting over people she should care nothing about, *Why did she care?* Did she, her mind scanned her inner self and yes. Yes, she did care about what these people would think and say. Would they know that she was a fake...Know that she was an imposter, only playing a role?

Please give me strength. I need your guidance...

She was in the middle of her prayer when the door that joined her room with Nicholas' came open. There was no lock otherwise; it would have not been an access for him to come in unannounced.

Quickly she got off the bed and snagged her robe tightly around her small waist but not before his eyes feasted upon her body, liking what they saw. His blue gazes ate up the soft pink cotton panties and matching bra with lace cups.

"Etch hum..." He cleared his throat. "Sorry."

"I have asked you and asked you," She scolded him in anger. She'd been there a full week and still he did as he pleased and it infuriated her.

"I know." He raised his hand to silence her. "I wasn't

67

thinking. I'm sorry." Jackson caught the sudden anger that filled him. Sorry! He'd been saying it all damn week to her and she didn't give a damn! He never apologizes, and here he was making a record of it in just the past few days.

Nevertheless, his eyes scanned her delicate softness, recalling what he'd seen before she was able to cover herself up. Damn it, she was hot! She inflamed him without even trying and it was driving him crazy with want for her. He was a man *damn it* and he is a sexual, pleasurable man that needed a little release before his head came off his damn shoulders.

He has been very, very careful around her. Hadn't she noticed? It was the hardest damn thing he has done ever and it was starting to take its toll on his nerves but the last thing he needed was to scare her off. He needed her to say *I do* before he could show her just where he, as a man stood in this relationship.

He smiled inwardly. He couldn't wait to show her where she stood in this as well. Because he could feel the heat reverberating off her body, which, wasn't helping his ignored desire to plunge into her warmth, and feel how her body would wrap around him with delicate velvet softness that would be wet from her own desires.

"I have something for you," He told her. She had been in his life a little more than a week and when he told his parents he was getting married, they didn't hesitate to ask questions. Too damn many, if you asked him, but he answered to the best of his knowledge and he even accepted his mother's invite for dinner despite his inner soul telling him not to.

Lord only knows what will happen and he really didn't wish to strike any problems with Evelyn and his parents. She just would not understand, and he feared that *maybe she would,* which put an unusual sense of turmoil in his heart. A little more than a week and he was feeling protective of his bride to-be. She was too nice of a girl to thrust her in front of his parents. She didn't have a hardened heart, she was easily upset, and she'd scare off easy if she got the wrong impression; which would be the *right* impression, of course.

She watched him like a field mouse would watch a snake as he approached her. He held out his offering and watched her eyes take in the reflective gold band and then widen to the sparkling diamond. "Nicholas." She gasped softly as she eyed the diamond he was showing her, using his given name.

Ever since their meeting with his private lawyer and she discovered his full name, she no longer calls him Mr. Slade but Nicholas. It was a step in the right direction but still not his name. He tried to explain to her that Nicholas was not his name; no first males in his family were ever called by the first name.

Every first boy had Jackson as his middle name and called by that name, it was tradition, unless you had a room full, then and only then were the first names used. Nicholas was just there. Jackson was his real given name, handed down by fathers of fathers many years ago. His father was Elliott, but his brother who died young, named Gavin Jackson Slade, Jackson nonetheless.

He would have been the Slade to pass on the tradition of marriage and a son had he lived and Jackson was the only son, only child to Elliott, so was named as tradition calls for and is now forced to marry and bare a child, an heir before he turns thirty-five.

He stepped closer to Evelyn, taking her left hand, softly holding it up so he could slide the ring on her small finger. She'd given him her ring size earlier, so she really shouldn't be surprised about the ring, but she was and he was fascinated by her awe. Her eyes sparkled almost as brightly as the four-carat diamond did.

It was small, smaller than his mother's and Jackson was sure she would comment on it, he didn't care.

Before sliding the ring all the way on her finger, he noticed she was shaking. He stopped, looked away from her trembling hand to see her brown eyes glistening, trying hard not to reveal how this small detail was affecting her. Her cheeks quivered gently as she looked away from his gaze. He knew she was trying to keep the moment real.

He broke the silence between them, "Nervous about tonight?" She rolled her eyes and gasped. He smiled, happy to relieve the tension that was building within her.

She shook her head. "I can't even find a decent outfit." The hand that was holding her robe loosened up and the soft pink bra and panty outfit peeked out from the gap that was slowly getting larger as she moved about.

"I don't understand it." She closed her eyes.

Jackson let his eyes take in the beauty he was seeing beneath her robe. His crotch grew three times larger creating such pain he gasped and slid the ring home as his body rocked forward with the jolt that ripped through him. Catching himself, he steadied his stance before her eyes opened to look at her hand where the ring, *his ring* rested upon her finger.

The moment turned magnanimous for Jackson. The ring, meant to bind his inheritance suddenly seemed to be binding something else and he wasn't prepared for the sensation that coursed through his heart. It was *his ring*, she was wearing *his ring*, which suddenly meant *she* was also *his* He'd never given it a thought about really wanting someone else to belong to him in any way fathomable, but right at this moment, he couldn't see anyone else but Evie belonging to anyone but him and vice versa.

His eyes darted down to the pink bra that was poking out of her robe conspicuously.

"It fits perfectly." She murmured.

Jackson looked up from her breast to see her bedroom eyes pulling him forward. He felt his fingers wrap around her hand, gently caress her as he pulled her towards him.

His mouth barely touched hers, just a light brushing. His mind screaming for him to stop before a light brush was going to be more like a quick devouring of her sweet tasting mouth that he has been craving ever since that day in his office.

He grunted like an animal, barring all of his strength, not to take the sweep of their embrace into a bolder more impairing hold, before he took her in his arms, throwing caution to the wind and her to the bed where he could plunder more than her mouth.

Slowly, he brought his hand up tenderly graze her bra, touching very delicately over the lace, squeezing her firm breast in his palm. His lips kissed the tip of her nose, keeping this seductive embrace at arm's length. His eyes danced around, taking in her sensuous gazes, noting she was submissive and eager to allow his mouth to touch hers, wanting him to kiss her. Wanting to kiss her… he moved away, stepping back to assess what they were doing. Taking charge for the first time and hating himself for it.

He touched the tip of her nose with the same hand that had held her firm breast in his palm and then his fingers splayed out, running softly across her face. Her eyes closed to his soft touches. His hand wrapped around her head, dipping just below that tight bun of hers, pulling her forward. Her mouth opened just a bit and he took it with a hard kiss because he could *not* deny himself just a brief taste of her, and that was what he took.

His lips crushed hers. Her body came forward, touching his. The robe completely forgotten, opened up. He struggled with what he wanted to do, which was to take his free hand and wrap it around her small waist. He wanted to touch her legs and open her core to feel just how heated she was for him, but he didn't. Instead, he slipped his tongue inside her mouth, tasting her warmth and savoring it with a groan.

His inflamed groin throbbed with anticipation of feeling her warmth as well. *Would her heated core be as heated as her mouth?* He wondered and then images of *both* taking his flesh deeply and what it would feel like flooded him.

He pushed away from her. He had to break contact before his body took charge of his mind's thoughts. *God, to have her warmth surround him!* He didn't care which one took him in, at this point he wanted both. Needed both for his sanity but … he did nothing to appease his mind or groin.

His eyes opened just in time to see Evelyn bringing up her hand to smack him for the impure act he had put upon her. *Lordy…* if she could read his mind and knew everything he wanted to do with her, she'd kill him!

Jackson grinned softly, catching her hand with his, stopping her from hitting him, as she had done before. He expected her to want to hit him for all of the feelings he was bringing to life. The one that caught his attention was the desire deeply embedded in her brown gazes. Even now, angered, she still wanted him. Her flesh quivered beneath his hand where he gripped her firmly but not painfully. The last thing he wanted to do was hurt this minx.

He watched her eyes grow intense with wanton as he pulled her hand against his lips and proceeded to kiss each finger seductively. Then to her horror, he opened his mouth, and took her first finger inside and circled it with the tip of his tongue.

"Do me a favor," He whispered over her finger, his tongue still circling the digit provocatively. "Wear the pink outfit for me." He requested dropping her hand and moving away from her, meandering towards the door.

Evelyn's chest heaved without care as she tried to settle her nerves. Her heart raced, painfully pounding against her breastbone. Her breathing was shallow. She closed her eyes to help settle her impetuous thoughts.

How dare he! She wanted to scream out from all the insolent things he had done and the way her body refused to listen to her mind. No matter how hard she tried, she could not forget how it felt when his mouth grazed hers teasingly. She recalled how her heart had quickened at the idea of him putting more force into it, and then to her horror, wanting him to do just that. Wanting to taste the whiskey she knew he'd have on his lips…he drank way too much.

Her belly fluttered in an unfamiliar way when his hand slid the ring onto her finger. Absentmindedly she stroked her finger, the ring that swirled with ease. Her eyes quickly scanned the hand where he'd placed the ring. Her heart thundered in her chest. It was a beautiful ring. Huge but pretty. Not too big, it dwarfed her hand. The clarity in it was the best she'd ever seen, not that she'd seen many rocks the size she had on her finger.

A harsh gasp filled the room when she caught her opened robe in her sighting. She dropped her hand to look down at her breast, the one with a hardened nipple poking through the lace in the cup. The *same breast*, that Nicholas had actually caressed with his large hand. Her heart stopped dead and she closed her eyes again. Her whole body trembled with delight at the touch of him. *What would it have felt like if the bra was not there?*

Another loud gasp filled the room and her eyes snapped open, spinning to face herself in the tall mirror by the closet she watched as a tear ran down her face.

What made her think of that? What was making her think of his taste when he did finally kiss her? ...*Not really a kiss, more like a plunge.* His mouth devoured hers and took charge of the impassioned kiss as if he could *not* control himself. That kiss was pure man not whiskey. Heat beyond any she'd ever felt came out of his mouth and slithered into hers. His tongue, which *drove* her insides to a boiling point, she couldn't grasp much less control. She wanted him, wanted his kisses and... *so much more!*

Breaking into an all out sweat, she dropped to the floor. Watching her reflection as she brought her arms up, clasping her hands together. The sparkle of the diamond was the last thing she saw as it twinkled in the mirror before closing her eyes to pray.

7

Jackson tried with all his might to keep the smile from showing up when he saw her on the stairs in that tight pink suit she'd worn the day he'd met her. He felt his creased mouth grow bolder as he watched the already short skirt ride up her lovely thighs while she stepped carefully in those tall-heeled shoes also the color pink. Without much thought he stepped to the bottom of the stairs to wait, and didn't ask to take her hand when she reached the bottom, both he did and she accepted quite well.

"Stop that grinning," She scolded him. "You're despicable Nicholas and I will not tolerate your behavior any longer."

He smiled more, with a turn of his head. "I'd apologize but..." He leaned in closer to her. "We quite enjoyed ourselves earlier." His eyes danced over her features, daring her to argue the matter because if she did, he was going to take her down memory lane.

Jackson delighted at her gaze as she held his stare. Her eyes spoke to him without words. She was angry but she didn't show it. She was burning up being so close to him. *That...* she showed and was angered more for doing so. She was a smart woman, knowing when to play her cards and when to hold back and he was highly impressed to learn she knew already how far she could tug that chain of hers before it was no longer a request but a dare. Jackson *never* backs down from a dare!

He let his eyes crease softly as he cascaded them down the full length of her. "It fits perfectly." He mumbled. Their eyes met and for a while, he fought with himself. He wanted to kiss her again, she wanted it too but they had to leave, they were going to be late. *What better excuse staying home and not go at all?* He thought to himself. She didn't really wish to go, and he certainly did not want to.

His father, now there would be a mixture of emotions that would consume him. Confusion would probably be the first. He wouldn't understand a desire that big for his wife, for <u>he,</u> himself does not have such feelings towards his own wife. Then after that would settle in, he'd see his son's marriage will be much different than, his.

Jackson was actually going to like his future if the woman he chose could actually, feel something for him and if by some miracle he felt for her as well...

"You really should close that gaping mouth," Evelyn said turning away from him and sauntered to the front door. "I didn't wear it for you." She cut with sharp words but they did nothing to the electricity in the room, it was so thick he was afraid they'd cause an arc if they weren't careful. He watched the sway of her hips as she walked. He shook his head as he approached her with her jacket in his hands.

"I don't care why you have it on, just that you do."

"It's my best suit." She told him, allowing him to help her with her jacket. "I have to look my best. Act the part the best I can." *Lies,* all of it was nothing but lies and she hoped he couldn't see through the veil she tried to place between them. She'd spent hours trying to find something in her closet but every time she decided on something, her eyes darted to her pink suit and she'd hang it back but refused to get out her pink one, only to repeat the process over and over again until finally she relented to what he had asked for. *Why,* she had not a clue.

...but she did favor his expression as she walked down

the stairs. His eyes scanned the soft cashmere white sweater with pearls and lace sweeping downward towards the breast line. He lingered there, his eyes devouring her firm breasts with adoring fondness. Nicholas even swallowed to get a grip of himself, before his eyes went southbound, to her tight skirt and the way it rode up her thighs as she stepped down.

"Glad I have great taste." He surmised and opened the door for her to walk out before him.

She laughed openly, "More like a hair trigger libido that is working overtime."

Once more, she walked away from him, leaving him to watch her as she did so. *My, my, my… what a fabulous view,* he deduced right then, and there. He really liked this side of her. The sway of those hips told him just how right she was and he literally bit his tongue to keep himself from adding, *you keep this cat and mouse game up sweetheart: you'll see how close you are about that hair trigger.*

"Are you offering a release of such dilemmas for the future?" He asked her as Walter the driver, opened the door of the car so they could get in. Evelyn paused to turn to Nicholas.

"I'm afraid you'll have to sate those dilemmas with someone else Nicholas." She responded then got inside the car.

"What if I said I didn't want anyone else sating my libido?" He asked running his finger over her knee as he sat in the seat beside her.

Quickly she snapped her leg away from him and glared at him. "I can't possibly sate your appetite Nicholas."

"How do you know?" He questioned with soft eyes. "And why do you call me Nicholas? I told you that is not my name." Their eyes danced back and forth before she turned away.

"First off, I am not that way. I am a lady and could never satisfy a man like you." Her tone was demure although she found argument in her statement. She hadn't meant to sound harsh, or even imply he was rouge, she was trying to get those hungry gazes to turn away they made her uneasy. Made her curious to what she *could* do for his hunger, to what extent could she possibly please him and... *would he please her?*

"Your name *is* Nicholas Slade. I saw it." She argued vehemently. She wasn't about to claim just how uneasy the name *Jackson* made her feel. Nicholas wasn't quite as dashing or even empowering as Jackson was and the way *Jackson* simmered her blood in a way she did not understand or want to understand, she refused to use it.

Evelyn slid closer to the door and looked out at the passing scenery. It remained quiet for a few minutes until he said, "So... let me get this straight. You think you're out of your league when it comes to sating me and you hate my name." Evelyn kept her eyes straight, continuing to watch out the window as the car drove on. For some reason, the man sitting beside her did not force the conversation any further. She sighed softly as the trees and green grasses cleared away for the bright lights of the city.

Jackson wanted to talk this out in a very bad way but knew she wasn't up for that kind of talking. He let his gaze scan over her taught frame. She was as rigid as a damn tree, afraid. She was afraid of him and that set a tone for the rest of the evening. She was scared witless and didn't know how to change her course without losing what she'd been struggling with, to keep her family's farm.

He'd forgotten just why she had agreed to do this. He looked away from her, trying to settle the beating in his chest. Damn! How had this gotten so messed up so quickly? They were doing this for each other, not for romance and certainly not for life. At least, she wasn't and that was what scared her. Things were changing and she didn't like it one bit.

Movement from her side of the car brought him back to her. He slowly looked at her as she trembled. Her hands were in her lap, tightly wringing back and forth, her fingers as white as snow. Her eyes were huge with fear, afraid about the unknown, afraid about this evening. He continued to watch her hands until he couldn't take it any longer.

He reached over and laid his hand over hers. He hadn't meant anything by it but to warm her troubled heart but the moment his fingers felt her soft flesh beneath his, he actually caressed her hand before grasping it and giving it a gentle squeeze. He heard her sigh of relief but didn't say anything. The rest of the ride was in silence.

The house wasn't like what she had expected. Evelyn looked up at the small brownstone in Queens with uncertainty. Had he taken her to his parents? She looked at him but couldn't word her suspicion because a man came out to greet them.

"Harris," Jackson greeted his parent's butler with a strong tone. He was about to take this game to the extreme and he hoped that Evelyn was ready to play.

"Mr. Slade." The man addressed him and then addressed Evelyn with a calm tone before closing the car door. Jackson led Evelyn up the front steps but stopped her before going inside.

"I won't leave you alone." He winked at her and smiled. "…Promise."

"I appreciate that." She told him as the front door opened to reveal a tall woman with wavy auburn hair that touched the middle of her back.

"Jackson," She cried out gleefully. "It has been too long." She hugged him with her eyes looking directly at Evelyn in question.

"Quit fawning all over the boy, Trisha." A deep scolding tone followed the hug that looked to be quite genuine. Evelyn was pleased to see the woman in the portrait on the stairs did indeed love something in her life.

Evelyn looked down noticing Nicholas had grasped her hand and was now holding it for dear life. Her fingers grew numb quickly as the blood severely cut off. She gasped softly making him turn slightly to look at her.

"Nice to see you again, Jack." The man addressed his son with a robust voice. Pride deeply embedded in the tone, but not upon his face. Nicholas scanned Evelyn's gaze, looked downward and then weakly grimaced, his eyes saying he was sorry, his hand letting up on hers but not releasing it. It was apparent that she wasn't the only one that was nervous about this evening.

Nicholas introduced her to his parents and before they turned to enter their home, she tugged his arm until he stopped walking pausing to look at her. Evelyn searched his wavering blue eyes and smiled softly as she leaned in, grazing his cheek with a light kiss. His gaze scanned her facial features before a hint of a smile appeared upon his lips.

"I won't leave you." Their eyes danced back and forth while she added,

"...Promise." To her heart felt offer.

**

A promise made, only to be broke right after the dinner that was nothing but an inquisition between the Slade's, and

Evelyn.

"Why don't we let the women talk a bit?" Elliott questioned, as all four of them meandered into the parlor. Their house was half the size of Nicholas' with less rooms and less art and décor. The parlor offered a bar, three chairs and a sofa all leather and very elegant. The rugs were of the orient and the Ming vases were of the same. A few paintings donned the walls, but there were no family portraits anywhere, not even ones of Nicholas through his years of growing up.

Evelyn found the house to be very sad and dark, it bothered her, but she didn't know why.

At the older man's suggestion she felt her body jerk in shock. Her eyes immediately met Nicholas' soft gaze.

"I'd like to go over a few things in the office." His father added to make his son move in the direction he wanted.

Jackson didn't want to leave Evelyn alone with his mother, but he had no choice. To offset her fear and his own hard beating heart, he stepped to Evelyn, pulled her head up and kissed her warmly, softly upon her mouth. The embrace was so elegant she felt her heart stop and her belly fill with butterflies.

Nicholas had been a gentleman all evening. Sat beside her at the table, but did not touch her not even to kiss lightly on the cheek. Evelyn was beside herself when his mouth caressed hers in a way that hadn't happened thus far. The kiss was soft and very respectful, but full of passion as it drew to a close. His blue eyes danced around, the left side of his mouth lifted and he touched the tip of her nose with his finger.

"Be right back." He told her in a whisper.

"Nich…" She called out but his finger stopped her short.

"Right back," He promised and then stepped away from

her.

Horror filled Evelyn as she turned to face Mrs. Slade.

"Jackson mentioned you work." Mrs. Slade slowly entered the parlor.

"Come on in," *Said the spider to the fly.* "Sit down. Would you like something?"

Evelyn shook her head. "No, thank you. Yes. I own my own company. Satin & Lace," Evelyn stated trying to save face, gain a little points, she could tell that Mom was not impressed at all. In fact Mrs. Slade appeared to be appalled by her working at all but instead, the woman was looking sharply over at her with scored eyebrows that almost touched.

"Underwear," Her bright eyes darted around the room before looking right at Evelyn once more. "You're…an underwear salesman?" The undertone in her voice was crystal clear to Evelyn.

"Lingerie," Evelyn corrected.

"Bread is *still* bread, no matter how you slice it dear."

Mrs. Slade walked elegantly to the bar, pulled the top from a liquor bottle and then looked over at Evelyn who hadn't sat down yet. The negative energy in the room was too much for Evelyn to sit idle in a chair. "Would you care for a drink?"

"No thank you," Evelyn stated and then added, "I'm not much into drinking." Hoping that would be something worth passing on. It was obvious not much pleased her.

Evelyn eyed Mrs. Slade's long flowing gown. The pale blue did wonders for her dark hair color and high cheekbones. Trish's face was lightly colored. She stood at the liquor cabinet for some time, pondering something before she poured out her drink. Her flaring eyes then turned to Evelyn. Had Mrs. Slade taken offense? Evelyn hadn't meant that she looked down on those who enjoyed a drink now and then.

"My son drinks a lot. Do you look upon him as an alcoholic as well?" Evelyn tried to remain as calm as she could to answer the woman. Her *son* uses alcohol for release, to help settle his nerves. It was a vice she had hoped he'd kick before it became something more. He certainly was *not* an alcoholic!

"Nicholas needs another form of release is all," She turned away from Mrs. Slade while she continued softly, "I never implied he was or is an abuser of alcohol." She then faced the woman with caring eyes. "I'm sorry if you thought I did."

"You think you can control him?" Mrs. Slade snickered evilly, shaking her head all knowingly. "Jackson has done what he wants for a very long time. *You can't change him.*" The last, spoke with unequivocal assurance that was set in stone.

"I don't *plan* on changing him. He's fine, just the way he is." Which was the truth there wasn't much about her *son*, she didn't like. *There in itself, lies the problem.* Evelyn thought briefly before she looked up at her soon to be mother in law.

"How long have you known Jackson?"

Evelyn took a deep breath as she walked over to the farthest window away from Mrs. Slade trying to get space between them so she could breathe better but it didn't matter where she went, the undercurrents that lingered between them were thick and dark.

Evelyn eyed her own reflection in the glass before she answered. She and Nicholas had spent a lot of time together hashing and rehashing out the details of their relationship. Talking about personal things one would know about their lover and soon to be spouse.

"It's been just a little over a year." She replied to the woman. Evelyn didn't like the lie but Nicholas insisted that was the only way. A cab ride, like she suggested would never do. So she gave her answer and let it go. Hoping Mom would do the same but…Obviously *Mom* had wanted more details.

"Where did you meet?" Once more, the woman's underlying tones thickly laced with dislike.

Evelyn bit her tongue closing her eyes to go over the story once more before it came out of her mouth. "We met at a convention." She answered softly.

Mrs. Slade chuckled vehemently, "An underwear convention…no doubt."

Her snide reply bit into Evelyn and anger she didn't even know lived in her soared through the air as she came right back with, "Actually it was a modeling convention. He'd mistaken me for a model." Again Evelyn was trying to make points, but suddenly realized the error of her ways when Mrs. Slade laughed aloud, making fun of the thought she had just imagined in her head.

"A model," She gasped harshly. "You *must* be joking!"

Evelyn turned to watch as the other woman scaled her from top to bottom with heated gazes and then burst out with laughter once again. "With *those* thighs," She shrugged, evilly eyed Evelyn and then added, "Jackson must have been ill because you must have 20lbs. over *any* model I've ever met!"

Her words cut deeply into Evelyn's chest. The woman just called her fat! In retort she snapped right back feeling heated from head to toe and not really comprehending why. Why did she care what this woman thought, but… *she did care*! It hurt and angered her to think this woman could be so cruel and hurtful.

"Nicholas doesn't seem to have a problem with my thighs!" Evelyn announced rhetorically. In fact, he seemed quite pleased with her shapely legs, she'd noticed as she came down the stairs earlier that night just how pleased he was with her appearance.

Mrs. Slade laughed again but this time with malice. "He's a man. He likes women. *Any* woman will do." Her bright eyes flared at Evelyn as to add affliction to her words. "Don't be fooled into believing he cares of you, Evelyn. You're just a means to get him what he treasures and that my dear is his money."

The last of that statement was double sided and placed carefully so that she would not get the idea that he would somehow treasure her more than his namesake. She even gave pause to help emphasize what Mom truly trusted of her son. Maybe Mrs. Slade was hoping for a response from Evelyn but not getting one and then went on to further nail the stake into Evelyn's heart by asking,

"Did he tell you he was marrying you for his inheritance? He doesn't love you."

Mrs. Slade's powerful gaze grew wicked with darkness, giving Evelyn a cold chill. She wrapped her arms around herself to keep the shivers at bay. Confusion filled Evelyn fast, making the room spin uncontrollably.

"He never will, my dear." She assured her with an all-knowing grin that sunk deep into Evelyn's soul. "Take it from someone who knows." She added gruffly, bringing her glass to her thin lips and drank down the liquor inside. She quickly poured out another, pausing to look Evelyn's way with tender, caring eyes, which seemed to knock that stake she was so determined to put in Evelyn's heart; all the way through.

"Sure you don't want one?" Evelyn again shook her head

in answer, uncertain if she should say anything to the woman who obviously was in pain. "Given time... you'll need this as *much* as I."

"Things look great Jack," Nicholas' father had walked into the parlor right about that time.

"Numbers should be much better, but..." Jackson was saying as they entered the doorway. Noticing the tension in the room the moment he and his father walked inside the door.

His mother was at the liquor cabinet, drinking as usual. Evelyn was standing in the corner by the window looking severely abashed.

"What have you two been talking about?" Elliott asked full of concern, obviously feeling the tension as well. Evelyn didn't even acknowledge they'd come into the room but her eyes shot up and Jackson felt his chest tighten up when her brown eyes glazed over.

"I'd like to go." Her voice cracked and her legs quivered slightly when she took a step towards the door, towards Jackson.

Immediately he reached out for her arm and nodded in answer without question as to why she suddenly wanted to go, sensing her need to depart.

"Thanks for dinner." He told his parents.

"Yes!" Evelyn stopped midway to the front door, her manners coming in to play. "Thank you it was nice meeting you." She told both of them, not meaning it in the slightest.

8

Evelyn accepted his hand as he led her to the car that was out front waiting for them to emerge from the house. He didn't ask what took place inside with his mother. He wasn't sure he wanted to know. He shut the door and then leaned against the front seat.

"Hey, Walter..." He spoke softly as the driver sat behind the wheel. "I feel like something sweet. Let's go to 'Freddie's Dippin Spot'." He told the driver then settled back in the seat.

Evelyn closed her eyes the moment Nicholas was right next to her taking her into his embrace, holding her. The heat of his hand running up and down her arm felt good. He felt good. Instantly her mind went to his mother's cruel words of warning. Had she been warning her? It felt that way.

Mrs. Slade's words really shouldn't bother her. Which confused Evelyn the most because, they did. His mother's words bothered her very much, despite having already known what had been told, Nicholas didn't love her, wasn't going to love her, it was not news. They were lying, to everyone and suddenly things were being tangled up in the weave of lies and she wasn't sure which way was up. *Why did she feel like crying her eyes out? Her chest was so heavy with burden. He didn't love her...Never love her...*

**

They watched as the bright yellow ball, rolled up the embankment and down the slide, across the bridge and slowly roll to the hole in the green.

"It's going, going..." Jackson watched as the ball rolled right to the edge of the cup and then abruptly stopped.

"...Uh!" Evelyn gasped as she stared at her dead ball. It was so close, right on the edge. "Do you see that?" She asked him. "How close can one get?"

Jackson walked over to the ball and softly popped it with the end of his club sending it into the hole. He smiled. "Great shot..."

"What'd you do that for?" She questioned him biting on her bottom lip.

"It was a great shot." He told her picking up her ball and handing it to her. "Don't expect me to let you get away with that every hole." He warned.

They'd been at the ice cream parlor well over an hour. They ate some ice cream at a table, watching a group of kids playing on the playground in front of them and now they were at the tenth hole on the mini golf course.

He was a stroke down but he kept giving her a break, on the last hole her ball ended up in the water. Nicholas gave her only three strokes rather than four. Playing golf had never been her favorite pastime as a child and hadn't had the desire to play as an adult. He wasn't very good at the game, telling her he wasn't much of a player either, but they were having a great time.

"Are you cold?" He asked her as they settled on the bench after their game.

He finally gave up the ghost and pulled off a hole in one on the seventeenth hole, and passed her by three strokes.

"Not really." The air was breezy but not chilly. She looked down at her pink dress and giggled. She recalled the looks the attendant gave them when they walked up for their clubs. Her pink dress was not quite the attire for golfing.

She looked up when she felt him touch her chin softly. When her eyes fell onto his deep blue stare, she felt warmth fill her that hadn't been there. It started where her mouth turned up into a bright smile and traveled down her body, all the way to her toes.

"Should have never taken you there," He said softly.

"I'm fine." She replied to his concern. *And, she was fine.*

He nodded. "Now," He shook his head.

"I had to meet them." Evelyn stated truthfully.

"Yeah, But I should have waited."

Evelyn got up, removed her stiletto heels so she could walk along the trim on the golf course in front of them. "It's over. I'm kind of glad it's over. I won't have to do that again, right?"

Jackson watched her small feet slowly walk the wood trim. Her toes hugging the side of the wood as she went along. He wanted to tell her no, ease her mind, but it wasn't true but he didn't want her smile to disappear and by telling her the truth, he was certain her smile wouldn't be the only thing to leave. He didn't want to face the truth just yet. When the time was right, he'll ease her into the truth... *when* that time comes.

In the next few days that passed, nothing seemed different for Evelyn. She woke up, went to work, did her daily routine and then went to a different home to sleep. He didn't interfere with her work and she didn't interfere with his. They sometimes ate together in his large dining room, sometimes they ate alone.

**

"Why don't you come with us?" Keli asked Evelyn Friday before leaving.

The girls were going out to a nightclub and wanted her to

go. She used to go with them but… what can she do, she was getting married. Surely, Nicholas wouldn't want her in a night club. She had to act like his fiancée.

"I can't." Evelyn declined even though she wanted to go.

"Call Jackson, have him meet us there." Keli suggested.

"I'll think about it." Evelyn told her watching Keli leave and then proceeded to remain right in her chair just staring at the phone. Would he want to go out? Finally, she lost the battle and lifted the phone.

Oliver answered the house phone and told her Mr. Slade has not yet gotten home. Disappointed she hung up and started for the door when she wondered if she should call his cell.

"Yeah," Nicholas answered in a deep drawl. He sounded tired.

"Nicholas?" Evelyn spoke softly, not wanting to interrupt his work. There was a brief silence on the other end of the line.

"Mm, Evelyn." He chuckled. "Please call me Jackson. I had no idea who it was at first." He laughed more. "This is a surprise."

"Are you busy?" She asked. "I don't want to interrupt your work."

"It's close to six. You aren't interrupting anything that can't wait. Are you home?"

"No, I was just leaving the office. Keli asked me out to a club, Well…" she paused. "She invited us to a club."

Jackson eyed the model in front of him with her silver beaded swimsuit and long sexy legs that flowed well over the runway she was walking on. She had a natural step that worked well with her swaying hips in her stiletto shoes.

He eyed her bouncing breasts as she strutted along, the suit dancing right along with her long strides in time with her long blond hair. Her long legs, thin, tanned and silky smooth, but too thin in his eyes. Her round bottom in the bikini didn't seem full and firm. Her bobbing breasts didn't appeal to him either but... maybe she would do better in a dress rather than a swimsuit.

What he was looking at just wasn't good enough. She needed firmer breasts, a plumper bottom to fill out that suit much more than she did. He suddenly waved her off the stage and stood up to leave himself. It was a long frustrating day that didn't get better, only worse. It was time to pack it in and go home.

"...Club?" He asked Evelyn over the phone as he recalled her words just a few moments ago.

"If you don't want to go..."

"No." He cut her off without thinking first. He normally didn't like the club scene at all. The girls were too clingy and the music was disco tech most of the time. He ended up drinking excessively and taking the prettiest thing he could find to the nearest hotel, *maybe with her*...

"I think that is just what I need right about now. The day has really been horrid. You want to meet at home or..."

"Why don't we just meet at the club?" Evelyn asked him. "We're already in the city." She coaxed him softly.

"Yeah, ok. Where will you be?"

**

Jackson finished up with work, sending models home. He then went into his office to change into something less stuffy. He briefly glanced at his reflection in the long mirror in his bathroom to make sure he fit the part of a clubber, before leaving altogether. His mind filled with ideas of canceling out, he really disliked clubbing. The only reason he found himself in the limo heading for the address Evelyn had given him was pure curiosity. She struck him as even less of a clubber then he was.

The music from the club was loud enough to hear from the streets. Jackson stood outside looking at the line of people trying to get inside. Most of them– girls with clothes that appeared to be bed attire they were so flimsy and sheer.

He took a deep breath, still debating whether he wished to go inside, telling himself this won't be the same. Evelyn was inside and she will buffer any unwanted solicitations. He'd be safe from the she lions he was witnessing out front.

Taking a deep breath, he headed for the line, smiling to the redhead standing at the end of the line in a tight shirt and vest outfit that trimmed her robust chest and curvaceous hips.

"Hi, I'm Brownie, would you like to sample my treats?" *Let the night begin*!

Inside the club were crowds clumped into groups. Some on the dance floor, some at tables, and others were at the bar and surrounding floor, all keeping within their group. If you were alone, then you were a target for unsavory offers such as Brownie's.

Jackson tried to find the group he would belong to but it was hard, he knew only one face and he wasn't sure how many was in the group he was searching for. He scanned the smaller groups at the bar and then jumped around at the ones at tables before finding her at the least likely spot... on the dance floor.

Evelyn was with a group of girls, laughing and dancing her heart out. Her face glowing with sparkling makeup that he'd never guessed her to wear a day in her life. Tight jeans hugged her swaying hips, her legs rocked back and forth to the music, not missing a beat with those tall heels she wore and then there was her top... Silver accents sewn to her royal purple blouse caught the flashing lights above, shimmering down her body like a spot light flashing on and off, signaling each, and every move she made with dances of their own. The bottom of the blouse danced precariously around with the waistband of her jeans. *What a sight!*

"Wasn't this a great idea?" Keli asked Evelyn while they danced to Prince's '1999'. Evelyn nodded her answer. It had been a long time since they'd gone out and she'd forgotten how much fun it was. Evelyn was a different person in nightclubs, it was a transformation that frightened her, the first few times it happened, but now, she welcomed the changes with open arms.

She felt the shifting the moment she was in the taxi. She felt her heart race at the sound of the music when she stood outside waiting to get in but, the second she was inside the club the transformation was complete, she was at home. Her inhibitions fell at the wayside and she felt free as a dove flying in the night. She was able to forget her past and the future and just, be.

She enjoyed her friends and the way they made her a part of their group. She hadn't had many friends growing up, not the kind of friends you told deep dark secrets to. She had plenty of those, and while out on a night like this, she was able to release some of them and not feel chastised in the slightest.

She felt much like she did when she'd made the first biggest decision and had gotten married. She was convinced she was doing the *right* thing back then and she felt so carefree and complete. Much like now, and it was strange that she compared the two when they were flip sides of a coin. Complete opposites of each other as any two things could be.

…But, *this* carefree freedom she felt was exactly the same and it felt wonderful all over again and she welcomed the sensation without recourse.

"We need to do this more often." Monica stated as she rounded Evelyn, bumping rear ends as she came up behind her.

"I agree!" Evelyn responded joyfully.

"You look much better." Keli revealed.

"And I feel better." Evelyn turned and bumped her bottom as they turned against each other.

Jackson felt his Adam's apple lodge right in the center of his throat when he saw Evelyn gyrate her hips against two other girls' fannies. Was that *his* Evie? He wondered as he watched her dance around without a care in the world. He scanned her from top to bottom with a strikingly onset of emotions.

First of which was to run up there and give a stop to those swaying hips that were triggering some other kinds of emotions not only in his lower regions, but in a few of the other men that were standing close to him.

"That one with the tight bun has got some awesome moves." One guy standing by the rail spoke to his friend.

"Yeah, I'm feeling her *all* over." His friend replied, grabbing his low riding jeans that were sagging at the hips and giving them a yank to correct his thickening body and licking his feverish mouth like an animal ready to pounce on its prey.

Jackson was about to spin and deck the man that was blatantly talking about his bride to-be when the music changed and people were coming off the dance floor. In the group just happened to be Evelyn and he was able to snag her before the other man who, was looking at her like she was a slab of meat, was able to.

"Oh Nicholas," She cried out with a smile he'd never seen on her face before. It was wild, carefree and very becoming of her. Her eyes lit right up and he found the anger that had been building, dissipating as her softness leaned right up against his hard frame. "You made it."

Wanting nothing more than to stake his claim upon her, Jackson pulled her in and kissed her softly upon those wet heated lips of hers. Letting the man next to them know that this filly was taken, hoping that the stranger was *feeling* that as well.

Evelyn pulled free from Jackson's hold. Her eyes scanned him briefly before turning away from him and heading to her table where her friends were waiting for introductions.

"Nicholas," Evelyn addressed him standoffish. "This is Keli, and Monica." Evelyn pointed to the right of the table.

"Ladies," Jackson smiled and nodded in a gentleman's way.

"Mr. Slade, it's really nice to finally meet you." Keli said with a big smile.

"Over here is Jasmine and Angie." Again, Jackson greeted them. "And in the middle sitting next to my chair is Raymona."

"You can call me Ray, all my friends do."

"It's nice to meet all of you." Jackson told them. "Please call me Jackson." Angie slid over to the empty chair, with Jasmine following right behind her.

"Have a seat." Jasmine padded the chair with a soft hand.

At that moment a waitress came to take some orders, but Jackson was the only one who passed on drinking anything at that time, he was busy looking at the White Russian that Evelyn was sipping through a straw while she and her friends ordered tequila shots.

"Wow, I love this song!" Angie gasped as she stood up.

"Let's go!" She tugged on Jasmine's arm to head to the floor for another dance session. Everyone but Jackson and Evelyn rose from their chairs. Keli stopped and eyed Evelyn.

"Coming?"

Evelyn had been sipping on her drink so she just shook her head, swallowing before saying, "No I'm going to sit this one out." Keli then moved her eyes to Jackson who caught her in his side view while he still eyed the liquor in front of Evelyn. He'd been watching the way her thin fingers twirled and circled her straw subconsciously. He snapped his eyes toward Keli who was waiting for him to notice her watching him.

"You want to dance?" She asked and Jackson shook his head, taking his arm, wrapping it around Evelyn's waist. Mentally noting how soft she was.

"I think I'll stay here with Evelyn."

"Ok." The moment Keli turned around and headed for the dance floor, Evelyn grabbed Jackson's hand and threw it off her waist. She spun around and glared at him.

"Stop it." She demanded. Jackson eyed her curiously. "Don't play games, Nicholas." She warned him. She should have never invited him! He was crashing in on her good time!

Jackson leaned in and said, "Call me Jackson." His eyes danced back and forth while they looked at each other.

"Stop it." She finally told him.

"We're in public, nothing wrong with what I'm doing." He cautioned her in a low warning voice. "Do you have a problem with it my dear?"

His blue gazes were bright with the devil inside. Evelyn knew better than to say anything about his forwardness in front of her friends. It would just make things worse, but she couldn't just let him think he was free to do whatever he wished.

She pointed her finger in warning. "Be careful, Nicholas." She told him with strong heated eyes.

He should have taken her words of advice, he told himself later in the evening. Because he should have been very careful, but he decided to play with her instead, he leaned forward, and took her pointed finger into his heated mouth and proceeded to suck on it.

Evelyn snatched it back saying, "You're the devil."

Jackson raised his big eyebrows and smiled making Evelyn turn away with a flushed face.

From that point on, the night was something like a roller coaster ride from hell. Evelyn couldn't concentrate on being herself, she was forced back into her shell which literally ticked her off. She refused dancing with Jackson when he asked her. She played tired with aching feet.

"I'll dance!" Jasmine announced. Happily, she got up and headed for the dance floor. Jackson was going to say no until he caught Evelyn's glare at her friend's back as she walked away from the table. He smiled and stood the rest of the way up and without pausing, strolled to the floor and proceeded to dance with Jasmine.

Once that dance finished, every time Evelyn said no to him someone else said yes and Evelyn grew more and more frustrated at her friends. Traitors! She grasped her head and took in a sigh.

"Can I get you anything?" The waitress asked her. Evelyn looked up.

"Shot of tequila." She responded in haste.

She shouldn't have, but she needed something to settle herself down. Her friends had abandoned her. All of them had danced with Nicholas and, were having a great time. Her great time was gone the moment he kissed her.

Instead of dancing and having a good time, she only thought about those sweet velvety lips, how wonderful they felt. He hadn't kissed her since that day in her room. A whole week and he didn't even touch her. *Was she* sorry? No! She was *craving* that's what she was and she was so angry with herself for abandoning herself in matters dealing with Nicholas.

How could she be so wonton about her body and hunger for things that should not be? She prayed endlessly with no answer in sight. Even God has abandoned her when it came to the affairs of the wicked!

**

"You went with Evelyn?" Raymona asked in the midst of their conversation. They were talking about the previous week getting things ready for the wedding that was now just a week away.

"Sure, why not?"Jackson asked.

He actually enjoyed watching her try on long elegant white dresses. It was a long and frustrating week, watching her beautifully fill out dress after dress. Satin and lace favored her delicate pale skin and he couldn't get the woman in her magazines out of his head. Would Evelyn look as sexy as her model did in her own lingerie? Once that question came to mind, many others accompanied it. He couldn't look at Evie and not picture her in satin and lace underwear, with the soft material kissing against her pale flesh. ...Absolutely beautiful... *absolutely agonizing*!

"Men usually don't help out." Angie told him.

"Oh." Jackson looked slightly amiss then said, "I enjoyed it." He then shrugged his shoulders.

"How long did it take to agree on colors and invitations?"

Raymona asked.

"Flowers," Jasmine added.

Evelyn and Jackson looked briefly at each other.

"Was a piece of cake," He replied, and it *was* she thought. Everything she suggested, he either agreed right away or would say, I think a lighter shade of that would be more fitting and he *was right!* The golden invitations she liked he toned down to beige with gold lettering and was the *perfect* touch. It was just what she had wanted only, couldn't see it with beige but, he was right and they looked fabulous with the embossed lettering and white roses with their long green stems. He even helped her address them.

He was also right with the flowers. She again wanted to do something bright with autumn colors. He pointed out the white orchids and said, "You wanted a white runner, with light yellow gold trimmings all around the church to coincide with the invitations, right?" She nodded in agreement.

"Why not go with something delicate and add lace to the trimming around the church. Orchids have a soft elegant fragrance and are very pretty in both white and gold."

His idea was not so bad after they sat down with the florist and actually looked through photos of different kinds of orchids until they found Bow Bells, an orchid with white petals and a golden throat. The shades will perfectly blend in with the church colors she had already chosen. She and Nicholas had actually bonded together and found common ground with what they both wanted. It had been a pleasant week as far as that went.

"It went fairly quickly." Evelyn added as she and Jackson eyed each other.

At that moment, a soft tune bellowed down from the big speakers. Jackson stood, taking her hand in his.

"Dance," It wasn't a request, it wasn't a question. It wasn't even a demand. It was a single word; uttered out of his mouth in a nonchalant form that made Evelyn stand and slip into his embrace on the dance floor.

"Thank you." Jackson spoke first. Evelyn shook her head.

"I figured if I didn't, one of the others would have jumped right up." She'd meant the dance, and he'd meant the last week they'd been talking about. He didn't clear the air.

"Is there something wrong with me dancing with your friends?" He asked her.

"Not at all," She replied hoping he didn't detect her lie. He looked like he was having the time of his life dancing with her friends, especially with Jasmine! At one time, he and Jasmine had danced a relatively somber dance that required a little body language and Evelyn hated to admit it killed her to watch them on the dance floor.

It was no secret that _all_ of her friends thought Evelyn had fallen off the onion truck, right into the lap of prince charming. They all thought he was the next best thing since the wheel. They all envied Evelyn, heck; even Evelyn envied herself! The man was knockout gorgeous, this she knew from the day they met. A day, she sometimes would like to kick herself in the rear for allowing him to share her ride, and other times, thanking the Lord above for her kindness.

Evelyn tensed right up when she felt his arm circle her waist and pull her against his tall frame. She wasn't sure if it was what she had been thinking about, or if it had been his actions that made her uneasy. When she felt his hard body graze against her while he led her over the floor, she pushed back.

"Nicholas…" She bit through her clenched teeth.

"Jackson." He replied in earnest, his bright gaze twinkling with delight.

"Stop being perverted. Can't you see you make me nervous when you do things like that?"

"I noticed." His eyes danced over her features while pulling her back into his space.

"Then why do," She began to ask.

"…why do you call me a name that, is not mine?" He cut her off. She gasped and looked away from his searing eyes that were burning into her skin.

"If I stop, will you stop?"

She humbly begged him and then flinched when his warm breath caressed her ear when he whispered, "I like to make you nervous. You're eyes dance with sensuality and desire I can't sway from, no matter how I try Evie." He shook his head pushing away from her, but still holding her tight while, they danced.

"You're the devil." The torte in her voice rang true of the anger she was holding back. She wanted to smack him, but couldn't here in public and his sneer told her he was counting on that.

"I've been called worse." He whispered in her ear, feeling her body tremble from his heated words. He wished they were home, in her room where he could end this torment she was putting him through. He'd spent most of the past week hard as a damn nail because of her.

"I'm sure you have. You're a despicable man. I can't wait to be rid of you!" She spat, pulling out of his arms and heading for the women's room.

Jackson remained on the dance floor watching her retreating frame as his body shook while he laughed inwardly. Rid of him, indeed! More like rid of the hungry gazes and lustful demands, he can't seem to harness for very long.

He felt the way her body swayed and melted in his arms

just then, and the shivers she experienced, when his whisper traveled the whole course of her spine like molten lava from a heated volcano. She was about to erupt and rid of him was the last place she desired to be.

9

"...Body shots!" Angie gave a yell and then strutted herself to the bar with a long line of pursuers hungry for what she was about to offer them. Evelyn was once again on the dance floor, but she was dancing with Keli while Jasmine again was dancing with Nicholas.

While Evelyn danced, she couldn't keep her eyes from straying to the couple on the dance floor right beside her and Keli. Jackson's silky black shirt clung to his back from the sweat and body heat he was creating with his dancing. The front, Evelyn couldn't keep her eyes focused on anything else. In fact, just about all of the women were getting an eye full of Jackson's hairy chest that shifted in and out of view through the opened shirt that was buttoned only midway.

She should have been happy that Jasmine was eager to dance with him since she herself didn't want to. Better her, someone she could trust then a complete stranger.

Once the dance was over, Evelyn hurried to the table and drank the last of her White Russian. While looking for the waitress, she spied Angie sitting on the bar, men all around her, taking turns at removing a shot of liquor from between her breasts. Angie's chest heaved out, her blouse opened up just a bit so the men could get to the shot a little easier. Angie's head hung back, laughing at the feel of the man's mouth against her flesh.

The crowd around them all chanting him on and then clapping when he actually retrieved the full glass from her bosom and tilted his head back to drink down the shot in one forceful gulp.

Evelyn gasped as she watched in a perplexed state of mind. Watching Angie's face light up when the man's lips touched her flesh in a very intimate way. Evelyn shifted in her seat as a heat built up within her, which confused her. She didn't understand where it came from or how to control it.

"Another drink," The waitress asked her and she nodded not taking her eyes from Angie's delightfully aroused body and suddenly felt a tingling sensation in her breast.

"I'm going next!" Raymona stated and jumped from her chair. "...Body shots!" Evelyn watched as Angie stepped down so Ray could take her spot. To her surprise, Ray did three before another girl took her place. By the last one, Evelyn's drink had arrived and she'd drank down more than half before the waitress could leave the area and she ordered another.

"Don't you think you've had enough?" Nicholas questioned so softly no one else heard his comment.

"Excuse me?" She argued standing up. "I don't tell you to slow down on the whiskey." She glared at him. "You will not tell me." She then raised her hand. "Body shots!" she announced as she approached the bar.

Angie grabbed her arm. "Are you sure?" She questioned.

Evelyn wasn't fond of the game her friends liked to play. She always frowned on the way it looked and how it must feel to be that close to a complete stranger.

Jackson's chest tightened right up when her voice rang out her announcement ...*what the hell was she up to, there was no way he was going to let her...*

Jackson almost stood right up from his chair but then stopped suddenly. What game was she playing now? All night she had glared at him for dancing with her friends and

104

even started glaring at Jasmine for getting too close to him, as it seemed. She was jealous. He'd seen it many times before. Women were always fighting over him, which was one of the reasons he hates clubs.

He'd been enjoying Evie's fits of jealousy and even chuckled at the thought. Her friends were nice and all very adequate in pleasing his sexual appetite but none of them really turned him on. Not like their friend did. *Not like, she did…*

He remained in his seat, watching Evelyn walk up to the bar in her cat like strut. She was trying to prove something, but to whom, him or herself. He fought with himself as she did so. *Calm down*, he told himself. *She's not going to do* it! He watched as she adjusted the front of her blouse as she settled on the bar, like all the others. *She is going to do* it!

Jackson wrenched himself from his chair, when the two men that had been watching her dance when he first arrived, got in line. Scathing with anger he started for the bar to stop her but he paused, watching the bartender hand over a shot glass. Suddenly he had a plan…

"This is not going down!" Jackson began hauling the men aside to get to the front of the line.

"Hey, jerk!" One fought him, but Jackson ignored him.

"If you don't back off," Jackson pushed another man out of the way. He was angry with Evelyn for giving these men reason to touch her in this manner. Angry, because he: would kill to be able to touch her, as she was about to allow a complete stranger to do but tonight… he was going to get his shot!

"Wait your turn." The bar keeper told Jackson.

"I am not allowing them near my fiancée." Jackson glared at first towards Evelyn and then to the men all standing around grumbling and ready to fight.

"She offered!" One shouted from the back.

Jackson nodded. "I don't care buddy."

"Stop it." Evelyn scolded Nicholas with hatred, her eyes questioning him. "How dare you!"

"How dare I?" He asked in surprise. "We're getting married next week. I should have a right,"

"Well you don't!" She snapped angrily although she was oddly happy he'd stopped her stupidity. What was _she_ thinking? This was crazy and here was her hero, rescuing her!

"You really want to do this?" His blue eyes danced back and forth with anger and something else she couldn't quite define. There was a catch in his tone, a threat of some kind. Would he call off the wedding? Her heart hammered in her chest unexpectedly. _Did she really want to call off the wedding, lose the family farm?_

"Yes." She found herself answering him in spite. He didn't have to be such a pig headed man!

"Fine," He replied defeated. His tone should have had sorrow or even a hint of rejection in it, but it did not. She didn't notice.

Instead of stepping away, he nodded and addressed the bartender, "Set her up for cherries jubilee."

Jackson stepped back while the bartender asked her. "Are you sure you want to do this?" Getting approval before things progressed.

Evelyn nodded. "Yes. Set me up, like he said."

Determined to pull this off despite her thudding heart, Evelyn allowed the bartender to lay her out on the bar, pull her blouse up a hair to reveal her belly button.

"Push your chest up and out." He told Evelyn and she did as directed and then bit on her bottom lip as the bartender handed her a maraschino cherry. "Place that between your breasts." He instructed her. Evelyn slowly slipped the fruit into the crevice that was wider than normal because of her unusual angle.

"Deeper." The bartender told her and then nodded when she had pushed the cherry deep into her bra. "Now, place this on top, cover the cherry completely." Slowly she placed the cold glass against her warm breasts, cradling the shot snuggly between her firm mounds. She then looked at the bar tender, breathing deeply while her heart started to hammer in her chest.

"Like this?" She asked him. Moans filled the area of the bar. Music still blared from the large speakers, but the crowds by the bar were silent.

The bartender nodded. "Lay still, don't spill it." He warned and then took the tequila, turning it upside down, pouring the contents out onto her flat stomach Evelyn giggled at the way it trickled down her skin.

"Careful." Angie told her. Evelyn looked over at her wondering if she could hear her thundering heart. Angie leaned down. "I like your new man." she whispered to her. "He's taken the shell right off your back."

Evelyn didn't have the time to question what her friend meant, because she jerked in fright when something cold was being placed into her belly button. Quickly her eyes went to the bartender in question, but he was busy filling up another shot glass. Evelyn darted her eyes to Nicholas who was standing right beside the bar, taking all of this in not too far from her. He was about to watch this from a front row seat.

Suddenly she no longer wanted to do this. Would he be angry with her? Would her desire to be herself kill her chances with him? Was *this* really worth it? Fear taking charge of her soul she started to move.

"Nich…" She cried out fearful for what she was about to do. He leaned forward.

"It's just a cherry, love." He answered her unasked question.

… *Just… a cherry*! Her heart hammered hard now and she felt faint. Why was he allowing this? *Please!* She closed her eyes in prayer. *Please don't let me do this! Please I'm sorry…*

Evelyn's eyes shot open the moment she felt something cold against her stomach. Three shot glasses full of liquor, was being placed on top of her navel, one glass right over the cherry and the other ones, on either side of it. Chanting began as it had all the other times. Fear made Evelyn's eyes close in heavy prayer once more, begging for a miracle to stop, this crazy, impetuous idea of hers.

"Nn…" Evelyn began to cry out when she felt a warm slick touch upon her stomach right beside the middle shot glass, trying to say no to the man who was touching her in this fashion, there was only one man…she wanted.

She closed her eyes tighter against what was taking place, shutting out the chanting still going on, but unable to shut out the twinge of heat that rode along her side, starting where the man had touched her. It was low at first, but grew more intense when the touches became more ardent and firm. A familiar groan sounded close to her ear. Soft and intimately focused upon the sudden tension that was filling the air around the bar.

Evelyn fought the wild sensations that started to filter into her body, this can't happen! *Nicholas was right there watcher her! Oh God, what had I* done? She cried to herself, trying desperately to block the wonderful tingling that was tickling her side now. Her breasts were starting to harden …*Was she liking this…OH MY GOD!*

Her eyes shot open and immediately went to the spot

where Nicholas was standing. She wanted to see nothing but his sweet handsome face. She wanted to whisper how sorry she was and *please, please forgive her!*

The spot, he'd been standing, was now occupied by someone else, watching, with hungry eyes. Nicholas couldn't handle it and had walked out! Had he walked away from her as well? Suddenly she lurched forward about to get up, go find him and beg for his forgiveness.

Sudden urges surged through Jackson so quickly he couldn't hold them all back. He clenched his fists at his side to prevent them from reaching out for her. Damn, it was hard to remain still! Not grab her off the bar and throttle her with his tight fists he was so angry at her stubbornness, but at the same time it was…*ambrosia!*

…she tasted so damn good! At the first touch with his tongue, he was lost in her taste, the liquor was nothing compared to her. He was so lost he concentrated on her flesh more so then the damn shot he was supposed to be taking. He dragged his tongue firmer against her side, up to the edge of the bottom of the shot and then let out a groan so deep and lustful, only she could have heard it; *and she did.*

He felt her body react to his touches despite her fighting it all the way. She didn't want to show how much she liked the way his tongue felt, didn't want to show the hunger he was bringing to life.

"No." She whispered. "Nich…" She cried and that's when their gazes met. At first disbelief, and then her eyes grew so big with understanding, her heart pounded against her chest at the thought of Nicholas' tongue dancing over her side and, not a stranger's. *It had been him all along!* Her heart sang in jubilee! *Oh… thank you Lord!*

Evelyn caught his dark blue gaze as he ran his tongue along her side, up to the glass, opened his mouth and slipped it in. The slow motion action made her heart stop, her legs twitch with yearning of being licked, just like her side. She watched him tilt his head back and swallow the liquor within. She ran her tongue over her dry mouth.

She'd never seen anything as hypnotic as when he slipped his tongue inside the clear glass, circling the shot, getting all of the contents before dropping it into his hand. He then smiled devilishly to her as he slipped downward, raising his eyebrows as he turned his heated stare to her writhing legs that still tingled with interest.

Damn! Jackson cursed as his eyes watched his minx move in front of his hungry eyes, tempting him with her sexy movements that drove him wild with want. ...Another week.

He wasn't sure he was going to make it.

Turning his hungry gazes away from her beautiful legs and the rocking vortex between them, he eyed the second glass, lifted it up in his mouth without touching it and downed the liquor, dropping it into his hand right beside the first.

Then quickly moving away from her musk-scented womanhood, Jackson went right to the first glass in line, the last that was still on her flat stomach and he repeated the act, drinking the liquor with one gulp, the glass clinking against the others when he dropped it in his palm. Carefully not touching the bar or Evie, he eyed her stomach and the treasure within.

"Nich..." Evelyn gasped when he planted his mouth right over her belly button. She clenched her throat tight to keep the moans that threatened to erupt from deep within. Her hips jolted upright when his tongue slipped into the liquor-filled hole, slipping around the cherry and deliciously caressed the flesh inside.

His touch inflamed her soul, she struggled to reach out for him but held still, unsure of how she was supposed to react to this wild act of emotions that were assaulting her from every angle there was. *Oh, she was on* fire!

Jackson took small liberties at her navel and then swept the cherry right out of its hiding spot.

The plucking of her cherry was her undoing. Twitching sensations filled the heated spot between her legs with uncontrollable spasms that triggered her whole body to respond. Her nipples grew instantly hard and ached for some kind of relief but neither was answered, because Nicholas was now moving up to the next shot, touching the skin around it once again with his tongue.

Jackson felt her jerk once more, knowing her body was reacting to this erotic way of getting her attentions. He'd done this with many girls but never had he ached, like he did for this one. He clenched his hands tighter fighting the urge to bring them to her body, to her breasts that were begging for his touch, to her quivering belly that hungered for more of what he was doing.

What he ached for the most, was to reach his hand up to those shapely legs that were laid out right in front of him, caress each one with equal attention and then yank them open so he could eat the center of her fruit scented core, until she screamed out his name. His *real...* name!

Jackson didn't waste a drop of this last shot as he lifted it up with his teeth, his lips grazing her flesh softly. Her scent, vanilla or something close to it made the ache in his groin a full-fledged throb, dull and oh so painfully hard to move.

He couldn't hold back the groan that filled his throat, a response similar to the one she made just moments ago. A groan generated from hunger, triggered by her beauty, a desire that can't be fed by her scent alone he could no longer withhold how she was affecting him. Because having her this way, was a better aphrodisiac then a crate full of damn oysters!

The glass fell to his hand just like the three before it and hunger fed his movements from there on out. He didn't pause a second. Not even to look at the woman lying in front of him. He leaned down, smoothed his mouth over her pale delicate skin and caressed ever so softly while his tongue darted out, licking the flavorful flesh like it was a lollipop. He heard another flutter in the back of her throat. She was purring for him again and he smiled over her warm breast while his tongue danced over the silky whiteness.

"So hot..." she breathed right into his ear. Jackson felt his groin take on a few more inches as her soft breath filtered into the crevices of his nerves and made him shiver with a chill. Damn...*why can't we be home? This was just a damn tease but it was so good... so hot.*

Jackson took a deep whiff of her vanilla scented skin one more time before he expertly slipped further down into the valley between her breasts, sliding his wet tongue over her flesh, around the treasure he sought and then with his teeth pulled out the cherry by the short stem. Without a moment's hesitation, he stood up, pulling Evelyn upright into the sitting position. Instantly she swayed from lightheadedness, but he was fast to catch her and wrap her into his embrace.

Clapping and whooping was all about them, all he could see was Evie, her flushed face and those damned bedroom eyes of hers and he was gone... He slid downward, touching her chin with his fingers, raising her head to look deep into her beautiful gaze. She smiled softly as he lowered to place his waiting mouth against hers.

"Mm..." Evie groaned, leaning against his frame for support as she willingly opened her mouth to deepen the kiss and was greeted with the cherry he'd kept for her. Her mouth creased as her smile widened, taking his offering without care. She pushed away, looking slightly amiss as she felt her face heat up, knowing that her whole body was at the boiling point. She chewed the fruit as she chuckled in a giddy way. "That was so unfair." Her eyes creased a little more when he raised her chin up.

Her eyes danced over his handsome face when he smirked and replied with, *"You telling* me!" He shifted his pants to adjust himself without caring that she could see his particular problem. She giggled again. "Glad you find my pain hilarious." He retorted in jest.

The crowd around the bar began to dissipate leaving them alone to continue their private talk. Evelyn couldn't take her eyes from the bulge in his pants if God himself had struck her down. His predicament wasn't in the least bit funny, but it was completely thrilling for her. It was a first, not that she was ever going to admit to that. *Especially to him!*

"Will you excuse me?" She asked him trying to get off the bar. Jackson grabbed her by the waist and helped her to the floor. Her eyes scanned his face as she struggled in standing before she started towards the women's room.

"Hey." Keli grabbed Evelyn by the arm and walked with her. "Are you ok?"

Evelyn nodded. "That was…wild."

Keli laughed. "Yeah, it sure was. I think you've had way too much to drink. I'm glad it was Jackson who took your body shots." She told Evelyn as they rounded the corner where the lighting was a bit dimmer and groups of couples were against the wall taking advantage of the privacy the bathrooms allowed. A small partition closed off the bathrooms giving each door a secluded entrance.

"You seemed to enjoy it enough." Keli told her as they

walked into the bright bathroom. The light hurt Evelyn's eyes and she squinted.

"It was so embarrassing." She told Keli as she took the nearest stall.

"I was skeptical about him and you at first, but you make a real cute couple. It's cute how you get all jealous of us when we dance with him."

Evelyn scrunched up her face in thought. Was she jealous? She shook her head, unsure of anything, but the way Nicholas' mouth seemed to ignite her entire body, not just the skin he'd been touching. *My… she could still feel* it!

The heat of his tongue felt so silky hot it made her burn inside. She wondered how it would feel if he touched her where she tingled the most. She shuddered at the mere thought. She felt heated to the core and looked up towards the ceiling. *I'm so sorry for acting this* way! *What in the world has gotten into me lately*? She wondered but knew if she kept it up, she was going straight to hell! She closed her eyes and started to pray for her sinful acts of late. Maybe it wasn't too late and she can redeem herself.

"I'm heading back out, are you ok?" Keli asked her.

"Yeah, I'm fine."

"You sure… not queasy, gonna get sick?" Keli asked leaning against her stall door.

"No." Evelyn shook her head, was she drunk?

"Okay then." Then there was silence.

Evelyn looked around the stall. Her vision was slightly blurry and she wasn't queasy, lightheaded but nothing more. She wasn't drunk, just very giddy. Her fingers deftly touched her belly where Nicholas' mouth and tongue had scorched her. She closed her eyes recalling the way it felt. Heat, unbelievable heat came from the spot.

She'd been branded! Her fingers dipped in between her

114

breasts where he'd also touched her with titillating caresses of his tongue that sent chills all down her spine. Both spots were heated and hungry for more of what she knew he could do for her, if she asked. *Should she* ask? Her heartbeat quickened and a loud banging from the big speakers gave her answer.

"...Oh...To have that mouth on my body..." a woman's exasperated tone filled the silent bathroom, making Evelyn jump in surprise she almost called out when another voice answered the first.

"I *have* had the pleasure once..." A higher pitched tone responded and then two stall doors slammed and bumped to a close as the occupants took their closed in chamber.

"... When my boss was going out with him..." The woman continued with her confessions of sin.

A short gasp filled the stall to Evelyn's right. "You were seeing him when he was dating your boss?"

"Honey... he is way too hot to *date* anyone...If you get my meaning. They went out a few times."

"He is so dreamy..." Came from the other stall and then the doors opened up and they both came out giggling.

"Why do you think I said yes when he asked me out that one time?"

The running water as they washed up filled the room but didn't block the words Evelyn heard last.

"It was years ago but man... those lips on my body left an after burn that lingers today. So hot..."

"That girl on the bar is so lucky."

"Yeah...Luc...ky!" More of their giggling erupted into the room before they walked out leaving Evelyn alone to ponder over their conversation, who they had been talking of.

10

Jackson had propped himself against one of the unoccupied walls of the 'private room' just outside the bathrooms and waited for Evelyn to come back out. He began to get worried when a lot of time slipped by and still she hadn't come back out. Just as he was about to go get one of her friends to check on her... there she was.

"Are you all right?" He questioned taking her arm with his fingers. Evelyn nodded feeling heat generate from the slight touch of his hand. She looked at him. The room was dim but not dark enough where she couldn't see his concern.

She smiled. "Afraid I'd slipped out the window on you?" She giggled softly, covering her mouth as she did, recalling the way those woman giggling just moments ago.

"Course not. Are you okay?"

Again, she nodded. Her eyes looked into his blue stare and suddenly she heard his mother saying he cared not for her in the slightest and never would. She couldn't believe how that made her sad. It was obvious they had some kind of attraction or else that little bar scene would not have happened. Even though she was cautious about that same attraction, it's what made her sincerely look at him. *He was incredibly gorgeous! It was no wonder what he did to her body!*

She shivered at the thought of lying in his bed, as she had on the bar and her memory working her senses as his mouth had worked over her entire body. Would she still feel the heat years later, as that one woman suggested?

"Are you sure you're okay?" He asked her once more. She

looked peaked and fretful. Maybe the alcohol was starting to take serious affect. Maybe he needed to take her home.

"What we did on the bar."

He heard her murmur softly. Jackson paused as he looked at her. He swallowed as he saw how fidgety she suddenly became.

"It was wonderful." She whispered and then giggled even though she hadn't meant to. All of a sudden, she felt like a fool and turned away from him, heading back to the safety of the women's room.

Jackson snagged her arm in a tighter grip and whirled her around, sidling her into the corner. His eyes scanned her face then slowly slid downwards. His fingers followed his eyes, running a soft trail over her blouse until he was lightly touching her side. The spot immediately ignited and she gasped, taking a deep breath.

"I agree." He whispered against her cheek. "It *was* wonderful." *He'd never experienced anything like it.*

He flicked his tongue out and touched the tip of it to her face. He closed his eyes at the taste and scent of her as she filled his senses.

"To feel your trembling body as I tasted you made me quiver myself." He gasped as he spoke right against her, his mouth moving and tickling her skin. "I could hardly keep my hands off you." He paused again, allowing her to take in what he was saying. What *was* he saying?

All he knew was he was glad their paths had crossed and he was struggling in ways to keep her, no matter what he had to do.

"Do you know how much I want to kiss you right now?" He asked her. She shook her head. "Let me taste those sweet lips like I have already tasted your body." He requested as his mouth lightly caressed her face. He brought his hand up to graze her chin, lift it so he could reach her beautiful mouth without effort. His fingers played softly across her throat...*and she* purred!

Jackson groaned and leaned against her in agony. "God, please let me taste your mouth."

Evelyn turned her head closer to him, her eyes searching him as he closed in to take what she had offered. Ever so slowly, he lowered to meet her lips. The softness of his mouth touched hers briefly, before his hands grasped her shoulders, and rake her in, taking the kiss to a deeper level.

She closed her eyes against the sweet taste of his lips. Her belly twisted around into tight knots. Her knees weakened, but he held her against the wall, in the corner and proceeded to pulverize her mouth with his own.

Kiss after sweet kiss and when his tongue grazed her lips her body began to sway, leaning more into him and her mouth opened for his entry. Her belly twisted some more. Bringing her arms up to his shoulders and before she knew what was happening, she was drawing him closer to her frame.

Pulling, tugging on his shoulders until there was no room between them. His frame leaning against her while she remained glued to the corner. Her hands spanned out, flexing over his wide shoulders and then...tightened their grip as Nicholas laid completely on her in the corner.

Every inch of him was touching every inch of her with legs rubbing against legs. His hardened body gyrating against her inflamed midsection, moving in unison to his soft probes unlike she'd ever done before with a man. *She was on fire... AGAIN!*

...But this time, he was touching her with his hands and his mouth. The sensations that rippled through her were *fantastic*!

Evelyn purred again when Jackson smoothed his hand over her belly, and in minutes brought his hand higher. Wanting to explore the firmness, take her fullness into his palm and gently squeeze, but unable to control himself, his fingers sought out her hardened tip and gave it a soft tweak. The instant he felt her against his hand his mouth covered hers with severe kisses, dipping his tongue into her mouth repeatedly.

Heated down to the core, needing to taste her skin, he released her mouth so he could tantalize her throat. Jackson nipped and sucked at her flavorful flesh all around her neck, nibbling on her ear with impassioned strokes of his tongue while he also sucked the lobe into his mouth, thankful for once that her hair was up in a bun, he didn't have to fight with it to get it out of the way. Her neck was free for the taking, he took much liberty there.

Evelyn felt her body react to this man as he sampled what he wanted. She did not stop him, *couldn't* stop him at this point. She was so *hot* and it felt so *good*. She arched slightly against the hand that knew exactly how to bring sweet relief to her aching nipple, wishing he would switch to the other that was begging for the same release.

His fingers twisted just right, pulling perfectly it sent a jolt all the way down to her core and her hips moved in reaction. It was a brazen act for sure, one that did not go unnoticed, thrusting his hips, meeting her with the bulge between his legs. Her body grew hotter in that region.

"Did you feel my tongue graze this area right here?" He asked in her ear, his finger softly tugging her hard nipple.

"Mm." she responded.

"Wish I could flick my tongue over it right now." He gruffly stated.

"Taste you, take it in and suck it like a lollipop." He

119

kissed her ear and drew the skin right behind it into his mouth, demonstrating how it may feel to have his mouth on her nipple.

Heat roiled her body. Consuming her from head to toe, there was no getting around what he was doing to her. She tried to push it away, but his sweet touches and kisses only made it worse. She stiffened her throat, but the moans still found a way out.

"So hot..." She murmured into the space between them. His teeth grated against her throat while his mouth continued to torture in sweet agony.

How on earth, can one body feel heated and chilled at the same time was beyond her but a succession of chills enthralled her when his hand dropped down between them, his fingers slipping over her jeans. His hand cupping her in the center of her heated core where she thought, the touch of her would scorch his hand but instead of pulling away from pain, he pushed in, applying sweet pressure against her.

"Careful." Jackson whispered into her ear when her knees slightly gave out.

He hadn't meant to take this interlude so far but he couldn't resist. She felt and tasted so good and he needed her so much. Damn he wished they were home! Home and in his bed where he could thrust his hard flesh into the heat he was feeling with the palm of his hand.

Deftly he slid his fingers against the denim and sighed right with her at the feeling they both got from it, *Instant* heat._ She shivered at the pressure he applied between her legs, thrusting upwards, trying to break through the material to get to her.

"Evelyn?"

Her name echoed into her brain, but all she could concentrate on was Nicholas' hand between her legs. If it weren't for her jeans, his fingers would have been inside her…if only the pants weren't there! She never wanted anything more than to feel him inside her!

"There you are. Oh. Sorry." Jasmine turned away in respect of what she had interrupted between Jackson and Evelyn.

Nicholas' body completely covered Evelyn's, *thank you god*!

Jasmine couldn't see what he'd been doing, only that they were necking. Making out, with his mouth planted onto her throat, her hands gripping for dear life onto his shoulders, but Jasmine did not see where Nicholas' hand was.

"We're getting ready to head on out." Jasmine was telling her as the two of them suddenly came apart. Evelyn felt as if she had been doused with cold water except for the tingling that continued to excite her heated core where he'd been touching her.

"Okay." Evelyn nodded.

Jasmine raised her upper lip and grimaced. "Sorry to interrupt."

Evelyn came out of the corner in a snap. She shook her head but Nicholas was the one to speak.

"Ah. No worries."

Evelyn's head jerked up and her angered stare penetrated him deeply, she then stated gruffly. "We need to head home as well. I have had way too much to drink."

"We had a great time." She told them both. "Loved the bar scene!"

Jackson grabbed Evelyn's hand, stopping her from following her friend. Evelyn spun on him and glared. Without saying a word, he released her, watching, as the two women strut away.

**

"You're upset." Jackson had waited a few silent minutes after getting in the car before he decided this was not the way he wanted the night to end, he'd rather they go home, take up where they were so rudely interrupted and end his torment once and for all.

"How can you tell?" She snapped.

"Cause you haven't spoken since we were,"

"Stop," She told him, her eyes hazed over with such anger. Was she mad at him or herself?

"I'm not going to apologize." He told her...Hell no!

"I'm not asking you to!"

"Then *what* do you want me to say?" He questioned in anger. Evelyn's eyes lost all anger when they suddenly filled with tears. Jackson felt his chest rip open ...Damn it!

"I can't control it anymore." He finally admitted. Their eyes met and he wanted to pull her into his arms and just hold her. He watched a single tear run down her cheek. "Don't Evie." He reached out and rubbed her cheek, she pushed him away.

"Talk to me." He whispered to her. He watched her body pull away from him. He was sitting across from her because he knew she didn't want him near her when they left the club. *Man* he wanted to shove her over and slip right in beside her, hold her. Kiss her...

"You didn't stop me." He remarked and then begged, "Talk... to... me." He caressed her knee as he watched her look out the window.

Minutes passed while they rode in silence. She refused to talk about it, he wasn't about to force her. He sighed and sat back, removing himself from her and her space as much as he could without getting out of the damn car.

"This can't happen again." He heard her whisper. His eyes left the window to look at her. A big tear fell down her cheek. He swallowed hard as he watched it roll downward.

"You must promise me." She raised her eyes to look at him with sincerity.

Evelyn struggled with her demons until she no longer could hold them in. What she'd allowed this man to do to her in public appalled her to the extreme. *This* was *not* a relationship! He was not her real fiancé and she was not to act as such in any way!

All of this was a lie. A game, of which if she started playing for real, she will lose much more than her heart. Mrs. Slade's voice screamed out at her. 'This was only for his money. He won't love you. Take it from someone who knows.' The woman had practically warned her of her son's in-discretions.

"Please." She begged him. "Promise,"

Jackson couldn't agree any longer. No matter what the outcome he wasn't going to lie about this. He shook his head. "I'm sorry..." and for once, he truly was. He'd finally found him a woman he couldn't keep his mind off of much less his hands. He wanted her, end of it *and he was going to have* her!

"You *must* promise Nicholas." She begged him. "I can't,"

"No." Jackson cut in. His eyes danced over her sweet face. "I'm not going to agree to that." Her tears came effortlessly now. "I can't!" He yelled at her.

"No, it's me that can't!" she argued right back. "A lady shouldn't allow," She tried to say but shame filled her, stopping the words, cutting off her throat. "It's not real." She cried out. "This is *not* real. I am a lady!" She told him.

"The hell you say!" He replied as the car came to a stop at the house. Evelyn's gasp filled the space between them the moment he'd said his retort. The air filled with dismal emotions and she snapped a horrified look at him for a brief second before jumping from the car before Oliver had the chance to open the door.

"Shit!" Jackson growled as he also left the car. "Evelyn!" He called running to catch her.

She avoided the house, trying to keep him from catching her, she ran out into the yard deep into the gardens that hid her well into the shadows. Gasping he stopped by a cypress tree.

"It's not what I meant..." He called out. "Evelyn?" He started to look under the tree to see where she might have gone. There was only one-way into the gardens so she was trapped, "What I feel when I touch you *is* real." He spoke softly "That's what I meant..." He coaxed, "Come on out, Evie. Please..." but she did not. "I'm not leaving until we talk about this." He told her.

"I don't want to talk, Nicholas." Her voice traveled little, he grinned. She wasn't too far from him. Slowly he walked around the rose bushes and sighed when he found her leaning against the marble statue of a horse.

"What we both feel is real." He told her as he approached the horse.

She turned her head to look at him. "*We* are not *real*, Nicholas!" she yelled at him. "You and I and this *game* we are playing, is *not* real!" She choked back her sobs. She felt so drained. She wanted to feel his mouth upon hers again and feel the realness of his passion. Yes, that was real, but this, she looked around, was not. She was only here for a short time. Truth not fiction, it was killing her inside to know the truth.

"The way we ignite each other is real, Evie."

She shook her head no. "That's not real, that's lust." Sweet and endless lust that made her crave the things she couldn't have. "Please," She begged him. "I'm not strong like you."

"Who says you have to be?"

Oh God! She closed her eyes.

"It's okay to want me. We will be married next week." He pointed out. "Is that it?" He asked softly. "You want to wait until we are truly wed before you give in to me?" That *was* it, he decided for her. She was put out from all of these emotions because they weren't really allowed to have such desires yet. She was ashamed about the way she felt and shamed to explain herself completely.

"Okay." He put his hands up in defeat. "You win. I will back off." He promised ...*Until after the wedding*! Surely, he can wait just a few more days!

* *

"Right now?"

Jackson should have stepped away from the library when he heard her voice but he didn't. Desire rooted him right where he stood. They both had avoided contact with each other all damn week. She worked late and he ate out just to avoid being close to her. He'd promised, but it was hard. He laid in bed every night, thinking about the way she would melt in his arms on their wedding night, a night in which he awaited patiently.

His memory worked overtime forcing him to rehash everything about her. The way she shuttered beneath his hand when he palmed her heated core over her jeans. The way her body flamed up at the touch of his mouth to her neck and the way she arched when he pulled on her hard nipple kept him awake every night with wanting her. It was a damn miracle he didn't slip into her room and just take what he needed, do what they both wanted, but he didn't, he was a man of his word and he promised to leave her alone.

Now standing out in the hallway he listened to her voice, closed his eyes as he imagined the way she would sound in the throes of lovemaking.

"Yes, but Steven." He heard her call out. "No, we can't, you're right...No time at all like the present. I'll be right there."

Jackson quietly stepped away from the door and back into his office. His mind in heavy thought ...whom, the devil is, Steven? He'd made it almost to his desk before Evelyn was standing behind him.

"I have to go out, don't wait up for me." She started to leave when he lifted the letter he'd received. Suddenly getting away was more than a passing fancy of his.

"Hey, I was hoping to talk with you. Do you have a minute?" He asked before she left.

"Sure." She stopped at the door. He turned to face her to find her in that pink outfit. He really liked that outfit. Was she going to change before going out, at... he casually looked down to check the time.

"Eight...?"

"Excuse me?" She questioned him.

He looked up. "Huh? Oh, nothing, Ah," He settled on the edge of his desk, lifting his leg up a bit and swung it in indifference to the way his chest suddenly got heavy. "I know we agreed on not doing a honeymoon but I got to thinking..." Evelyn was already shaking her head no. "Wait..." he raised his hand. "You haven't even heard me out."

Evelyn sighed softly as she looked down at her watch.

Eight...? She won't be getting done until late and she dreaded every minute of it, dreading it almost as much as her wedding night. She'd actually talked him out of taking a honeymoon. Why did they need to do that when they really weren't married? Why indeed! All she worried about was keeping herself unavailable to him on their first night as man and wife. After that, it will be easy to sway him.

"Everyone has been asking me where I am taking you." He explained softly. "I don't want to lie about it but have no answer for them." He smiled, "Until I got this. I forgot all about it."

"What is it?"

"A trip; per-say," He answered. He then stood up, "I would really like to go, and I'd like you to go with me."

There was something, in his tone that warmed Evelyn down to the bone, he wanted her to join him, it sounded cozy and interesting.

"Before you say no, listen to me and then decide. Okay?"

"Okay." She agreed with a nod.

"I take this trip every year, just different times and places. This one, I plum forgot about." Truth, he was so preoccupied.

"Thing is, it's not your average trip." He rounded the desk keeping eye contact with her as he did. "It's to Maui." He told her and instantly Evelyn began to argue ...*What*? How is she going to ignore him on the most beautiful island there was?

"I can see no in your eyes but wait, hear me out." He told her with his eyebrow raised. "It's not like you think at all. We won't be staying in the hotel, not on a beach, and we won't have any down time for each other." ...*Intrigued*... She continued to listen.

"In fact, we will be with about fifty or so others in a very

127

small space. Think you'd want to do that?" He sighed as he sat down in his chair. "I have to take you somewhere, granted it won't be a fabulous trip, but it will be to Hawaii and no one will question it."

It was a win, win situation... One that she definitely could live with "...How long?" She asked, trying not to sound eager in any way. "I have to tell Keli how long I plan to be gone."

"That's the best part, just the weekend. No need to take any time off work."

Get Married on Thursday; take a flight that night...*sweet*! It couldn't have been better if she'd planned it herself.

"Okay." She agreed and walked out before he could change his mind.

11

Sitting on her bed in her white dress Evelyn couldn't believe the amount of emotions that coursed through her. So many, they were all jumbled up, intertwining around other feelings that she couldn't get a grasp on any one thing. All she knew was that her stomach was in knots because of it! She felt as if she was losing it.

Trying to get a grasp of her surroundings, she spied the pill bottle on her night- stand. Medicine she knew she'd need before the day was through and…she was right, which was why she'd left it sitting out in plain sight, so she wouldn't miss it in a moment of dire need; Like now.

Quickly, she got up, snatched the bottle and popped two in her mouth. She took a deep breath, waiting for the slowing of her heart that was drumming a steady beat. Her heart rate was just as crazy as her thoughts were. It was beating fiercely against her chest bone making it hard to breathe.

This was so crazy…A panic attack! That's what was happening and she couldn't get a grip to save her life.

Sitting back on the bed Evelyn took another deep breath, exhaled and then repeated the act until the tightness in her chest loosened up. She then laid back and closed her eyes. If she didn't settle her nerves, bad things were going to happen. She closed her eyes briefly so she could just take in the moment of stillness. Silence made the fluttering subside in her stomach, she sighed again. Her chest started to decrease its rhythm as the pounding weakened slightly.

Yes… This is what she needed, peace and…

"Evelyn?" A soft knock sounded on the door joining her room with Nicholas'. "Are you ready?" Evelyn felt her stomach lurch forward and she immediately sat back up to settle it.

"Sweetheart," Nicholas called out as he opened the door.

"You aren't even dressed." Jackson announced in shock. "You've been up here for hours."

He went to the bed, noticed her tremble and knelt in front of her. He ran his hand up and down her legs, his eyes cascaded the front of the lacy bodice and then to the silky ribbon waistline. The dress was beyond beautiful and she was an image to bestow. Man was he lucky to have found her…

The veil was on the bed beside her. Her hair tightly tied up like normal, her cheeks pink, her eyes frosty white above her dark brown gazes as she looked at him in a daze.

"Evie…" He whispered, searching her eyes for distressing signals. Was she in pain? Her soft wisp of a smile settled his pounding heart.

"Hey." He whispered, standing up on his knees to kiss her forehead. "We did it." He smiled searching her face, catching every detail he could. He then kissed the end of her nose. "You can breathe, sweetheart. It's over."

Jackson swallowed when her eyes finally adjusted and settled upon his face. Her bottom lip quivered and a single tear dropped to her cheek. He pulled himself up and kissed it away.

"Nich…" She began but her tight throat cut her off.

"Yeah," He replied lowering to see her brown gaze as she looked at him.

"Did we do the right thing?" She asked and then trembled. Her eyes searched his for answers.

He nodded. "Yeah," He swallowed again.

"Are you sure?" She looked down at the floor gasping. "I keep asking myself that very thing, but can't answer it."

Jackson cupped her face and looked deep into her eyes. "When we get back and I hand you that deed to your farm, you will know then that it was the right thing to do."

Evelyn shook her head. "I'm not so sure that paper was reason enough Nicholas. Are we going to hell?" She burst into tears. He grabbed her up into his arms and rocked her.

"No." He told her. "We're not. I may..." He added as an afterthought,

"I'm not the greatest guy in the world, but you..." He kissed her wet cheek.

"You are not going to hell." He pushed her away to look in her eyes. "You hear me?" He questioned her. It took her a moment of thought before she nodded.

"That's right." He wiped her face. "Let's get ready to head to Hawaii, huh?" He started to get up.

"Nich...?" Once again her throat tightened up, cutting off her voice. He stopped to look at her. Her watery gaze delved deep into his heart. He scanned her sweet face with his eyes as his finger traced her bottom lip.

"What?"

"I forgot to tell you..." She gasped softly. He noticed her chest heave with haggard breaths she appeared to be sick. Her eyes rolled slightly as if she were about to pass out.

"Evelyn?" He called out softly shaking her. Her eyes snapped open in surprise and she looked at him. "What did you forget to tell me?" He watched her struggle for the words.

"I don't fly..." She whispered and then closed her eyes.

* *

Evelyn's first conscious thought was warmth and something silky smooth against her bare legs. She took her body, curled it up and savored the feeling. All wrapped up in a warm soft bed, with huge pillows that were fluffy soft. A luxurious stretch suddenly struck and she extended her legs and arms all the way, pushing the covers she'd been enjoying, off her body and over the edge of the bed.

A huge yawn followed her cat like sprawl and then she sat up eyeing the unfamiliar room. Noticing her silky covered breasts that were jutting out, she curiously looked at the thin slip and recognized it as the one she wore beneath her wedding gown. Her eyes grew huge, quick to understand that was all she had on...Oh...My...!

At that moment, Jackson walked in with a bag in one hand and a tray with coffee in the other. The smell of food filled her nose before he actually was all the way in the door.

"Good morning sleepy head."

"Mm" She grumbled softly. "My head hurts." She ran her hand over her face.

What happened to her, where was she? Then she sighed. The pills! She took two of them to quicken the effect and it knocked her for a loop. She looked around in awe. This was not her room. Was it *his*? What had she done? *What did he do?*

She then glared at him. What kind of man took advantage of an unconscious woman?

"Hungry?" He asked coming closer to the bed, handing her a breakfast sandwich. His eyes scanned the front of her slip, her firm breasts that were completely free of a bra, her nipples poking at the thin material as if trying to escape. His smile told her he was enjoying the view quite nicely. She bolted away from him, throwing herself to the other side of the bed, in search of the covers she knew were there and proceeded to grab them, pull them back over her half naked body.

"Do you mind?"

Jackson giggled. "Not really, and you shouldn't either." He winked seductively at her and then asked, "Who do you think got that big gown off your body?" Evelyn gasped in horror, which made him laugh harder.

"You beast...!" She snapped in anger. "How dare you take advantage of me? You had no right bringing me in here. I want to go to my room this instant!"

Her demands only made him laugh all that much more. "For me to do that," He stated and then grinned for her benefit. "...that would be a true miracle, Evie. That'd be like having sex with a blow up doll." He leaned in, touched her forehead with his lips. "You were a little under the weather, my dear. I don't take..." He lowered his head and smoothed his mouth over hers. "...Advantage." He mouthed over her lips and then carefully swept his mouth completely over hers.

"Mm..." Evelyn moaned. His sweet mouth was warmer than the bed she had woke up in and she reveled in the sensation that rippled all the way down her body.

"Besides..." He kissed the tip of her nose. "I got plenty entertainment trying to get that damn gown off!"

"Oh, you...!" She smacked his arm, thrusting him away from the bed. She didn't want to know how he got that tight gown off of her nor did she want to know about what he got out of it himself.

"Eat that, it will make the headache go away and then we can get a move on."

"Are we still going to Maui?" She asked him thinking they'd missed their flight. She started on the sandwich with little bites, but then began to eat it for real, it was so good and she was famished.

"We're there." He informed her. She raised her eyes to meet his pacing form as he walked about the room.

"We are?"

"Yes, arrived last night."

She watched him lift a coffee cup to his lips. The swirling hot steam kept her attention as he drank from the foam cup. In slow motion, much like the steam rolling off the hot liquid, her eyes roamed over his rigid form. A pair of jeans and a polo shirt that hugged his muscled torso replaced the normal outfits of silk suits, ties. Attire she had never seen him in, but looked very refined. The jeans fit him like a glove against his frame. Her eyes found his bottom end to be more than desirable. The slacks he normally wore weren't quite as tight as the jeans. The material molded right against his fanny and accommodated his long legs without a flaw.

Evelyn had to swallow down the lump in her throat trying to recall his hands, the ones that her eyes were now watching with hunger. Wishing she was awake to have felt them upon her flesh as he undressed her.

She shivered. Those kinds of thoughts were going to get her into a heap of trouble. She flinched when she suddenly did feel his hands upon her. Heat filtered into her flesh along her shoulder and then she shuddered with a chill. Both sensations making her flesh pimply and sensitive. The tips of her breasts ached from the tightness the chills had produced over her body.

"You know," His voice whispered right by her ear. When did he get so close to her? "If you put some clothes on, that chill might go away."

Evelyn closed her eyes, trying to shut out the fact that he was standing right beside the bed making her heart jump for joy. Nothing would shake the trembling feeling she got when his deft fingers found their way to her aching nipple and lightly pinched it, stroked it and then left her flesh, leaving a melting cesspool of nerves behind its wake.

...Or...maybe...not... she said to herself. *No* amount of clothing or warmth was going to take these kinds of chills away.

"Unless...." His voice trebled softly as he continued to speak right by her ear. "You want me to join you and we can forget meeting up with the group." *...YESSSS!*

It took every ounce of her strength to shake her head the opposite direction then her heart was speaking. Night after night she'd find herself awake, her body shaking, heart pounding. The memory of how his proficient hands felt upon her body was driving her insane! There was no other way of describing what he was doing to her. It had been days, almost a week, yet it felt so real and so alive it could have been just the night before!

"All right then." he scolded her. "Get up and get some clothes on before *I* change our plans." His eyes danced over her thin slip, his eyebrows twitched as his mouth creased with a silent murmuring. "We have some shopping to do before we ride out."

**

Ride out...Words that didn't mean much at the time when spoken. It wasn't but an hour later when she realized they were a play on words, a huge play on words, that found herself speechless, as she stood in front of the big black and silver motorcycle. She couldn't get her eyes to remain on any particular part of the bike that Nicholas was packing up.

He stood at the rear of the metal monstrosity tying down

their larger bags to the luggage rack. Inside the saddlebags were their other bags, some with the clothing they'd just bought for her.

"It's not going to bite." He told her moving close to her. She wasn't so sure about that… "Ever ride before?" he asked her. Shell shocked that he had…she looked at him.

"And you *have*?"

His laughter seeped into her bloodstream heating her right up. He nodded nonchalantly. "As a matter of fact yeah," His eyes danced with a sparkle she'd never noticed before. "A few times,"

"A *few* times," She questioned him and his ability to ride her around. She watched him grab a helmet and push it on her head. She remained a statue while he locked it down. She can't get on that…*thing!*

"Once a year for the last ten," He answered dressing his own head and then straddling the wide girth of the bike. He turned his head, his eyes dancing with delight as he reached to the seat behind him, "Hop on."

"I don't know how!" She exclaimed.

Jackson reached his hand out, took hers as he laughed. "Put your foot on the rear peg," He pointed to what he meant and waited for her to do so.

"Grab my shoulders." He smiled as she also did that. "Swing that sexy leg around and hop on." But, his thoughts died right out when she actually did just that and then some. The feel of legs against the back of his, stopped his heart, but then kicked it right in when she pushed her hips forward meeting his rear with her flat abdomen was more then he could handle.

He took a breath and turned the key to start the bike. Her grip tensed the moment the motor between her legs fired up… Jackson closed his eyes as his mind went straight into the gutter.

"This is crazy!" Evelyn spoke over the bike's roar.

Jackson nodded. "I know but it's a *GREAT* kind of crazy!"

They met up with a group of other riders and off they went down long winding roads that led deeper into the dense forest. The ride was actually…nice. She was able to look around and enjoy the scenery, but the best part of the day was being able to hold Jackson. Evelyn had died and gone to heaven, didn't care if she never woke up. When it did finally end hours later, she shook out her legs the moment she was on solid ground.

"Well?" He questioned pulling off his helmet. Evelyn fumbled a few minutes trying to release the tie beneath her chin when he took her fingers and pushed them away. "What did you think?" He asked her as he unlocked the strap.

"Better than I thought it would be." She replied as she looked around at the terrain that changed with every move she made. In one area, a dense forest thick with trees. A few paces from that, flat meadow where some of the bikers were pitching tents. Where they stood… more level land, but hilly with trees that shaded the ground and smooth surfaces at the base of each tree, that area also had a few tents. Straight ahead, across the road was a lazy river. It was so majestic and natural to the naked eye. Quiet… except, for human voices echoing in the distance. Camps were blossoming in all directions.

"How much further are we going?" The words were in her mind and out of her mouth even as she watched him release the tie downs on the luggage rack. One of the large bags dropped to the ground with a thud as he replied.

"This is the end of the road."

Not knowing what to say she quickly got busy, asking

him what she can do to help. Soon her troubled mind was too busy to worry about sleeping out in the middle of the forest. It was soon replaced with the single two man tent that she helped him erect in a matter of minutes, then a fire was built and dinner was being cooked. They talked and chattered about nothing in general.

After dinner, which was eaten in the meadow where tables, chairs and a big fire pit where all meals were fixed. They talked with fellow campers, mingling and getting to know the other riders in the group who come from all walks of life, doctors, lawyers, farmers all sitting around a fire sharing life stories.

"Better than you thought it'd be huh?" He asked on their way back to camp.

"I have never ridden a bike before."

"I know it's not the most glamorous honeymoon…"

Evelyn can't complain, she got to hold him all the way here. "We didn't want a honeymoon." She reminded him.

No, you didn't want one. He thought sharply but let the issue drop. This wasn't bad, it could be worse. They could be home, in separate bedrooms…like his parents.

Evelyn felt the chill in the air that surrounded them, but was certain it wasn't the night. Nicholas withdrew himself from their stroll, something had pulled his thoughts away and now they walked in silence as they headed for their tent. He grabbed the flap for her to get in the small tent first.

"You go ahead and change, I'll wait out here."

Honorable of him and Evelyn appreciated his kindness. She took a short time stripping her jeans off and slipping out of her underwear, putting a t-shirt on as a nightshirt. There was no way she was going to share this small space with him in her nightdress. Thank goodness, he'd brought separate bed rolls.

The beat of a drum echoed in the chambers of her heart, her chest rose and fell to those beats and her breath actually caught when she heard the flap as Nicholas lifted it later in the night. He'd given her plenty of time to get settled. She tried to summon the sleep gods to knock her out before he came in, but she hadn't gotten drowsy. Her eyes snapped open when the bedroll next to her shifted as he took the spot beside her on the ground.

The moment he settled and he was facing away from her, she released her held breath. The sound filled the silent space like the drop of the blade on a guillotine. It reverberated off every wall of the tent. Evelyn closed her eyes dreading what he must think.

Jackson fought the urge to reach out for her. Her smell permeated the whole tent by the time he'd gotten the nerve up to go in. He didn't even take off his jeans knowing the temptation of pulling her into his warm roll would haunt him all night if he had.

Lying there beside her, knowing she wasn't asleep made him wonder what she was thinking of. Did she think about the night in the club? He did ... *All* the damn time! The way she purred, made his own throat swell up with a growl so intense he felt like a lion. Was she *even* thinking about him? He wondered then sighed. If she was, she was probably praying he wasn't going to try anything tonight. He wanted to, *Lord* did he ever!

Images of the night before filtered into his head. That damn dress was murder to get off her body it was so tight around her waist it clung as if it'd been glued to her frame. Every time he moved it, that flimsy slip she wore shifted right with it, exposing her alabaster flesh.

A battle soon ensued between his desire and his morals. Wanting to take his wife and explore the depths of her beauty despite the huge siren going off in his humanity. Evelyn was dead to the world unaware of the devil that rested upon her husband's shoulder all the while he undressed her but in the end, Jackson's gentleman side won. It was wrong to think the things he was and the pain that he was now trying to ease through… was his just desserts.

"Good night Evie." He was a damn fool if he thought sleep was going to come for him. He hoped she'll trust him enough to let her guard down a little bit more so she could sleep.

**

Sleep must have come to her at some point in the night, but it wasn't a long sleep. Something stirred within her soul and made her heart quake with trepidation. She felt scared instantly upon waking in a strange place, she turned to find Nicholas gone, his bedroll empty. She couldn't believe how the vacant space where he'd laid seemed to leave her as void as the spot.

Slipping the recently bought sweat pants over her lower half she popped her head out the tent. Outside under the bright full moon and the star lit skies, she could see almost as if it was daylight. She scanned the nearby area but not locating him…*Where the devil did he* go?

She spotted the bike under the nearby tree, stepping out of the tent, drawn to the big black metal beast. She slowly sauntered over to it, deftly reaching out to run her fingers over the seat. Picturing Nicholas Slade on this monster would have been impossible if she hadn't seen it for herself. The man was a Wall Street connoisseur that blended in with the tradespeople on the Stock Market floor. He wore expensive Italian suits, tailor- made while he was in Italy. He

140

has five sports cars in his garage, none of which he drives. Evelyn touched the black gas tank and grimaced to herself.

Jackson was a puzzling man. She was intrigued half the time she was around him. Names that were not his, parents that lived in a catatonic state of mind: What else was she to learn about him? With every new thing she learns, she finds a deeper emotion making a home within her heart, and worrying on how she was going to remove it when the time came.

12

"It's a beauty, isn't it?" Nicholas stood right behind her, how he'd gotten there was beyond her. She jumped slightly. They both chuckled. "Sorry." He told her. "Couldn't sleep?"

Evelyn shook her head... not alone. She felt the cool metal of the tank as she continued to touch it. She looked down at it.

"Why do you ride?"

She rounded the bike as she gazed at the whole frame.

"At first I started when I was young, when life was so...fast." He paused. "Carefree." He leaned against the bike, Evelyn doing the same on the opposite side, their backs against each other, and bottoms on the larger part of the seat.

"And...now,"

"Now, I do it for the ride."

"I find it hard to grasp you on a bike. Do your parents know?"

His deep laughter echoed through the dark night. "They are why I started riding. To get away,"

"From," She asked running her finger along the tank once more.

"Them," He replied. "Me." He then sighed. "Hell, I was just running."

"Sounds sad," She mumbled. It was something they had in common. "You weren't a very happy child, were you?" He chuckled softly. She could feel the rumbling in his back as he held some of the laughter inside.

"What about you?" He asked side winding the conversation on to her.

"What about me?" She repeated.

"A happy child," She giggled but didn't answer.

"What's so funny?" He asked.

She shook her head. "Nothing really, I was just thinking about how different we are."

"Ah." He sighed.

"Were you a happy child?" He asked after a brief pause.

"We had just us three, but a big family with many cousins and uncles and aunts. Holidays were always a good time for us. My parents wanted a big family, but weren't blessed. They ended up with me. And I was spoiled, pampered and truly loved."

Jackson listened to her story and noticed sadness in her tone as she spoke. She may have been loved and pampered, but something wasn't quite right about her tale. He recognized a sad tone when he heard it. He got the same way when he talked about his childhood and his family life. So how can a loved spoiled little girl grow up to feel so, repressed.

"Do you miss them?"

Evelyn wasn't sure how to answer that. Of course, she missed them! She missed them a lot while they were alive too. She missed many things that she regretted now. Almost hated herself, for being an impetuous girl who thought nothing about others and everything about herself. She'd been so young and careless about her parent's feelings and wished she could go back and change the way things had been but...it didn't happen that way. Can't happen that way, all she can do now was live with her actions.

"Have you ever done something really stupid?" She asked him.

"I'm afraid more than *a*... something." He laughed softly. "...You?"

She nodded. "It was so stupid and I hurt them so much." She sniffled softly.

Jackson turned around abruptly and caught her before she fell due to him leaving so fast. With the bike between them, he ran his thumb over her cheek, wiping away the tear that ran down her face. She pulled away embarrassed to have opened up to him.

"Sorry." She gasped. Jackson allowed her to move away but before she got too far from the bike he straddled it and wrenched her back with his hand around her waist. "I haven't talked about this to anyone." She laughed off her shame as she settled in his arms, relishing the warmth he was providing her. It felt good to speak of her ill minded past. Felt good to let it out finally, and be sad for the first time and not feel guilty about the choices she had made back then.

"What did you do?" he softly questioned her, touching his mouth to her forehead for support. He couldn't think of anything she might have done to get this upset about.

"I was thirteen." She began. "My parents had ideas about what I should do with my life and I had my own. We fought a lot about what I wanted to do and I felt as if they were crowding me, changing me, making me into something I feared wasn't me. We couldn't agree, on anything." She cried out, her body shaking as she wiped at her face.

"We all fight with our parents." He told her. "I fought, and still do with mine!" He tried to make light of the matter, to break up the tension that was building.

Evelyn shook her head. "Not like we did." She sighed again feeling depleted of all energy. "I was horrible to them. Screamed at them, *they didn't love me, didn't respect me.*" She

144

gasped. "I couldn't get them to understand me and the way I was feeling. Nothing..." she paused with a deep sigh. "Nothing worked."

"So..." She started but then let her thoughts drift off. A long pause ensued.

He touched her cheek with his finger. "What happened?"

"I left." Her reply was pointblank and then silence filled the space between them again.

"Left," He whispered.

"Yeah," She closed her eyes.

"We all do crazy things when we are kids." He told her assuredly.

"Say stupid things we don't mean. Parents know that." His finger caressed her cheek a little softer. "What did they say when you came back?"

Evelyn shook her head, turning into his arm and trembled as if suddenly chilled.

"Evie?" He whispered against her ear.

Evelyn shuttered with uncontrollable shakes that started on the surface, but took only minutes to dig deeper into her flesh as it bore all the way to her soul.

"Hold me?" She begged him. Man, she needed to feel his arms all around her. She knew nothing else would do to shake the chill she was now getting. Nicholas didn't ask why, he scooped her up and sat her on the bike side saddle style with her right in front of him. Her fanny rested between his legs, on the seat, and his arms circled completely around her frame, closing her into his warmth.

Evelyn rested her hand on his bare arm, noticing the thick muscle and no shirt. She closed her eyes and remained that way, sitting on his bike for a while.

"What happened, Evie?" He kissed her head. "When you went home?" He couldn't help himself in asking. He was interested in what took place. Had they argued more? Was that why she was so upset?

Through his chest, where her face rested up against him she heard the thunder of his heart, it was a constant beat that drummed into her ear, it was soothing. She snuggled up closer to him, listening to the wondrous sound as it lulled her quaking frame.

"I didn't go back." She whimpered through tight lips, her tone a mumbled confession of just how stupid she had once been.

Jackson had millions of questions he wanted to pummel her with. She was just a kid! Where did she go? Where did she stay…Certainly *not* on the streets! He just couldn't see that or… maybe he just decided that *that* was not what had happened to her. He couldn't grasp the notion of this beautiful creature all alone like that at any age much less thirteen! How did she survive on her own like that?

All of these deep impending questions disturbed him in an unfamiliar way, but what his heart was feeling had nothing to do with any of that but, the way her head felt up against his bare chest… She cuddled, into his arms with her lips, touching his flesh in a tantalizing way that stopped the beating of his own heart. He was lost with what felt so natural. Afraid to move, pull her closer only to have her pull away. He sat motionless while she took liberties in his warm embrace.

They were having a moment that defined all reasoning. Sharing an important part of her past, hardly touching. Definitely not in a sexual way if they did touch, yet Jackson couldn't have felt more sated sexually then if they'd been back home, in his bed sharing more than words.

She was so warm against him. There was no room between them to slide a piece of paper. She found herself puckering her lips to his shoulder, was it a kiss? She wasn't sure. It was too light to be anything remotely like a kiss, but it was thrilling nonetheless. The feel of his skin, the taste of him filtered through, musky, salty and all man.

Time seemed to stand still, slowing down for them alone, but the constant beat of his heart told her time was definitely passing by. Hearing the beat falter every time her mouth brushed against him…he felt it and then her heartbeat would increase.

Not allowing herself the pleasure of the feeling too long, she suddenly shifted, turning around, straddling the bike in front of him, needing to put a little distance between them. It was safer that way.

"So you love to ride?" She asked him, her voice cutting through the thick layer of contentment.

"Every chance I get."

"You ride every year you said." She leaned her head against his chest, her bun rubbing his chin.

"Why, only once…"

"This is between us," Nicholas spoke right next to her ear sending chills down her frame. Evelyn nodded her promise. "This is how I get away. No one knows I do this, no one on the ride knows who I am off this bike. To them I'm Jackson. A guy who, like them enjoys the ride." He sighed softly.

"I can't…afford to do this more than once." He paused and then added,

"You know what I mean?" She nodded again.

"Did you like it?" He questioned her. "Did you feel like you were flying? Free as a bird."

"Is that how you feel?" She asked him.

"Every time I get on," He replied. "Didn't you?" He questioned leaning her forward, taking her hands and placing them on the handles. The wide expanse of his chest brushed her back as they both stretched out to reach the handlebars together.

"The pulsating motor between your legs… the wind in your hair…"

She turned her head to look at him. "My hair was up in a bun."

They shared a brief smile and then he changed the last to, "The wind on your face…"

They held each-others stare for a moment. His hands caressed hers over the handles and then they were moving closer, in sync, until their mouths touched softly. Evelyn kept her eyes open while rising to receive his kiss.

All life around her stopped the moment his mouth touched hers. Her lips responded to his as if they were water to a heated throat. They were petal soft over her mouth as he touched and then slightly taking them away only to come back and repeat again, and again. All in slow motion, as if the world had stopped and they had a lifetime to enjoy the sensation their two mouths were creating.

Evelyn finally closed her eyes at the brief touch of his hand against her waist. Her hand he'd left on the handle bar was now cool from his departure, but the heat was now scorching her stomach.

As slow as his mouth was sweetly pummeling hers, his hand slid upwards, slow… *tantalizing*. Then his fingers were on her tight throat, which, she had stretched out to the limit to reach his mouth, her flesh tingled from his touch. His warm kisses remained indefinite.

Softly his other hand released hers that still rested on the handle bar. Following his movements, leaning backwards, using him as a rest. Her eyes sprang open when he took the opened space that was now free, touching her hard nipple underneath her shirt. Her breath caught in her throat, his fingers smoothed it out for her.

"Purr for me, baby." and she did in a long agonizing groan. She watched his face while he continued to kiss her in the same manner as he had been. Untouched by the act they were sharing, or so it seemed.

The night around them started spinning. Her eyes closed in sweet ecstasy. No one has ever touched her like this and she was, transformed into the carefree person she adored in the clubs. Could he... she wondered to herself.

Jackson thrilled at the new entity he was creating within her soul. She was opening up like petals of a fragile flower. He felt her shutter, but not from loss of control. This was a new feeling for her, a togetherness they hadn't felt and she thrilled in its presence. Accepting it, thriving in it, and mostly needing it, needing him.

He softly twisted her nipple between his finger and thumb, rotating it gently then moved to the other hungered peak and repeated the act. He slowly opened his mouth to deepen the kiss, slipping his tongue over her lips, into her hot mouth and grazed her tongue with a caress. The kiss was endless. Taking her breath away, it felt remarkable!

"Did you feel like you were flying?" He mumbled parting from her warm mouth, making the kisses light and feathery, taking her full breast into his palm, squeezing it, and fondling it.

"Yes." She answered over his parted mouth, accepting his wet offering once more; sucking on it like it was a piece of candy. Tasted like a piece of candy it was *so sweet so delectable!*

Evelyn turned her head when he started to nibble on her cheek, traveling to her ear and then finally to her throat. His fingers played on one side while his lips sucked and licked the other.

Down lower, his hand moved over her flesh, caressing her breasts, then her stomach, only to go back to her breasts. The rotation of all he was doing sent her body on a downhill spiral that felt incredible!

Bringing his mouth back to hers, she rose her hand up, grasped his head and pulled him to her. Opening her mouth for him to delve right in the moment their lips touched. Her eyes sprang back open when Nicholas slipped his hand into her pants, his finger grazing the fine hairline. Her eyes rolled back into her head when he touched the heated spot between her legs.

Once again, she turned her head when he began moving his lips to her throat. He stopped at her ear.

"Free like a bird?" He whispered, his lips caressing the lobe before sucking on it.

"Yes." She shivered from the chill his breath created.

"Feel carefree?"

"Yes, much like..." Her breath halted in mid sentence when his finger slipped inside her warmth. Her body jerked with heated desire running through her veins. Her hips moved forward, taking him into her.

"Much like?" He questioned, kissing her throat.

"...when I became a nun..."

"Hey, Jack?" A man's voice called out from the road at that moment cutting off what she said and stopping what was taking place. "You hear someone by the bike?"

Jackson's back stiffened as he moved, looking over his shoulder. Evelyn's body literally peeled away from his. Her sigh sounded into the night, Jackson could hear the depravity deep within her tone as he withdrew his finger from her heated core. A movement that seemed to have pained *her* more than it did him, which really made him angry about the interruption.

"Oh…" Louis had started to come toward them, but then stopped giving notice to the fact that Jackson was not alone. "I didn't see you had company. My apologies Jack…" Louis turned away from them.

"You're all right, Louis." Jackson found himself calling out to the man he normally rides with. He was another single man that was out for a good ride. Jackson couldn't believe how even toned his voice was despite the agitation he was feeling.

"I come out here, thinking I heard something." He chuckled, "Looks like my ears are just fine. I sure do apologize." He said as he approached them. Jackson watched as Evelyn hopped off the bike and turn away from the approaching man.

"I'm going to bed." She spoke to no one in general and then slipped into the tent without even a glance towards him. Jackson sighed and tried to give Louis a genuine smile.

"It's getting late anyways, Louis." Jackson shrugged his shoulders and shook his head at the same time, acting as if being interrupted in quite an intimate situation, was more then all right. In fact, it was downright acceptable.

"It is at that." Louis answered. "You all set for the river in the morning?" *Damn, damn, damn!* Jackson meant to say something to Evelyn earlier and forgot all about it. It was too late now to spring it on her. He wasn't about to go into that tent, so he hoped she liked water sports.

"You," Jackson asked as he nodded his answer.

"Yep," There was a short pause before he went on with, "Well, since it's safe to go back to bed, I guess…" Louis turned back to the road. "Hey, sure am sorry about… well, you know."

"Not a problem, Louis, have a good night."

Jackson stood still, eyeing the tent. The blood coursed

151

through his veins like the river they were about to run in the morning. He took a big breath and then spun away. It was going to be a long day on the raft without sleep tonight, but that tent could catch fire right at the moment and he wasn't going to go near it.

13

When the sun was starting to rise, it brought a mixture of realities for Evelyn. Sleep had not been her friend the night before. She used the time to see things clearer then she had before. Mrs. Slade's voice hammered her thoughts all the while she cried out her frustrations. Nicholas didn't want her for anything, but an inheritance that he was entitled to. She wasn't sorry about helping him out because in the end, he will help her, just as they agreed, nothing more. She knew that right from the beginning. She'd fallen into that fairy tale nightmare that all girls dreamed of and she couldn't believe how quickly she did so. Granted, Nicholas was a superb specimen and any woman would fight for the honor to be his wife. A position she now held and with that honor, came pride.

He was a fabulous lover, this she was learning of recent, but had to keep her mind focused on the larger picture. This was a merger of two people who made a *temporary* pact, it wasn't supposed to last no more than a month or two and she will have to deal with the loss she was sure to feel, when that day came. It would be much easier if she could just leave her heart out of the matter entirely. Last night...*Was a bad mistake.* One she will now have to live with and face him with her dignity still intact, if it were possible...

...But it wasn't possible. This she discovered the moment she stepped out of the tent, almost running into Nicholas. He grabbed her arm to steady her. When she looked up at him, her heart slipped from her chest and plummeted to the bottom of her stomach. She felt her whole body flush with embarrassment. She couldn't hold his gaze. She looked away as she stepped around him heading for the warm fire pit and something to eat.

"Did I hear something about a river?" Evelyn asked him looking down at the fire. "I thought I heard that man mention it last...night."

She sat on the rock by the fire, but didn't look at him. She tried to keep her eyes on the fire, which reminded her of the flames that had scorched her the night before. She swallowed, telling herself that if she could just forget that ever happened...

"River rafting," He replied standing right beside her. She jumped at his closeness. She looked at the plate of food he was handing to her. The aromas awoke every sense in her nose.

"Last night..." He began to say when she took the plate.

"You folks ready to head to the river?" Frank and Martha Henderson approached from across the road. "We need some help getting the gear ready."

Jackson turned to wave at the couple. "Be right there." He then looked back at Evelyn.

"Do you like river rafting?" He questioned despite what he really wanted to ask. What he wanted to do was to remain right there at camp and finish what, his body eagerly hungered for. He'd walked miles last night just to get the ache out of his groin. Had he gone in that tent with the rock hard erection he had, he would have consummated this marriage whether she wished him to or not.

"If not... we can stay." He suggested hoping that she in fact couldn't raft.

Evelyn shook her head quickly. She'd never rafted, but wasn't about to stay here alone with him! That was more dangerous than any river. "I love rafting." She smiled at his defeated look.

"All right," He nodded. "Eat, I'll go help pack up the gear.

River rafting turned out to be the most exhilarating thing she'd ever done. Riding the strong current up and down on God's natural roller coaster was so vigorous and exciting! The entire day they traveled down the wildest adventure Evelyn was sure ever to have the pleasure to partake. Some parts were smooth and slow moving. That's when she was able to take in the beautiful nature all around. During the rougher patches, there was no time to look around.

The strong currents tossed the raft around a bit, but it was invigorating to the extreme measures. Her heart a few times leapt right out of the raft as she watched the waves take over the sides with crashing strength, the raft almost turned over a couple of times, but she didn't question the abilities of her fellow rafters and what their capabilities were.

Everyone in the rafts helped maneuver and steer. Those who weren't sure what to do were often helped. There were six people to each raft, she and Nicholas shared theirs with two other couples and the ride was better than the bike ride the day before, and as that ride, Nicholas took charge of the raft as if it was second nature for him. It was obvious, he had a carefree side that no one knew about, he fit so well inside Mother Nature's habitat it was surreal.

The ride completely drained Evelyn of all the stress she was shouldering at the beginning of the trip and kept it away all night long. She was too exhausted to care about anything, but laying her tired achy bones in her bedroll and sleep with Nicholas right beside her, as dead to the world as she.

**

Oliver met them at the door upon their arrival back home. The house that usually offered great comfort to Jackson, today, only seemed to add to his frustration. He wanted to talk with Evelyn about the night on his bike and he tried to catch her the moment they were awake, but she avoided him like the plague. Before he knew it, it was time to get things packed up and be on their way.

Once they got back to the hotel there was no time. A limo was already there to meet them to go to the airport. Evelyn, who had taken one of her pills, was down for the count. So there had been no time for him to breach the subject. Not that he knew exactly what it was he wanted to say or ask. His mind was cluttered with desire he hadn't felt in a very long time. It was hard to hold it in, but the word *NUN*... keeps coming back to the surface and douses the flame to a mere flicker...Nun? Had he heard her right? He was married to a nun. He thought nuns couldn't marry. Weren't they already married...*to* God?

What was hardest to grasp, was he'd touched a nun in a real *bad* way but, what terrified him most...he wanted to touch her again! He wanted to kiss her sweet lips, and...

He was going to hell! No doubt about it he was as doomed as a sinking ship out in the middle of the ocean.

Evelyn went right upstairs heading for her room that was no longer there. He'd told Molly to take all of Evelyn's personal things and have them put away in his room, in the room they will be sharing. Jackson almost called out for Evelyn to stop, but decided *this* was how he was going to snag her. He quickly took his bags to his room and started to unpack the clothes he never wore.

He looked up when the door between their rooms slowly opened up and Evelyn stood in the doorway just glaring at him. She didn't hold his eyes for very long before she looked away, embarrassed.

"I can't…" She began to say but her throat cut her words off. She looked around his room. Thinking about sharing his large room filled with nothing but him and his smell, her heart started to beat against her chest in fear.

"Yes." He answered her dribble. "You can… you will." He added lastly without consideration of her feelings.

"No." She shook her head. "No, I won't." Her brown eyes flared at him.

Jackson returned her anger with, "We are married and that is what married people do." His tone held a slight amount of anger, but the tension between them doubled.

"It wasn't in the agreement." She snapped back. "I am not sleeping in here…" Evelyn's throat clenched tight a second time when she spotted the big four-poster bed with lacy curtains attached to each post. Somehow sharing that big comfortable bed seemed much more dangerous than sleeping in the small tent they'd just shared.

"It's what's expected. And you will…"

"You lied." She bit harshly. "You said nothing about having to share a room, nor a bed!"

Jackson threw his bag to the floor in anger. "And you said *nothing* about being a damn nun!" He hadn't meant to cross that bridge in that manner, but now that he had, he stood there returning her glare. He was married to a damn nun…how on *earth was* she going to give him a son…Any children at that matter? In addition, there was not a damn thing he can do about it now. Now, wanting to throttle her, or wring her damn neck ranked high on his agenda!

Evelyn tried with all her might not to cry, but she always

did when she was upset. She wanted to disappear and forget this whole mess. She wanted out of the fiasco she'd gotten herself into. She can't do this. She wasn't strong enough to lie to others the way they had been. They weren't married! For God's sake, they weren't supposed to be fighting like a couple. Nothing was at stake here. She was helping him and in return… but somewhere along the line, it got all tangled up and she wasn't sure which way was up anymore.

One thing she knew, for certain, was how her body had betrayed her and all she can think of; is how she will feel after all is said, and done, when she would actually leave this charade and become herself once again.

This had started out as a venture for her farm but it has turned into one for her heart. A desire for a man has somehow gotten in the way and she can't for the life of her figure out how that had happened.

Nicholas Jackson Slade was never a venture in any of this. She knew that right from the start and had she not… she'd been informed quite effectively by his own mother. Somehow, her heart had tripped and fallen. Now she was struggling in efforts in keeping her virtue intact while her betraying body continued to crave the sinful things it should not.

She turned away from his harsh stare as her thoughts continued to stray, facing the window hoping the gardens in the back would appease her nerves. She closed her eyes as her legs still quivered from the touch of him. Her mouth dried up while other parts moistened at the mere thought of him so close. There wasn't a prayer out there strong enough to keep her sanity from floating away. It was adrift much like her heart these days and remaining here under such intimate scrutiny was just too hard on her.

"I'm not a nun." She whispered keeping her back to him.

Jackson couldn't fight the surge of relief that coursed his veins. "You'd

Said … you felt free. Like when you became a nun." He questioned her.

"I was a nun." She scanned the gardens as she spoke.

"Was, as in, not anymore, right," Tightness took over his chest as he watched her, noticing her soft tremble. She was crying.

Evelyn spent her entire teen years serving and doing God's will, helping those in need of a spiritual guidance. She traveled the world saving women and children from despair in hostile environments. She lived in impoverished lands where people died of infectious diseases and has come close to dying three times herself, but not once did she ask why she was there, thrown into such miserable conditions.

Most did not understand why she chose the life she had, especially her family. She didn't talk to them, because of their non-supportive ways and she never visited them in fear of them trying to pull her away from what she loved doing. Until she'd learned her mother was in the hospital in comatose-state after being in an accident.

Evelyn was able to visit, but it had been devastating to her. Her mother never woke up to know that Evelyn had remained by her bedside the full three months she laid sleeping. Evelyn was able to say goodbye, but she found the calling that had summoned her so deeply before, was gone from her heart. It affected her so she spent her last year back in the convent.

It had been a long hard struggle trying to recapture a desire to remain but it had vanished from her heart. All she wanted was time to heal from the loss she felt and to be with her father in his time of need. Evelyn's need to stay by her father's side was the new heartfelt calling she welcomed with opened arms.

While getting her business degree, her father received a devastating blow with cancer. Evelyn helped her father out as much as she could and when he died, she had thought maybe she'd go back to the church but, the calling never did come back.

The years she spent in God's care, she never regretted. Her services were too grand of an ordeal to regret. The faces she saw in those years and the smiles she had seen when she gave hope, all kept her heart in the right place of mind. She had done the right thing. She just wished that sometimes, she'd done things differently, like going home, instead of being pigheaded. And the one thing she did regret, was the caring and understanding she gave without question to complete strangers, but couldn't to her own family.

The calling she had, had changed her. It took her heart and soul, leaving a shell behind to take on what was left of her life. Clubbing was the only thing to bring it all back and she loved every minute of it.

Evelyn nodded her reply and then said, "I'm sorry Nicholas..." She tried to sound indifferent, but she shuddered despite what she wanted to sound and appear like. "I just can't..." She tried with a little more strength in her tone.

"Stop calling me Nicholas!" Jackson fumed in anger. He went over to her, "It's Jackson, goddamn it!" He demanded placing his hands on her shoulders and turned her around. "Please, stop calling me that name."

Jackson hadn't been overly fond of his name and most of the time people called him Jack. Why it irritated him that she did not, he didn't know but, he was getting more and more irked by her refusal in the matter.

"Why are you so harsh all the time?" She asked him. "I

don't know you!" She snapped and then added. "I'd much rather call you Mr. Slade!"

Her big brown eyes flared at him and Jackson shook his head trying to keep the smile from forming, but the tips couldn't hold it all back and curled slightly.

"You are an evil man. You take much pleasure in my pain, why is that?"

Jackson sighed as he released her shoulders. He was losing the temper as he watched her face crease with the truth. She wasn't comfortable around him, hadn't been from day one, unless she was in his arms. She feared him and now, he understood why. No woman turned down his advances before and it daunted him until now. Evelyn wasn't like normal women…A nun…

"I don't mean to be so harsh." He found himself speaking before he had the words all thought out. "We have an agreement." He spoke softly.

"But I wish to end that, right now." She answered swiftly. "I can't do this." Evelyn looked around the room, took a deep breath and let it out. This was a good time to be honest, as honest as she could be.

"It's not that simple." …*Impossible*!

"But I… *can't*." She gasped turning those huge watery eyes onto him. Their stares locked and Jackson felt his hand come up and almost touch her cheek. *Oh, she most certainly can*! And…he was going to show her.

"May I ask why you agreed to this in the first place?" His blue eyes danced around her soft features, as he waited for her answer. Evelyn moved away from him as his words touched her in places she didn't want to be touched. Then again, maybe it was his heated stare, making her uncomfortable. He was playing unfairly…And he knew it.

"I was overwhelmed by your offer." She replied singed by

his reminder. "I needed money. I wasn't thinking of anything but, that."

"Well..." he paused, "You agreed to this, to pay off the bank." Evelyn didn't like the tone he was getting or the twinkle in his eyes. "The bank no longer holds your property." He stated nonchalantly. "I do." "You're blackmailing me?" ...The audacity of him! Not able to find a good response to him she darted for the door.

"Not blackmail Evie," He told her grabbing her arm. "Just an agreement to keep: *the* agreement." Evelyn looked at the hand that had halted her from moving. Her skin sizzled beneath his touch that was gentle, not firm.

"Take your hand off of me!" She snapped like a hissing cat, wrenching her arm away from his.

"You like the right or left side of the bed?" Jackson asked her, stopping her from actually leaving the bedroom. Standing in the doorway, she spun and eyed him standing by the bed. His cat-eating grin told her he wasn't backing down on this. He winked and said coyly. "I myself hog the bed but, I will try to remain on my side for the most part."

Her eyes darted away from the bed altogether and spotted the fancy sofa in the far corner. "I will take the sofa, *Nicholas.*" Then she turned and walked out, hearing his roaring laughter as she did so.

**

Evelyn ran her fingers along her temples, looking down at the pages in front of her. All week long, the numbers had been rising on the 'Sheer Delights' items and a few of the 'Dream Catchers' were going up as well. The closer to Christmas, the higher they will go. The new line 'Illusions' will be in the next issue, which Evelyn was sure would be a big hit by the holidays as well. She, herself had gotten a few of those they were so fabulous. She promised Angie a solid raise if they sold like, she had hoped.

Her deep sigh filled the large dining room. Shaking her head, she lifted up the number sheet again only to look harder at the items again. Maybe she should steer away from the 'Delights' and put more of the 'Cotton Candy' or maybe the 'Black Magic'. She was getting tired of having the same things in the magazines. She needed another way to entice those other lines. Get people to notice them more then the 'Delights'.

She threw the papers to the shiny table and sat back, rubbing her eyes. She'd spent hours and wasn't any further along. She had to tell Steven something by the end of the week.

Jackson noticed the dining room light on as he passed, slowing down to inspect what was going on, figuring Molly or one of the other maids was busy cleaning the chandelier, or maybe the crystal stemware. Sometimes they'll even polish the silver while the house was asleep.

He raised his eyebrows to the small frame sitting at the table, leaning back in the chair, her eyes closed. He glanced around and then down to his watch, it was ten fifteen.

He then sauntered inside thinking maybe she'd fallen asleep. She didn't look at all comfortable. As he approached he noticed the papers, but was looking beyond them, to the almost hidden magazine beneath them. He hadn't seen a Satin & Lace magazine for weeks, almost since meeting Evelyn. So much had been going on he even forgot she owned the damn company. His fingers pushed the magazine out and a pretty pink, satin and lace nightgown looked back at him.

"Can I help you, Nicholas?" Evelyn spoke in a hazy tone.

His cologne filled not only the air but her nose as well. It seeped into her senses like a slap across the face. It was sharp and left an imprint that stained her soul. It was harder to keep on task with him standing right beside her. Evelyn had to take a deep breath when he drew near and hold it when she heard him come into the room. Luckily her eyes were already closed and wouldn't be noticed when she did so.

When he reached out, her heart leaped into her throat only to have stilled, when she also heard the papers on the table shift. It had been a solid week since they came back. Seven days, and still she shuddered at the thought of him touching her. Her legs melted and her core sizzled with a yearning she'd never felt before. A week of suffering has passed, with a few more ahead, before an end would soon arise and she can go back to her normal world. A world she feared, his memory will silently haunt her with no mercy and no end in sight.

"Why aren't you in my office working," He questioned her. "The chair there is much more comfortable." He proffered. Evelyn shook her head no.

"It's your office. I don't want to intrude upon your life."
...*Too late!* Jackson gave thought with a shake of his head. Man, was it ever too late for that. He hasn't gotten one damn good night's sleep since they got married. He's been popping pain killers for the damn ache in his back from sleeping on that damnable sofa in his room.

His gentlemanly nature wouldn't allow her stubbornness impede his need to have her nearby. Evelyn wasn't sharing his bed with him and he wasn't going to have her sleeping on the damn sofa! They were at an impasse and he was determined to, not let her win their first battle. So, he was the one sleeping or _not_ sleeping on the small uncomfortable piece of furniture while she took the bed. Not that she cared a lick about his loss of sleep or, where he slept for that matter.

"It's late. Why don't you finish up in the morning? In my office," Again she shook her head no.

"I have to finish it up tonight."

"All right, suit yourself." He started to leave, but then he caught the magazine in the corner of his eye when Evelyn went back to work. Jackson then paused a moment, "Hey, Evie?"

"What Nicholas?" Perturbed that he was pestering her, Evelyn glanced up with dark rings around her eyes. She looked as much exhausted as he felt. Was she not sleeping well? She had his damn bed, why wouldn't she be sleeping well? Caught momentarily, he eyed Evelyn with curious wonder.

"Nicholas?" She called out when he was beginning to make her uneasy. "Did you want something?" She asked when he questioned her in silent stares.

"Ah..." He snapped back after she turned in her chair to get a real good look at him. "I was wondering, maybe... I can send you over a few girls to model for your magazine. I have a few that stand out, so to speak."

Evelyn's eyes narrowed in thought before she replied with, "Something wrong with my models?" taking his offer as a personal dig, even though it wasn't meant to be. How could it be personal?

"No." He shook his head trying to sound indifferent. Nothing wrong she just happened to be perfectly proportioned, in all, the right places. She was perfect for that kind of modeling and he _still_ wanted a shot at her. He could make her much more money, if the model would just break away from that small town business of Satin & Lace.

"I was just hoping that maybe we can share a little, I send some of my girls your way, and you send some mine, means more money for the girls and less cost for you and me, in the long run."

"Em." Evelyn turned back to her work unimpressed and not interested.

"Well, think about it, huh? Maybe you might have a few to call out." He headed for the door once again. "Give me a call if you find a need."

His smile stayed with her the rest of the evening. She tried to push it away, but every time she looked through the magazine, she pictured him on the bed with her. His hands lazily caressing over the soft sexy underwear she wore in the pictures, burning her all the way down to the bone, his smile wide, teeth pearly white…And those lips, those kissable lips. Waking up every inch of her body with a heat so rich and strong, it made her think of their camping trip; and finally when she jolted right out of the chair when her legs quivered because of the twinge she felt in the V between her legs that was moist and unbelievably hot. She knew work…had ended. She packed up her papers, threw them in her case and headed for the bathroom. She needed a long shower and a soft bed and… maybe a few hours of sleep.

14

The hot water felt so good, Evelyn ended up staying under the shower longer then she should have but, it felt so luxuriating she couldn't put a stop to it. Finally, dressed for bed she slowly padded to the bedroom to find it dark inside. Normally she was already in bed before Nicholas came home and he'd have to stumble his way to the sofa, but tonight she had that pleasure.

She bumped into the tall dresser with her knee and once she rounded the big piece of furniture, she ended up smacking into the tall post at the end of the bed. Her head cracked against the top and her toe collided with the bottom giving a solid thud and then a soft crack before she yelped out in pain.

"Evelyn?" Jackson had been listening to her fumble her way into the bedroom. He even snickered, knowing she had done the same when he had tried to get to the sofa without waking her. Only to find once he settled on the damn thing, she was awake watching him the whole time. He didn't acknowledge that he could see her eyes glistening in the soft moonlight coming through the window, which he had done all week.

"Damn it..." He cursed softly as he got to his feet. He switched on the table lamp by the sofa and turned to see her holding her foot sitting on the end of the bed. "What did you do?" he asked her, reaching for her foot. She moved away, not allowing him the slightest touch.

"I'm fine." She told him.

"Let me check it to make sure." He gently took her hand and moved it away as he softly inspected her foot. "Where does it hurt?" He asked but the moment his fingers grazed her big toe she yelped. "I see it." He whispered as he knelt in front of her. "You tore the skin." He ran his finger over the wound. "And it's bleeding…"

"It is?" She quickly looked down to check for herself.

"Just a bit," He winked at her, but then his eyes widened with more concern.

"Evie…" He brought his hand up to her forehead. "You've got a red splotch, right…." He gently touched the egg that was swelling fast. "There."

"Owe!" She cried out.

"If a light was on…" She snapped angrily. "I would have seen the dresser and that bed!" Her tone made Jackson's chest heave, but he didn't laugh. She was spitting nails and if it had been *any-* one else, he knew they would have cursed, just as she wanted to but, it hung right there on the tip of her tongue, unable to bring it out.

While he held in his laughter, he noticed the bedclothes she was wearing. The same t-shirt she wore their first night camping. Too big for her small frame, but 'comfy' which was why she wanted it. It was something easy to get on in the dark and not revealing in any way. It didn't have to be, to get the attention he was receiving now.

Quickly his mind was back on his bike, his hands up underneath that shirt touching her swollen nipples that he had wanted to taste, but didn't get the chance. The shirt hid her body well, but not in his mind's eye.

He saw the way her firm breasts swayed when she leaned against him, giving her full body to him without a single care. She was free and she was thriving in his touches. He didn't need to see through that heavy shirt to know just how beautiful she was beneath it. His eyes may not have seen, but his hands did on that night that feels like centuries ago, but was only last week.

"It's my fault." He heard himself say in the small space between them. His eyes darted from the front of her shirt, away from her full breasts. His hand was gradually moving upwards from her foot, over her silky bare legs, he couldn't stop himself. She had no sweat pants on tonight. She was nothing, but silky softness. "I should have left a light on for you."

Their eyes met in the dim lighting and danced while his hand continued a soft caress up her smooth leg. "I could kiss away the pain…" he was saying as he rose a little. "…if you like." Quickly she stood moving away from him, turning back to the bed.

"No. I'm fine." She glanced over at the sofa. "I'm sorry I woke you." He stood up behind her watching her while she pulled the covers back.

"I wasn't sleeping."

Evelyn abruptly turned, smacking into him. She almost flew backwards into the stand beside his bed, but his reflexes were good, he quickly caught her and steadied her. "You weren't?" Evelyn tried hard to keep her eyes away from his deep gazes that were speaking to her. His touches were scorching her again and the room was starting to spin out of control.

"I bet that sofa is very uncomfortable." She started to fluff the pillow next to her for something to do. He was too close. All of a sudden, she whirled around. "Is your back hurting?" She didn't want him in pain. She had moved towards him in concern and smacked right into him.

This time he caught her shoulders with his firm fingers and there was no way she could turn her eyes away from the darkness in his blue gazes that were the depth and color of the sea, murky endless waves of power.

"Would you like the bed?" She asked him with wavering eyes. "I can sleep on the sofa." She generously offered. "We should probably..."

At the moment, he didn't give a damn about the sofa or about his hurting back. With each word she spoke, he watched her mouth move. His fingers grasped her a little harder, feeling her softness beneath the thick shirt and suddenly, all he wanted was those sweet lips of hers on his.

Without a moment's pause, he pulled her towards him while she was talking and laid a soft kiss to her moving mouth that stopped immediately when they touched.

"Mm," Her soft moan filled his ears and pulled on his groin in such a quick second. He wrapped his arms around her, and pulled her against his lean body.

Evelyn stopped talking the moment his mouth covered hers. The sweet taste of his lips, that manly taste that was all him, she lost all words. Instead of talking, she began kissing. Long strokes... smooth strokes. Strokes that took her breath away, and then open strokes that made her heart sway.

Her hands splayed against his bare back, grasping him with all her might. She had never wanted a kiss as she did this one, and she wasn't sure if it was just the kiss or if the man had anything to do with it. Nicholas was such a good kisser. He knew just how to bring out her desires. Would he be as good a lover?

All he wanted was just a taste, a small sample of her lovely candied mouth and that was all... until he actually tasted those luscious lips. None was as precious, or so pleasingly plump. Ripe for the picking and damn did he ever want to pick those delectable lips until they were breathless and weak.

One slight peck was not enough for him and he knew it would never be again, it was a mere tease of what could be if enticed just a bit further. Knowing, craving to bring forth a desire within her so uncontrollable, she'd shutter beneath his touch. He'd never brought that kind of appetency in any of the women he'd bedded in the past.

He found a longing deep inside him, that was as strong as the yearning she suddenly discovered lived within her soul. He longed to be the man, the one man to give her a freedom she had never felt before. The kind that welcomes passion so strong, it leaves decorum standing at the door, the kind to turn her world upside down and leave her begging for more.

Jackson covered her mouth with severe kisses, tugging on her lips, pulling on her tongue, sucking the breath right out of her. Evelyn took as much as he was giving, then graciously giving it back with more fervency. Hunger ingulfed him, his hips thrust forward, pushing his groin up against her. His erection brushing against her belly, showing her just what she was doing to him…wanting to push her to his bed and fill her with that same heated flesh.

That's when he felt her stiffen, her entire body tensed up at the touch of him and immediately her flame snuffed right out.

He tried to capture her before she caught herself, pushing away from his warm embrace. Horrified but confused as to why she liked the wild sensation that was ripping through her lower half. Mortified even more, Evelyn turned away from his worried expression. She _did not_ want him to look at her as if she were some weakling, a babe fresh from the womb unsure about the world around her. More importantly, she did not want him to know she wanted him.

"Evie…" He murmured running his thumb over her chin, bringing her eyes back to his without much effort.

Turmoil filled her heart. She then shook her head. This was wrong, she could feel so many mixed feelings it was daunting. She wanted to run, she wanted to escape without any harm to her and she wanted to feel his lips against hers once more.

Her whole body was screaming with alarms that she needed to heed, if she wished to survive the nightmare she'd placed herself in: If she didn't run, escape from all the sinful needs he was bringing to life. The two things that once meant everything to her were in jeopardy, forced to live with her morality shattered and faith in despair if she continued as the doomed woman she was. The devil's works were at hand and she *must* heed the warnings or parish in a life-leading straight to hell.

"I'm sorry." Evelyn spoke. Her body trembled as she did so. Her whole frame shook as if she were cold, but she was so hot from head to toe, hotter in some regions that scathed her soul. She tried to hold his sweet eyes but found shame so deep in herself that she could not. She knew what she was doing to him. As a man, he had needs and she was giving him all the right signs, but then pulling back when he needed her the most...*A tease*! She never thought in a million years she'd been donned, a tease.

"Sorry...for what?" He questioned, still touching her chin with tender strokes. He didn't know how much that brief touch was soothing her quivering heart. He had no clue how torn she was. She had emotions that did not belong in this relationship and he'd laugh at her foolish heart for the way her naivety had taken over her soul. Evelyn was much like a young teen looking at a handsome heartthrob in some magazine. She was star struck and falling quickly for his charming charisma that exudes from him with ease.

"I don't mean to tease." She whispered. "I'm sorry I

keep…" Her throat tightened up, closing off her words. He shook his head, curling his lips in refusal.

"I don't want you to apologize." He looked deep into her eyes. "I need to give you space." His thumb caressed more firmly against her chin, his hand palming her face softly. "I should probably be the one apologizing." …But he wasn't going to. Jackson knew he was rushing her but damn it, he couldn't control his own needs. The desire took him by storm each time he kisses her. His whole being was eager to see what this cat will do when released of the bonds she felt tied to. He liked making this minx purr.

Space wasn't going to help this situation, Evelyn mournfully thought as she turned away from his heated stare, away from his tempting allures that drew her in without trying. Space was just a distraction of what the inevitable will bring and she knew bouncing back from giving him everything and getting nothing in return, was not what she was willing to do, her first encounter with a devil this strong has to be taken, forcefully and quickly.

"I need you to stay away from me, Nicholas." She addressed the devil himself, had to, to get his attention. She moved away from the bed, going to the far window just to be out of his reach. She turned to face her demon.

"What you seek in me, I can… not give. I will not." She added with pride in her belief in herself and her vows.

Jackson remained by the bed watching her as she tried to fight with her inner self. She was standing her ground. Her sense of danger was high and with good reason. Jackson wanted to crack that outer protective shield she'd been hiding behind for so long. She was afraid of what he instilled within her, a passion that raged and begged to be set free. She was the most passionate woman he'd had the pleasure to meet…*And, he'd married her!*

He was damn lucky to find her much less get her to agree to this charade. Should he tell her… he wondered if that would change her ideals about this 'fake' marriage. She is bound to him, vowed to God himself in a church and upon paper that he was never going to release until she was his. Not until he was certain, she was staying, until she was pregnant with his child. Until… the only answer was, to remain.

"The night on the bike…" He decided to remind her a little of what she feared, but wanted despite herself and her beliefs. Exploit her sensual side to help aide his cause.

"…Should have never happened." She argued vehemently.

"I was going to say… was incredible." He watched her body shutter at the mere thought, she agreed. "You want me to leave you alone?" He couldn't do that, and his tone, the vibrato in his tone helped his defense in that area. Because there was no way, he was going to be able to not, touch her in the future.

He slept with his hands over her naked breasts, touching and fondling them to perfect hardness that made his mouth water with wanting. That is, when he did sleep. The rest of the time, his mind was doing the touching and recalling what it was like, what she felt like and her damn purr…that was something he was *definitely* going to hear again. It was just a matter of time. Question was, could he hold out long enough to get her on those same wavelengths?

He had to… he decided. There was no way around that. He just had to bide his time. Play the game and play it better than her.

Her sigh of relief filled the room when he nodded his concession.

"If that's what you want." He slowly walked back to the

sofa.

"That *is* what I want."

Jackson slipped back under the covers on his makeshift bed, turned his back to her and said nothing else.

Cautiously, Evelyn made her way to the bed and slipped inside the silky sheets. The moment her head hit the pillow, the light was doused and the tears began. She turned into the pillow so Nicholas wouldn't hear her.

Jackson's back clenched at the soft sound he heard. He lay motionless, trying to pinpoint what it was. It was coming from his bed. Slowly he turned his head to look over at Evelyn. Despite her efforts, he could hear her anguished sobs.

At first he started to get up, but then paused. A devilish grin curved at the corners of his mouth. He didn't mind it when a woman cried, he knew that a woman's vise were her tears. They got anything they wanted when they cried. It was something that normally didn't affect him, which was why he was not married before all this mess came about. He disliked the wiles of women, women's lures, and manipulations, the crying games and lastly, the jealous rage that usually accompanied relationships he had no desire for.

...But having to hear Evelyn's sobs, put an uneasy tension in his chest. He didn't like it, and he forced himself to lay still and listen all night because within those sobs, were the sound of hope that one day he will be rewarded with her opening up. One day she will be free and in his arms where he knew she longed to be.

15

"I have Jeffries on line two." Keli's voice rang through the intercom on Evelyn's desk. She had Develand on another line talking about the increase in publications. Jefferies, her main stockholder, had scheduled to meet with her in the week after the upcoming shoot. She'd be gone for almost a week and hadn't told Nicholas that she had to be gone for Thanksgiving.

The last thing she wanted was, them arguing over a holiday feast with family that wasn't even hers.

Another week had gone by without mishap. He was gone most of the time and she had been so busy, avoidance was the name of the game they were playing now. And she was good with that. The less she saw him, the less opportunity for her to lose sight of herself. She was happy with this charade and soon…it all will be over with…A day *she* was so looking forward to.

"Develand, Jefferies is on the other line, can I call you back or will you hold?"

"I have some things to get caught up on, let me call you." Dev replied and then hung up without another word or a sound of farewell.

"Jefferies," Evelyn called out the moment she picked up the other line.

"Hey, just wanted to go over the prelims of our meeting. I have your flight arriving in LA around three PM. I can have a limo pick you up and take you straight to the hotel. I have two meetings set up for the next day. I really think Hastings is going to bite."

Evelyn sat back in her chair. "That's great!" Another stockholder, would be great, a few would be fantastic! Jefferies was doing a bang up job getting people lined up, but not many were interested in buying stock in a lingerie company. There was some stiff competition with bigger fish attached to them. If Evelyn could snag just one of those big fish…She wouldn't need Nicholas…or his money.

A commotion beyond her closed office door took Evelyn's attention briefly, with Keli's angered tone muffled just outside the barrier.

"You can't…." Keli's voice sounded roughly through the thick door.

"Stop, No!"

Evelyn stood up as the sounds became harsher, a man's voice could now be heard intertwined with Keli's. It sounded like an argument, which was not Keli's forte. Evelyn started to round her desk as she answered Jefferies without alerting him of a problem.

"Yes. I think going straight to the hotel will be fine." Evelyn answered, but was distracted when her door flew open and Keli rushed through, trying to hold back Nicholas from coming in.

"…should go pretty smoothly. Let me know, huh?" Evelyn only caught the last part of what Jefferies said and she really wasn't caring too much about it, her heart jumped to her throat at the sight of Nicholas.

"Yeah, I will. Let me call you back the closer it gets." She told him.

"Talk to you soon." She told Jefferies with her finger on the button to disconnect the line the moment the words were out.

"What is going on?" Evelyn asked eyeing both her

secretary and her husband.

"He wouldn't wait." Keli started.

"I just wanted to say hi and maybe take you to lunch." Nicholas argued.

"Why do I need permission to go in my own wife's office?"

"I'm sorry." Keli grimaced biting on her bottom lip, frustrated by the interruption.

Evelyn rounded her desk all the way. "It's all right, Keli. I'll handle this."

Keli nodded her departure, but not without a glare directed to Nicholas beforehand. Nicholas smiled as he turned his bright blue gaze to Evelyn, but then dropped his cheer when he saw her frown.

"You can't be angry."

Evelyn gasped. "I was in a meeting, Nicholas. No." She shook her head. "This is my office and you can't just come in whenever you see fit."

Jackson was about to argue the matter further but was caught off guard when his eyes took care in his surroundings. Leather bound furniture, sofa and matching set of chairs. Bookshelves donned with knick-knacks rather than books and the watercolor effect of the artistry all around the room. Paintings on the wall and the statues all were soft browns and beige with hints of sienna and oranges throughout that gave the room a masculine effect, but the glass figurines told another story.

The room… was as complex as its master. With every turn something different takes shape. A soft sensitive side reflected in the small animal and children figurines. Telling him a soft gentle side existed, but the brilliant colors and textures of the rest of the room, also gave a strong independent hue that drew much respect for the other side of her that he saw on a regular basis.

Seeing that he wasn't listening to her Evelyn sighed with a deep antagonistic shake of her head. This was *her* domain and she was a bit unsettled that he'd barged in without even calling. "What is it that you want Nicholas?"

Once Jackson got a fill of the surroundings, he turned his gaze upon her standing beside her desk. "Lunch," He stated, then added, "Now that I'm here though, maybe a tour?"

Evelyn felt his gazes before she saw the way he was eyeing her. Today she wore her black cashmere sweater with her silk slacks. It was chilly out and the sweater she knew held a lot of heat inside, knowing she would have to venture out for the shoot later in the day. She hated getting chilled and her long jacket was just too uncomfortable.

Gasping, she moved backwards, as if his eyes were pushing her towards the wall. The sweater was loose at the base but snug around her breasts, and the long string of white pearls lay softly in the dip between the crevice and dangling below, swinging freely with her every move, sending little morose codes out to him.

Jackson couldn't divert his eyes from that string of white distraction while it moved against her chest. Watching the way it was touching, rolling against her softness much like that of a caress of a fingertip, not just any ones…*his*. He wanted his fingers to caress her as those fine pearls were doing.

Uncomfortable with how thick the air had become, Jackson swallowed averting his eyes to her face. Her cheeks were colored nicely with a pale rose hue that almost looked natural, as if she'd been walking outside in the cool brisk air. The dark grey shade above her big brown eyes seemed to enhance her bright gaze. Her thick lips were the shade of plum with a high gloss that mirrored glass. He swallowed

179

again when he discovered her features up there only added to the sudden heat that consumed him. The only thing left was her hair that was in the same savage bun, high up on her head.

"A tour?" She questioned, skeptical about his interest in the building, but rather its contents.

"Yeah," He answered. "I'm engrossed with what goes on here. I may want to send some of my girls over." He paused, "Remember we talked about that?"

Evelyn nodded her understanding of why he was really there. It wasn't for lunch. He was up to something. She could smell it like month old socks.

"I recall I told you I wasn't interested."

"Yes, well. You may change your mind. I have several girls that would be an asset to your magazine." But none that was as exquisite as the one she already has.

"Why wouldn't you be interested in seeing what I have to offer?" Jackson took the liberty of walking around her large office, absorbed in what he saw as he did so.

"The magazine has all the girls I need. I don't have a big turn over. We are a tight unit here, small and very loyal." She watched him puzzle over her words while taking interest in her shelves of glass figurines.

"I understand what you're saying," Jackson replied. "What can it hurt to ally with each other?" He turned his blue eyes on her, shrugging his shoulders. "It can be a nice partnership in the years ahead. I have a lot of clout, Evie."

She hadn't given the future much thought after they part ways. She looked away as the notion of actually becoming business partners became a possibility. _He_ did have clout and a lot of money to back it up. Maybe they could figure something out after this nightmare was over.

"Show me around." Jackson coaxed her with a smooth

inviting tone. He then gave her a wicked smile that sent vibrations down her entire frame. Her heart raced in her chest when he took her arm in a way of lead.

So many days had gone by without as much as a glance at Nicholas. He was up and out of the house when she got up. Usually she was already in bed by the time he came home. They shared almost nothing, but the room in which they slept in. No words. No looks, nothing: *This* was the closest he's come to her since that breathtaking kiss.

She gave him her orders to stay away and it appears as if he was doing as instructed. So, why was she unraveling like a skein of yarn that a kitten was playing with? Frazzled and frayed all around the edges, about to break off any moment.

**

Evelyn's laughter filled the air around their table. The waitress had just placed their lunches in front of them while Jackson was finishing up his joke. The laughter that erupted from the woman across from him made him stop what he'd been doing and watch her face as it creased with delicate lines that didn't take away from her soft beauty.

He could tell she wasn't much for laughing. The sound had taken both of them by surprise. He was awed, she was embarrassed, turning red, lowering her face to hide the chuckles that continued to come forth despite her struggle with propriety.

How it had happened, he didn't know, but he was looking at the face of his future. He had been so lucky to find her. Jackson hadn't been looking for what this woman was bringing to the table and they were just beginning. He had a sudden desire to tell her everything. Everything, he'd left out of their agreement because he knew she would never have agreed but, things were different than a few weeks ago. More than a month ago, time has flown by. His birthday was just a few days away. Not that she knew that. He told her that event was next month to buy more time.

Would she be angry with him for not revealing all? She desired him, this he knew by just looking at her. Every time he touched her she pulled away, inflicted by the heat he produced. He vexed her in all the right ways, and if she knew their marriage was real and binding by laws and contract, would she be relieved because the sin she feels on a daily basis would be no longer an issue? Her virtue and vows would be intact, leaving nothing, but a yearning need to give in to the wonders of intimacy she has been denying herself.

Evie wasn't what he'd expected at all. When they met in the cab, she was all professional, with the right amount of sex appeal. She wore nice, alluring outfits with a demure surface to hide the sensual woman she truly was. At their first meeting at lunch, he discovered something about her that really lured him in for the kill.

He'd been apprehensive in the beginning, maybe he was making a mistake, *did he really want to be like his parents?* That was a definite yes. At that point, he did not foresee meeting a woman that he could desire for long periods. He tired way too early in relationships. A woman's sniveling act only daunted him making him loath their desire for material things. All women had been the same for Jackson, so he stopped looking. Hadn't desired a woman in many a years until… in walks Evelyn Mitchell stirring up every notion he'd ever conceived to know about women and their priorities.

Yes, he had wanted the kind of marriage his parents had. It seemed the only way. The idea of marrying with those kinds of shadows had really discouraged him about the whole matter, which was why he didn't tell Evelyn about the conditions with which she'd signed to. He hated the idea of being tied down. That is, until seeing Evelyn in his office, going over that damnable list. Touching her neck, soothing out her own disapproving heartaches he knew she was going through.

Evelyn wasn't drop dead gorgeous. She was a run of the mill attractive, not the kind he would date but turns out, one that he finds a desire too hot to contain, too strong to control, and too passionate to ignore. A passion that not only he is aware of and she tries to evade it at every turn, at all cost.

"You don't laugh much." Jackson watched her settle herself, gaining posture as she did so.

"I didn't mean to burst out like that…" She murmured.

"It's… so unbecoming of me."

"What's wrong with having a good time, enjoying yourself," Jackson leaned forward. "I like it when you laugh, shows your beauty."

Evelyn couldn't restrain her giggle. Her hand came up and covered her mouth as she laughed at his statement. "Don't." Her eyes pleaded with him to stop being condescending with her feelings. Not being beautiful never brought on the dissention she was feeling right then.

Normally, she didn't care about not being able to stop a man in his tracks by her looks alone. Since being out of the convent, she always had to have the aid of clothes or make up to grab a man's attentions. Soon she discovered it wasn't worth it. She was now thirty and was prepared to remain unapproachable by mere looks alone.

Today, though, she did find a smidgen of concern about Nicholas' ideas about her looks, and finding herself in a wishful state of mind. What would it be like if he did find her attractive? If their fake marriage didn't bring them so close, he'd never attempt to try being intimate with her, this she knew. She wasn't the man's type and vice-versa but she still wondered what if...

Jackson knew if he pressed the issue any farther she'd balk, so he changed the subject to the main one he had come to her in the first place. His parents called inviting them to dinner Thursday afternoon. Which he wasn't sure was a good idea. Evelyn didn't really cherish the idea of entertaining them. She was regal with his folks and very polite, but still shuttered from the first encounter with his mother. He suggested going over or have them come for dinner just to see her reaction, but not really intending to go.

"Mom called this morning. They'd like us to come over for Thanksgiving." He awaited a reply from Evelyn, watching her reaction closely, taking note of the slight wince in her face as her eyes creased with tension.

"I see," Evelyn responded. She wasn't sure how to approach the rest of what she wanted to say. There really was no way around this meeting. It had been planned, and she never gave the dates a second look.

"I know you aren't crazy about my parents."

"No, that's not it," Evelyn claimed. "it's just... I have to leave New York." She told him. "A meeting was already planned before we met. I didn't take notice of the dates I'd be gone, until just recently." Evelyn sighed, "I'm sorry."

"You're leaving..." Odd, how those words were affecting him.

"...that's..." He began but Evelyn's cell buzzed at that moment, cutting him off before he could say, all right.

His family really wasn't very big on the holidays. He was almost relieved that she would be gone. Maybe he too could come up with a plan to be gone. His mother would be unbearably harsh on him if he went alone. Evelyn was already on the hit list when she _was_ at the table; he dreaded the talk that would take place while she was gone.

"Right, I'll be there tonight." Evelyn was saying in her phone. "It's just a week." Jackson tried to not pay any attention to what she was saying until the next line she spoke tugged at his chest with anger he wasn't clear where it came from.

"Oh aren't you sweet, Steven. Will you hold my hand as well?" She asked then added, "In your lap… Oh, I don't think so." She smiled, her big brown eyes rolling to the back of her head, her face turned a light shade of pink. What was he saying …to make her blush like that?

"Yes. We leave early in the morning. I'll be going to the hotel right after landing, so maybe in my room later in the evening?" Evelyn turned away from the table as she spoke again into her phone. "Thank you so much, you're my sweetheart. See you tonight." …_Sweetheart_ … Jackson felt his blood boil at the sound of her voice as she spoke to the man on the other line. Steven, the name was familiar. The same Steven she'd talked to before leaving for a late night something or another? She called it a meeting, but she didn't get home until eleven thirty. What kinds of meetings went on until late at night? The kind he didn't like her going on, that was for sure. Again, he found himself wondering; who, the hell… was Steven.

He watched every move she made. Right after saying a short goodbye, she flipped the phone down and returned it to her purse. Undeniable anger festered at the pit of his stomach as he thought of the man she was meeting. Did she meet him all those times she was late coming home? Was he a boyfriend? Maybe he should have been more forthright with their agreement, what she had agreed to. Certainly, a boyfriend was not in it! Were they close? She called him sweetheart, did that mean…

Jackson stirred uncomfortably in his chair. Thinking about another man touching her was just too much to take. He leaned forward about to make a comment on what he'd heard when she spoke first.

"I will be back on Sunday, if you want to make arrangements with your parents then…" She proffered with a soft smile. "I just can't get out of this meeting. We have been planning this for a while now."

"We…" The single word caught in the back of Jackson's throat as it escaped his parted lips. He wanted to refrain from showing his discomfort about the call but obviously, his mind had other thoughts entirely and spoke for him.

Evelyn heard the anger in his tone, but couldn't do anything about it. Yes, she agreed to go to family gatherings every time they were invited. The more they were seen the better it would be for him, but there was no way out of this meeting and if there was…she'd never take it. This was her future. The future of her business relied on meetings such as this. It meant more money possibly. Surely, he understood that being an executive himself. If he didn't understand…then too bad!

"We," She started to say and then angrily added, "As in my company, _my_ business." She told him sternly. "So don't start with the agreement again." She warned him. "I know what we agreed, but this was already planned out way before that agreement ever came to mind."

"When do you leave?" He asked. She mentioned a week. Was she going to be gone a whole week? He tried to get a grasp of the situation at hand. The idea of being away from her upset him and he wasn't sure why. Was Steven going as well? He closed his eyes, relief filling him up when nothing came out of his parted lips. Thank God he didn't word his trepidation on what he was feeling and thinking at the moment.

"In the morning," Her whispered reply sank into his gullet and soured on the spot. As in: first thing in the morning? Slowly he brought his napkin to his mouth and wiped away some unwanted food. He'd began eating for nothing but a distraction, but a sudden wave of nausea hit him hard and food was the last thing he wanted.

16

"That's it... turn your head a little closer to Jay's. Great! That is fabulous hold it right there." Margot moved away from the set and the two people standing in front of the backdrop of a tropical island, at night with the moon glistening off the ocean. Jay was a male-bronzed model, with thick arms and legs full of muscle, with a tall physic to go with it. Wearing a tight pair of low riding red swim trunks that stuck to his oiled body, Jay leaned against the tall palm tree with his arms wrapped around the sleek and slender Ashley. They were facing each other in the throes of a magical paradise, about to kiss.

The studio lights were dim to give the effect of night so the drop looked more authentic. Jackson wanted to go to the tropics but this... He looked at the setting, wasn't half bad. It looked the part.

The whirr of the camera, as the rounds went off, filled the set and then Margot instructed the models. "Jay lean down a bit more, get right against her. Ashley, push that sweet body of yours right up to Jay...That's it." She remarked when both models moved as asked.

Jay was Jackson's model and Ashley was one of Don's great finds. She was attractive and what he'd been looking for, for this shoot but ended up with girls with baggy braziers and droopy drawers.

"Wouldn't have to tell me to get up close to that beauty," Don commented as he sidled up next to Jackson. Don Gentry; was renown, for his agency. He made many girls happy and they paid the price for their happiness. Jackson didn't play those kinds of games and maybe that was why he had baggy girls and not ones like Ashley. "Your guy's not too bad. Where'd you find him?"

"Mail order," Jackson replied. "Item number 435 in the husky section."

Don shook his head as they watched the shoot continue.

Jackson didn't divulge where and how he comes across new faces. Sometimes they walk right in the door looking for work. Others serve him lunch from time to time. He was always looking for a fresh new look, spotting the few that stand out from the rest, always on the job trying to be a step ahead of the competition.

"Lay your back right against that hard chest of his..." Margot was instructing Ashley. Jackson watched, as the young girl cautiously rested her small frame against Jay's muscled chest. Jay was leaning against the tree, with the backdrop behind him. Ashley looking up at him while his fingers caressed her neck, the tips just grazing her soft flesh. Their heads close, almost touching, while the camera snapped frame after frame of the romantic scene before them.

Sudden images flitted in front of Jackson. He'd been watching the way Jay's fingers had been caressing Ashley's skin and was taken back to the times when he had touched Evelyn that way. How soft her flesh had been beneath his touch and how heated she became with a mere caress. Had Steven touched Evelyn like that? Did _he_ get her heated with a soft touch? Were they together right now?

The two bodies in front of him suddenly changed. Instead of Ashley's neck Jay had been touching, it was Evelyn's. He no longer saw Ashley in the tight yellow bikini, but Evelyn. Evelyn was laying her body back raising her head up to

189

receive a kiss, and it was Evelyn's purr that he heard echoing in the chambers of his heart.

"That was great guys, thanks. Go change." Margot told the models. She then turned to Don and Jackson. "I'll send the proofs out to Dwight first thing in the morning. He won't make any decisions until next week." She patted her camera. "I think he'll have a hard time choosing which one he likes best. But when he does I'll send it on to you." Then she was gone, leaving the men to stare for a moment. Don then sighed, "Well, I have to take Ashley home."

Jackson remained in the studio for a few moments just looking at the backdrop still visualizing Evelyn and Jay standing on those sandy beaches and the moonlit ocean before them. His stomach lurched forward and that sour taste returned. He swallowed before turning away from the scene and stalked out of the studio, simmering down to the core.

It was Wednesday and she hasn't called once. Was she having so much fun she didn't have the time to call? Not even to let him know she'd made it all right?

The moment he was in the house he went to the family room, which was the closest room that had a bar and poured a shot of whiskey, drank it down and immediately poured out another.

She'd been gone five damn days and he hasn't heard a thing from her. He woke up in an empty room with a freakin' backache from the damn sofa. He tried to sleep in his bed, he doubted he would ever be able to sleep in that bed again since she'd lain between those sheets. Despite having Molly strip the bed, he could still smell the sweet scent of Evie.

The bed will never be the same. The room wasn't the same anymore. He would lay awake, watching the bed, wishing she were there to watch. Sometimes, he heard her breathing but now, it was just too damn quiet. Nothing was the same; even the house seemed too quiet. Food seemed to have lost all flavor, he hadn't been eating right. Not that he shared many meals with Evelyn. It was as if she'd suddenly dominated his whole world and without her, nothing made sense.

He laid his glass down on the closest table, even his drinking wasn't the same. The liquor had lost its kick and he wasn't interested in the dull flavor it left in his mouth. He'd much rather have a sweet kiss to savor hours later, which got him to thinking about Evelyn and wondering if she was sharing those sweet lips with Steven or maybe another lucky soul. Wishing she were there to steal such tasty treats.

Oliver walked into the room shortly after Jackson finished his second drink, holding the phone out, he stated, "You have a phone call, Mr. Slade. It's Mrs. Slade." Jackson sat forward taking the receiver from the older man's fingers.

"Thanks Oliver." Jackson took the phone. The grin that showed up on his face made Oliver cock his head in wonderment, but for some reason the stout man didn't comment about the odd way his employer was acting of recent.

Jackson didn't even wait for Oliver to leave the room before he called out through the phone. "Evie..." He meant to say a slew of things, but his throat closed right up and his heart fluttered beneath his chest. Why was he acting like a damn teenage boy, caught up in his first crush?

"Jackson."

The sudden pain he felt was indescribable. It hit dead center and then flowed throughout his whole body when his mother's voice responded on the other end of the line and not Evelyn's sweet tone.

The silence between them hung listlessly for a few moments before she finally began talking. "Lester tells me you aren't coming tomorrow."

"No." Jackson sat back against the back of the chair and watched the fire dance in the hearth.

"Why not," Her tone was curt and very sharp.

"Because I don't feel like it," He responded with the same tone. He snatched his drink and swallowed it in one gulp.

"Is everything all right?" She asked after a short pause. Her tone was wickedly sweet and demure. A tone he'd learned early on when she was saying one thing and meaning an entirely different thing.

"Just fine, Mother,"

"Are you under the weather because your wife isn't there for your first holiday?"

Jackson sighed, "No. We are _fine_ mother." He repeated assuring her that things were going well between him and his wife. "It's not a big deal."

"It's your first holiday." She hummed through the line. "Come have dinner with your family. It'll make you feel better."

"We hardly ever do the holiday thing, Mother." Jackson got up and poured himself another drink. "You and dad are always away for the holidays, and not together, so don't pull the wounded act with me. You could care less that Evelyn isn't here to spend any time with." He swallowed the amber liquid, waiting for the sting that didn't seem as strong as usual.

"I'll have you know we spent our first holiday together, Jackson. And, many after," She added agitated. Jackson shook his head. "And your father never once left me alone on my birthday."

Touché! She knew exactly where to hammer that nail every

192

damn time! Jackson poured another drink.

"Yeah… Thanks." Jackson hung up the phone and then threw it into the nearest wall.

The liquor in the glass sloshed around as he settled back in his chair, his eyes watched the dancing fire. His thoughts were on his wife. He trailed his finger over his left eyebrow as he did so. He was angered, but not because Evelyn hadn't stuck around for his birthday. She didn't know, he didn't tell her. She thought and thinks his birthday isn't till December.

It was his mother he was angered at, the woman knew just what buttons to push. Her dig wasn't for the missed birthday, he had plenty of those in his life. What she was digging at was the smug way she'd let him know, his marriage was worse than her own. Even in her miserable *arrangement* she had a spouse that cared enough to share her birthday, if nothing else, she had her husband on her birthday. It was more than her own son and she was pleased as punch to point that out. Revealing his unorthodox marriage, that replicated her own, almost, to a tee. *That* was what pissed him off the most.

He did not want to repeat their mistakes. He thought he did in the beginning, but the more he thought about it, he thought himself to have been crazy to want such a depressing, degrading relationship. Why on earth would he want what they had? He'd rather give his money away before he stooped to that level, to his father's level, because although he loved money and his position in life, he respected himself more than money could ever please. He respected Evelyn and was happy to say he actually missed her. Wished he had told her his birthday was coming up, he was certain she wouldn't have left had she known.

When was her birthday? He wondered. Would she like a gift or just flowers? What kind of flowers? If he bought her a

193

sweater, or maybe some jewelry, he had no clue as to what she'd like. He sighed as that notion put severe darkness in his heart. He was married but he knew nothing of the woman, except how she inflamed him without even trying.

Jackson gasped harshly. Where, was this relationship different then his parents? Elliott had no clue about his wife either and, that was, the way he liked it. Jackson watched the fire dance. Evie liked to dance. What else did she like? Instantly he snapped to attention. His eyes scanned the room briefly then he shot out of the chair, setting the glass down on the first flat surface he came to and hurried upstairs.

**

Raindrops hitting the tall window next to the bed sounded like drum beats. The room was so silent, the rain drowned out all other sounds. Evelyn lay in the bed, watching as the drops hit the pane and rolled downward to the bottom. Sleep allured her for the third night in a row. Normally she loved LA. This trip, wasn't so good. Her mind drifted away, not really keeping on task. She'd called the office to make sure everything was going well only to find out the girls were going out clubbing.

The moment she heard that, she couldn't say what the rest of the conversation was. Evelyn's mind quickly focused on the last time she went to a club. Her body immediately heated up where Nicholas had touched and laid his hot mouth against her skin. After that... work was the last thing she could concentrate on.

Frustrated, she rolled over on to her back and watched the rain dance on the ceiling above, wishing that sleep would come knock her on the head so she could get a few hours of rest before... what? She asked herself. She didn't have a thing to do in the morning, or all day for that matter. She could stay right where she was and sleep. No one would know, or even care.

A tingle tickled her cheek as a warm tear trickled down her face. The holidays had always been warm and cheery while growing up. She missed the laughter of cousins and her mother humming while she cooked in the kitchen. When she left, all of that stopped. Well, her parents surely still had relatives over she just never went. So many years of turning her back on them only to discover she'd be hurting herself in the long run.

Tomorrow was Thanksgiving and she was alone, again.

She'd lost all contact with the cousins she'd grown up with, all of them were from her father's side, none lived in Montana anymore and she'd lost all interest in speaking with them when she left. Back then, she cut herself off from her entire family. From everyone who cared about her, for the love of something they just didn't understand. She was so afraid they'd make her go home, so she never went home, period. Now...she wished she had at least over the holidays. Those she missed the most and wished she had fond memories of those days of old instead of empty space and a yearning for something different.

Wonder if Nicholas would be with his family tomorrow. She thought as she settled against her pillow and closed her eyes. Maybe she could call him.

17

The shrill of her cell phone woke her the next day. A blazing sun filled the room with its golden hues making her eyes squint with pain. Evelyn groaned, annoyed. Who the devil, could be calling her? She was sound asleep and probably would have stayed that way for several more hours!

"Arrg!"

She threw the blankets over her head, closing out the phone that rested on the dresser by the bedroom door. It kept ringing. Finally, she thrust the covers off and jumped out of bed.

"What do you want?" She answered expecting to hear Keli or one of the other girls eager to tell her how their night went.

"Are you gonna sleep the whole day away?" A man's voice inquired through the line. Immediately Evelyn stood up, eyeing herself in the tall mirror behind the dresser. Her nightshirt had twisted all around her body from her restless night.

"It's a beautiful day, sleepy head. Why don't you get dressed and go out to enjoy a bit of it before the day is gone?"

Evelyn sighed as she slipped back in her bed, pulled the covers up over her head.

"I don't feel like it Nicholas." She told him. "It's not a beautiful day at all."

"Oh. I just figured it was, you're in LA."

"Rained all night," She informed him.

"It's not now," He countered. "Come on, get up and go to the beach, get some sun."

"I can't." She replied softly, she tried to hide the sadness that was still lingering from the night before.

"Don't tell me you're working." His voice gruff, but interested.

"No." Evelyn sat up with her eyes looking around the room. "Why are you calling me? What do you want?"

"It's Thanksgiving," He replied. "...just wanted to say hello. See how things were going. Are you having dinner with friends?"

"No." ...Short, and to the point. She slipped back down, pulling the covers over her head once more.

"No dinner?" He questioned. Evelyn sighed.

"No."

"Turkey...stuffing...sweet potato pie,"

"No."

"Don't you like all of that stuff," He asked astonished. "...gravy, with mashed potatoes, and cornbread stuffing? Oh, Man, that right there is my fav...or... ite!" Hers, was the *cranberry sauce.* She loved that so much, she ate it right out of the can...Evelyn's heart quaked in her chest as the memory came to life. Oh...

"No, Nicholas. I don't want..."

"Come on, get up out of that bed before I come get you."

The silence that fell between them stilled Evelyn's heart. Her eyes flickered around the darkness beneath the covers, her ears listening...What did he say?

As if he heard her thoughts, his voice called through the phone. "Yeah, that's right. You heard me. Get up or I'm coming in there and getting you up."

She didn't know what to say in response. He was joking... right? He was in New York... He can't come in here...

curiosity getting the better of her though, she got up and slowly opened the door to the large sitting room. It was just as she had expected it to be… Empty.

"Very funny…" She chided him.

"I'm in the lobby… in your hotel… on my way up. Get dressed cause I'm coming in."

"Nicholas…?"

"Are you getting dressed?"

"I am not." She retorted.

"Then dinner will have to wait because…If I have to dress you, you'd better believe I'm going to have a little fun while I'm at it."

"You wouldn't dare!" She cried out.

"Get dressed…" The line went dead.

Frantically Evelyn rushed in the bedroom and pulled some clothes on, deciding to trust he was speaking truth. She didn't want to be standing in her flimsy nightgown when and if he came barging in on her.

Lucky she trusted him, because the moment her clothes were on, the pounding on the door began. She opened it to discover not only had he come to LA, he wasn't alone. Waiters from the kitchen accompanied him as he strode through the door, into her day room as if he owned the place. She wanted to speak him out for just barging in on her unannounced, but then she saw what the waiters were carrying and suddenly became unable to speak.

Jackson smiled as he watched Evelyn observe, as tray after tray of food came into the penthouse. Her eyes were huge with awe and the brown was so bright with confusion. Unsure she was seeing right and blinking back the tears that threatened to fall to her cheeks.

"What's all this?" She asked in a light gasp. Her eyes turned to him the moment the last waiter came in, deposited his tray and walk out, closing the door behind him.

"Dinner," He replied and then smiled brighter, seeing how surprised she had been made his whole day. It would be a first Thanksgiving that he could say he really enjoyed. "Happy Thanksgiving, Evie."

"All of this..." She spun to look at the abundance of food in the room.

"Is for us?"

"Isn't Thanksgiving without all of the food," He said dipping his finger into the sweet potatoes and sticking it in his mouth. "...Mm."

"I thought you'd be with your family." She stepped to the table and slipped her finger in the same bowl of potatoes. Her eyes slanted as she smiled, tasting the delicious flavor. Nicholas shook his head.

"Mother would never let me eat right out of the bowl." The laugh that came from him was soft and he leaned in to her and said, "She's such a prude!" His chest heaved as the roar of laughter came out with his statement.

He repeated his action the second time, but then took his finger to her mouth. "Are you glad I'm here?" He raised his left eyebrow in question as Evelyn licked off the potatoes from his wet finger. She giggled shaking her head. She was so happy he was there but it didn't have anything to do with the food or his sweet gesture. His kindness went deep, but his presence soared right to the heart and tersely stopped it from beating. *Was he missing her* or *was he just being thoughtful,* she wondered.

They actually had themselves a smorgasbord of delightful treats. It all was so wonderful and so filling. They ate, and they ate until they were both unable to move a muscle.

"The first year I was allowed to help my mom in the kitchen was when I was ten and I burnt the apple pies."

She snickered softly. "I was so upset. I was happy to be helping her, proud to be in her kitchen and I burnt the pies."

"She wasn't angry, was she?" Jackson asked her. Evelyn shook her head.

"Not even the slightest. My father actually ate a whole slice just to stop my crying." She rested her head against the sofa, watching him.

"They sound like good folks. Good parents." He looked out the glass window. All he could see was the blue sky above but it was better than looking at her sweet face while the unwanted murkiness of his own childhood took over his heart. He envied her and he didn't want her to notice just how much their life differed from each others.

"You don't have good memories like that...do you?" She asked him, seeing the truth flit across his face and his eyes twitch with damning emotions.

Jackson shook his head. "Not good ones, no. Dad never stayed home long enough to create any and when I got older, Mom started leaving as well. It was just me and the help."

Evelyn rested her head next to his shoulder. That really sounded pitiful, but she kept her thoughts hidden. "How old were you?"

"Nine, maybe eight... I was ten when I went to boarding school." He sighed. "It was before then."

"Where did you go for school?" She asked hoping that would lighten the mood. It was suddenly dark and depressing.

"Paris." Evelyn sat up and looked at him. Jackson turned his head to look at her. "Have you ever been?" She shook her head. She always wanted to, but never had the money or the time.

"I hear it's pretty there."

He nodded. "I grew up there, its home to me. I lived there straight out of school for several years."

It was quiet while they pondered a few things. He mainly stayed in France because his parents hardly ever went, he was free of them and he loved being free.

He gazed at Evelyn's face while she did the same to him. He didn't tell many about his childhood, about his family. It was depressing and he couldn't change it, so why talk about it.

Funny, how he felt uplifted and oddly appeased, despite the smidgeon of pity that seeped into her eyes but it was not alone, there was also a small hint of envy and he wasn't sure which took more control of her thoughts. Her eyes had swelled with so much interest when he said, Paris.

He wanted to take her there. The idea was sudden and accompanied with a strong sense of sharing something nice with her, much like the Maui trip. He wanted to take her to Paris and share his childhood memories, all of maybe a dozen, but they were good memories. The only ones that, _were_ good.

"You were real close with your folks." Jackson stated softly while his gaze settled on her soft smile and those kissable lips.

Evelyn nodded, clearing her throat. "I didn't realize that until they were gone."

"I'm sorry."

"No." Evelyn sighed looking up at the ceiling. "Don't be, I was foolish to take them and what I once had for granted. I have nothing left of them, except for that house..." She sighed deeply.

That house...

That house, thought Jackson was what had brought this remarkable creature to his doorstep and it was why she remained today. He hadn't signed it over to her just yet and he could tell she was anxious. Darkness invaded his insides. Once she had that damn house, he was going to lose her! The idea of her leaving upset him in many ways, it perplexed him and if she were to leave...

His eyes feasted upon her soft face. She hadn't had the chance to primp in front of a mirror. There was no color upon her cheeks, except the natural red, that happened when she smiled or blushed. There was no color above her eyes. Just those huge chocolate toned gazes that drew him away from all senses. Mesmerized by the innocent way she seemed to speak to him.

They had eaten their fill of food and drank enough drink to fuel most of the state, and feasted plenty of sweet deserts to keep a busload of children cranked up for hours. His stomach couldn't take on anymore but oddly, a hunger simmered continuously in the pits of his belly. Reminding him no amount of food could sate what his body ached for...

He scanned her high cheeks and moved his slow stare to her hair. Up in a bun as she always wore it. His eyes creased with wonder as to why she kept it so tight to her head.

Evelyn turned her head to look back to him and found his heated wondrous gaze, as he eyed her face, noticing the lack of makeup. She must look a fright, surely he thought her frumpy and plain! She took note as he took in her hair. She answered his questioning stares with a truth she shared with no one else, quickly looking away as she did.

"I was taught at an early age about coverings a woman needed to wear to hide her femininity." She shyly looked away from his gaze that seemed to bore down to her soul.

"Did you wear one of those...habits?"

She nodded. "...In the early years. We had to cover everything up. But when I traveled to India and Asia, it wasn't needed. As long as I wore my hair up, that was enough."

Jackson let his eyes flow over her hair. "You always wear it up?" She nodded again. "For the same reasons, to cover you..." His gaze darted back and met with hers. Evelyn watched his Adam's apple as he swallowed hard.

"It's become a habit of another kind now..." She smiled softly.

He nodded. "Do you miss it?" Evelyn wasn't sure what he was referring to.

"Being a nun?"

"Oh..." She gasped and shook her head. "Miss it...If that were so, then I'd still be one." She shrugged her shoulders. "I still go on retreats every once in a while and I attend church."

"Would you like some more to drink?" Jackson asked her, about to get up to get her something.

Evelyn shook her head as she moved against the sofa. "I just want to sit here and relax. I ate way too much." She then turned her gaze to the tables loaded with endless food that was going to go to waste. She then looked at him.

"Mm, me too..."

"What are you planning on doing with all of this food?" she watched his robust shoulders shrug with a blank stare in his eyes. Slowly while they looked into each other's gaze, she saw concern.

"What do you think we should do with it?" He questioned earnestly as he watched her closely, wanting to do whatever she suggested.

"There are so many going hungry..." She started to say but then he quickly shook his head in understanding.

"Right...Of course!" He'd never given anything to charity before but felt very compelled in taking part of what she had been suggesting. "Give me just a sec…" he whipped out his phone and Evelyn watched as he took charge of the matter. In a few minutes, the room was emptied out, the food to be distributed to all of the nearby shelters and soup kitchens.

"Thank you." She whispered.

Jackson moved close so she could rest her head against him. He closed his eyes and sighed. "Happy Thanksgiving, Evie." He whispered.

"Thank you for coming, Nicholas."

**

"What are we going to do again?" Evelyn asked Jackson as they got off the elevator.

"We are going to the Westmyer Country Club. I haven't been in years and I would love to get a game of polo in." Jackson told her as they got in the cab.

"I didn't know you played." She couldn't hold back the concern that fretted her tone. *Wasn't polo a harsh game?*

"I used to play all the time in France but since coming to the states, I've backed off. This country club has the best polo teams. I've played a few times with them."

Evelyn's slight agitation grew the moment the men were in position on the field sitting on gallant horses and smacking a ball back and forth. The game was played much like water polo but on horses. It was an aggressive sport, in which the jockey hits a ball, chases it upon his steed only to smack it again. Swift turns on a horse weighing hundreds of pounds more than its rider, waving a wooden mallet attached to their wrists like a bracelet. She'd heard of polo but had never seen it in action.

Quickly Evelyn realized she didn't like the game. It was much too harsh and she couldn't fight the wild emotions that coursed her veins every time the horses collided, as their riders jerked them back and forth, trying to capture the ball. Sometimes, the riders pushed and shoved their way to the ball, and sometimes both events would happen and Evelyn would just close her eyes and hope that all came out well.

Nicholas had said he'd played the game before and his riding ability showed just how much he played it. He was one of the most aggressive players on the field, there was another who was on the opposing team, who was as much if not more aggressive and the two dueled quite often over that stupid ball. In fact, Evelyn could have sworn they were looking for ways to meet up and fight over the rights to the goal. Enjoying their bouts each time they met.

In the bottom of the fourth period, Nicholas' team was leading and he had the ball in sight on the right of his horse, about to hit it farther down the field when the other aggressive player, from the other team made a dash for Jackson's horse. The two collided and Nicholas was jolted from the seat, his head bobbed up, still aiming for the ball just as the other player was aiming, but the other player actually got to the ball first and gave it a good _whack_.

The sound echoed over the field and reverberated off Evelyn's chest. The rider then kicked his horse forward and just as his mallet came around, it broke loose from the player's wrist, whipping through the air and catching Nicholas in the forehead, dropping him to the ground in instant blackness.

Evelyn couldn't believe what she had seen, as she watched Nicholas' limp frame fall like a lead brick off the back of his horse which was riding at full speed. Two other players were close by and didn't have the time or space to move and ended up running him over with the hooves of their horses.

Screams emerged from the crowds; Evelyn's may have been the loudest.

18

Wearing a spot on the shiny hospital floor in the ER Evelyn found it very hard to breathe. Her chest heaved with uncertainty. Her hands clasped tightly in front of her, twisting and wringing themselves into a sweaty mess. She tried, but couldn't control the shakes that her body was enduring. It was so hard to block out the way Nicholas looked lying on the ground not moving. Her heart pounded at the thought of him seriously injured.

She paced back and forth, sat down, trying to settle her nerves only to get back up and walk some more. *Please let him be all right*, she prayed over, and over again. She couldn't bear another loss, another loved one that slipped through the cracks...*Loved one.* The idea didn't surprise her as much as it should have. She'd known for a while just how much she cared and was trying to deny it. Love was the only answer to why she craved him the way she did, *wanted* him the way she did. How on earth, can she love a man that only wanted her as a pawn in a game? He wasn't *hers* to love...

"Mrs. Slade?" The doctor had approached her, Evelyn was so busy rocking and praying she didn't even notice. Her head snapped up at the sound of his voice. Her legs grew strength and she stood to greet him. "I'm doctor Jessup, your husband has suffered a mild concussion and a few bruised ribs."

Evelyn felt relief fill her heart first, before flowing to the rest of her body. Sending the notice that she could relax, everything was fine. Her heart jumped in precautionary mode and she asked with a tremble, "Will he be alright?"

"He will need some bed rest and a little TLC. He took quite a hit to the head." The doctor genuinely smiled when she sighed in relief. "He should be just fine in a few days. We're setting a room up for him to stay for a few days–just to be safe." He grasped her arm in assurance and gave it a gentle squeeze before turning away.

A flood of relief cascaded all over her body forcing her to sit back down and tell herself to take a deep breath before she had a nervous breakdown.

"You can go in now."

Evelyn once again turned to look at the voice that had spoken to her. The nurse that had been working on Nicholas was standing right beside her.

"Is he... awake?"

"I'm afraid not. The doctor has him on a heavy dose of painkillers. But I'm sure he'll hear you, it will comfort him to know you're close by." Evelyn walked in the room with the nurse. "You can stay with him until we move him."

Evelyn slowly approached the bed and looked down at Nicholas' bandaged head. He looked pale, and so frail looking despite his large frame and wide shoulders. A soft quivering smile fell over her lips the closer she got to the bed. Her trembling hand came out to wisp his hair that had fallen against the white gauze on his head. Her fingers remained on his soft hair, as she looked down at him. A renegade tear rolled down her face.

She was so relieved that he was all right but disarmed about what to do with her feelings. What will she do when he was no longer in need of her? She'd just discovered how it would feel if he was out of her life. Surely, she was excited about his injuries, but deep down she also feared losing him. What was she going to do when he is actually gone for good? A dilemma she did *not* want to face.

**

From the tenth floor window, the view was spectacular. To the right was nothing but ocean and the surf where vessels of all different kinds moved along. There were barges carrying freight and cargo boxes to the south. Sail boats, also dotted the scene below as they drifted over the crystal embedded waves.

Beyond the dazzling blue waters was the prettiest blue sky that reflected off the water in a mirror image that was breathtaking. The fine line where the horizon met skies to the sea, was hard to capture with a blind eye, it was so far away.

Evelyn had been staring at the view a few hours now. Her heart was there in the water, her mind, to the horizon. Turbulence shattered all the beauty before her. Her heart pained in dread of what was to come and how she must fight with more will power then she was sure to have but she must...

Sound from the bed made her abruptly turn and go to him. Finally, Nicholas was stirring. She smiled down into his bright eyes as she approached grasping his hand, giving it a squeeze. "Hey." She whispered.

"Hey." He called back. He closed his eyes in pain. "Why do I feel like I have been run down by a damn train?"

"Because you were," She told him in a tender voice. His eyes came open, noticing her apprehension. She tried to pull away, but his stare that was so full of color was also full of empathy for her and her troubled mind. She couldn't turn away from him.

She couldn't move as he brought his hand up to her face.

His fingers touched her cheek. Wrapping around her neck, and then pulled her closer to him.

"Come here." He murmured when she at first refused. The concern in his eyes made her move despite her fighting need to hold back.

Evelyn closed her eyes when his warm mouth kissed her forehead. His hand grabbed her by the bun and pulled her down closer, until her head was on his shoulder. The moment his arm came around her waist, the fight within her died right out and she let loose of all the fear and cried out in anguish. She sobbed on his shoulder, relishing the warmth she felt when his arm wrapped around her frame, pulling her almost on top of him. Both of his hands then went to her head and softly soothed her crying fits.

After a few minutes, she realized she was just about lying on top of him and struggled to get free so she wouldn't hurt his ribs.

"Evelyn." He refused to let her go. His hands gripped her head and pulled up until their eyes met.

"I shouldn't be…"

"Why not," He asked her.

"I don't want to hurt you."

He gave her a soft sexy smile. "You've given me worse pain then this." He told her and pulled her down to kiss her mouth.

"Mm," Evelyn lost the battle once more and relaxed in his arms giving in to his sweet ministries.

He tasted so good and felt so warm, Evelyn didn't falter when she felt the tip of his tongue graze her lips. Eager to taste more, she opened to him and took him in her mouth with a hunger that seeped its way into her heart. The craving she once felt was gone. Now it was a need that burned from deep within. To have him hold her, kiss her, love her as no man had ever before. She wanted it all; she wanted *him*.

Nicholas brought his hand to her face, caressed her cheek while they lay in each other's arms and kissed repeatedly. Her heart pounded against her chest in a thunderous storm that was out of control. *She* was out of control.

Breathless, they parted both taking in the needed air. Evelyn closed her eyes when she felt his lips against her neck. A tingling chill coursed through her senses making her weak kneed and unsteady. His hand dropped to her waist to hold her against the bed, while the other slowly caressed upward. Softly his fingers touched her leg, caressed her thigh, toying with the hem of her sundress. Noticing but disregarding her slight tension, he brought his hand up higher. Nicholas smoothed his hand over her breast, his fingers lightly grazing the nipple that was poking through the thin material of the spaghetti strap styled dress she wore.

The dress was a thin and tied at the shoulders. She wore no bra to deflect the wonderful sensation she felt the moment his fingers touched her breast. It was as if the dress wasn't even there and all Evelyn felt was the heat of his hand against her.

Moments passed, Evelyn was dazed, by the tingling ripples both his mouth and hand, created upon her flesh. Sensations she'd never dreamed of was taking charge of her ability to think.

Her hand grasped his thick head of silky hair when warmth touched her breast. Heat penetrated her core, trickled down her spine and flashed across her mind. Desire so passionate and warm caressed her body like a strawberry dipped into melted chocolate. When her core flexed in time with the tugs on her nipple, Evelyn jolted in fear of the unknown. A chill encompassed her. She pulled away abruptly, bringing goose bumps to her skin because of the wild emotions that flowed through her.

Evelyn's heart skipped a solid beat, as she glimpsed down to her throbbing breast and found it exposed and moistened. Quickly her eyes sprang to meet his watery colored gazes they were so blue, so full of desire. His mouth, she noticed was as wet as the tip of her breast.

Mortified, she pulled away tugging her dress right about her body, moving to the window to straighten more than just her clothes…What in the world?

"Evelyn." Nicholas called from behind her. She shook her head, trying to understand, gasping, when she felt him take her shoulders in his hands. "Evie," He whispered in her ear.

"This isn't right." Evelyn managed to say despite her shaky form.

"Shh." His mouth moved against her ear. "It is right." He told her, placing his hand on hers, moving it away from the breast she was covering. "It is right, let me show you."

Evelyn's body rocked softly when he touched her breast, closing his hand around her, caressing it, squeezing with tender strokes. "You tasted so good, I've wanted to for so long." He whispered. "It's okay…" he spoke right in her ear when she tried to move away. He kissed her head. "Let it go." He tugged on her nipple. Evelyn felt her knees give out slightly. "That's it…" He told her. "…I got you."

Sensations began to run through Evelyn involuntarily whether she wanted them to or not. Unable to stand on her own, she leaned back against Nicholas. Mixed feelings pummeled her, wanting to stop him and make things right, wanting him to never stop, *please*.

"I want you to open up for me, Evie." His hand slowly moved away from her breast and she made a sound, almost a whine. "Just a second, I'm not stopping." He told her.

Evelyn's eyes grew wide as she felt his hand caress down

the front of her. Intimately touching her abdomen and dipping between her legs, taking the thin dress with it. To her surprise, her legs parted giving him the access to what he sought. Her body shuddered against the smooth caress of his hand as he pulled her dress up and slipped into her panties.

Evelyn was beside herself, her mind was screaming *stop!* Her body was begging, pleading for him to end the sweet torment he was putting her through. An ache was beginning to burn steadily while his hand sought her moist heat and slipped inside. Evelyn rocked forward, as she did on his bike when he'd touched her there.

"Purr for me, baby." Nicholas whispered, nibbling on her ear lobe and sucking it into his hot mouth. *She did...*just as her whole body came alive. Choking back the thick sobs that came out, as her frame took every pleasurable stroke he gave and moved in time with him.

Jackson held her while her body rocked with spasm after sweet spasm. Her heart was pounding so hard, he felt it in his own chest, beating heavily through her back. Both of their hearts beat in unison while Evelyn experienced her first intimate moment. Their breathing had also linked up and became one sound as she rocked in his arms.

He pressed his mouth against her face, kissing her cheek. "Tell me how can this be wrong?" He asked against her head, his mouth kissing her face, over, and over again, as her body continued to convulse in his arms.

"And how are things going in here?" The nurse walked into the room at that precise moment. Evelyn gasped and Nicholas felt her body tense right up, she tried turning away.

"Sh. Sh. Sh." He breathed right in her ear, holding Evelyn tight against him, keeping his back to the door, still facing the window. "Relax…" He cooed.

When she responded to him, he turned his head to the nurse. Letting the hem of Evelyn's dress drop back down, he rested his hand over her stomach, caressing while he spoke.

"We're taking in the view, absolutely beautiful." Jackson told the nurse as he kissed Evelyn's head.

"Nich…" Evelyn watched the panoramic view through a cloudy haze. Her body slowly simmered down to small contractions bristling throughout her whole frame. Evelyn had just experienced something warm and wonderful and _private_… fabulous sensations trickled over her flesh but she was mortified.

Standing there in front of a large window in plain view while a man…How could Nicholas touch her like that? Why wouldn't he release her so she could make things right? The dress strap was still unfastened. Her breast was exposed, but slightly covered by his hand. His caresses to her firm mound kept the tingling sensations alive. Evelyn was completely beside herself in how to react to what just happened.

"Take it slow." His whispered tone swept over her torso like a flame licking the end of a log. Red-hot embers burned deep and long despite what he'd just done to her.

"Mr. Slade, you really shouldn't be out of bed. Let me help you get back in before the doctor sees you." The nurse advised.

Jackson stood straight up stepping away from Evelyn. His hands quickly pulling her dress right, and tying the strap back into place. Evelyn's husky sigh filled the space between them when his mouth scorched her bare shoulder, kissing her softly before he turned away.

Feeling amiss, Evelyn remained at the window watching the boats drift in the water. Her mind taking in what had transpired and knowing she was in for a very hard fall. No matter how she tried to tell herself, what she felt was normal after such wanton actions. She was certain though that being indifferent to them was not a smart idea.

"Did your meetings go all right?" Jackson asked her for something to talk about. They'd talked so much the other day while they ate and drank but it wasn't enough. He wanted to know everything that she'd been doing.

"They did." She replied.

"Come on over here and sit by me." He requested without really asking, although it wasn't an order either. He watched the nurse take his vitals before taking her leave to let the doctor know he was awake. "Do you have any more?"

The meeting she had set for today had been postponed due to his accident but she wasn't going to tell him that. She now has to make it up. "I have one Saturday and then we can go home."

It felt odd that they could conduct a normal conversation after… but the more they talked the more at ease she became. She felt drawn in to his words and his smiles. Evelyn settled right on the bed and they talked the whole afternoon away.

Jackson had few visitors before dinner. The other aggressive polo player came by to see if he was okay. They talked a bit and then they were alone again.

"I'm going to go down and get a hamburger while you eat." Evelyn hopped off the bed. She reached the door when he called out.

"I would really love a candy bar."

"What kind?"

He chuckled, "Doesn't matter. I love chocolate, any will do."

Jackson ate his meal of white chicken in a rosemary sauce with rice and broccoli. He was finishing his cola when

Evelyn came back. He'd purposefully left his cherry cobbler alone, to give to her. While they talked about Thanksgivings of the past she'd told him cherry desserts were her favorite of all the fruits. It was something they had in common, he too liked cherry *anything*, which was how he came to learn about 'Cherries Jubilee'.

"I got you two candy bars and look what I found." She pulled out a deck of cards. "Wanna play?" She also pulled out a bag of chocolate kisses. "I'll play ya for a kiss."

Jackson's laughter was so loud it had to have echoed down the hall. "Are you propositioning me?" Evelyn laughed sitting back in her spot on his bed.

"I wouldn't know how to begin…"

"I believe that was a hell of a start."

Hours sped by while they played poker. Evelyn sat Indian style with her legs tucked up under her dress. She was losing. She only had ten kisses left. Nicholas had taken all of her silver confections with just about a win to every hand.

They talked as they did the night before. Work and what they'd been doing recently. He told her about the new gig he got Jay. It was the boy's first *real* shoot and Jackson thought he was going to hit it big. She in return told him about the meetings she'd been having and how two really seemed interested in buying shares in her company.

"Are you having a rough year?" he asked her, concerned. Evelyn shook her head.

"Not at all, it's been going well, can't have too much support though. You never know what's around the corner." Jackson nodded as he bid his hand.

"You know, I could buy some of those shares…" When she didn't respond he looked up from his hand. The look of pure horror was all over her face.

"You wouldn't…would you?"

"For you," He explained, obviously she thought he meant to take it over. His heart started to beat again when her face started to regain color and smiling weakly. She then sighed in relief. "Anytime you need something…" he proffered genuinely.

"You would help me?"

His masculine laugh infiltrated her system and gave her a chill that ran up and down her spine. "Why wouldn't I?" He questioned. "We're partners, right?"

"That's nice of you to offer your help Nicholas but you don't have to. You are not obligated in any way to do that. That is not in our agreement."

Screw the damn agreement! She was his wife… he *was* obligated. Just as his father and the father before him was obligated. They all had been bound, by the oath they'd taken, sworn to the women they married. He hadn't much choice in the matter anymore.

After he'd won all her kisses, Evelyn bid him a good night's rest and went back to her hotel, showered, dressed for bed and then, laid there. Everything that could invade her thoughts did. Recalling the night before, the way they talked and shared a little about themselves. She felt bad for Nicholas. It was obvious he'd had a bad childhood. He didn't have a close relationship with either parent, where she had been close to both of hers up until she left.

She then started to think about how nice it was sharing Thanksgiving dinner with him. How sweet it was of him to bring the holiday to her and falling asleep on the floor next to him, feeling the heat of his body against hers, his arm wrapped around her, protectively.

As those thoughts faded away, the sweet tantalizing moments in the hospital came to life. Standing by the window while he'd rendered her powerless against his lovemaking. Never in her wildest dreams had she thought the touch of one's hand could take her to the clouds, soaring above all that she was accustomed to. It had been mindless, fantastic and so agonizing to think about and not want a repeated performance.

Tossing and turning without an end in sight, she finally gave up, dressed and headed for the hospital. Telling herself, that being closer to Nicholas wouldn't make any difference.

**

A soft sound woke Jackson sometime in the night. Sounds from the hall floated around the gapped door, but it was something else that had caught his attention, pulling him away from a soft slumber. He looked around the room, not finding anything of interest.

He tried to move to his side, but found his leg weighed down. He reached down to massage it to find a heaviness about it that seemed strange. He looked down to find the shadow of a hand resting there on his thigh. He followed up the arm to find Evelyn's head lying on the bed by his leg, her face in his direction. How long had she been there?

His slow inspection of her started with her creamy cheeks, which were a bed for each long dark lash that delicately kissed them as she slept. His gaze casually eyed the few freckles she had. Man, he wanted to sweep his lips over each one. He then moved his stare to her hair. It was up, *again*. Did she sleep in that ghastly thing?

Soft cheeks, long lashes, freckles, all features Evelyn carried so gracefully. She hadn't been stunning but for some reason, he couldn't keep his eyes away. Assessing what it was exactly that attracted him in because she drew him in like a moth to a flame and she did it in mach time.

"Evie..." He whispered into the stillness of the room. He reached out and touched her cheek with his fingertip. He then softly rested his hand over hers on his thigh and closed his eyes, drifting back to sleep within minutes.

19

A round of festivities produced themselves the moment he and Evelyn returned home. Christmas was on its way and Evelyn shared her desires to give to certain charities as she had done every year. Therefore, to help her out, Jackson happily sponsored several parties and dinners and the proceeds went to the charity of her choice. He'd been deeply touched by the warmth he'd gotten Thanksgiving, helping the homeless he found a desire to want to do more but used Evelyn as the reasoning. He'd never given to charity in the past and was concerned by the talk this new side of him may create.

An invitation to a Christmas party a friend of Jackson's was giving had been extended their way and they agreed in going despite Evelyn's displeasure of meeting his friends. There was no reason to do so, she wasn't going to be married to Nicholas much longer, why meet his friends, and complicate matters but, he insisted they went, he went every year and it would look odd if he didn't.

"Relax." Jackson whispered as he took her hand as she elegantly stepped from the car. He couldn't remove his eyes from the long red velvet and lace dress she had chosen to wear. A delicate slit up the right leg offered him a spectacular view of her sexy legs. She looked gorgeous, but had been fretting the whole ride over to Mason's home, Jackson tried telling her she will fit in perfectly with his friends but she refused to trust him.

Evelyn's chest was tight as they entered Mason

Lockhart's fancy home with elegant chandeliers and marbled floors. She tried hard to relax as Nicholas had told her but this was not her kind of fun. The place reeked of money and high society, she couldn't help being uncomfortable.

The greeting of his friends came right after entering the home and all seemed regally happy to meet her and Evelyn's worries slipped away until later when she was graced by the company of other *friends* of Nicholas' that made a deliberate effort to say hello the first moment she was alone.

"It's, Evelyn...right?" a tall red headed woman asked Evelyn as she approached her. The tall brunette woman beside the red head nodded with a demure smile plastered across her lips. "I'm Sophie and this is Gina." Evelyn smiled politely despite the sinking feeling in her gut.

"I expected something, well," Gina snipped as she leaned her head closer to Sophie. "...less frumpy." Both women giggled softly.

"Indeed, I did too..." the red head replied. "I mean none of us could get him to say 'I do'." Her bright green eyes slithered down Evelyn's torso as if she were eyeing a homeless derelict.

Evelyn tried to remain calm but her wandering eyes couldn't refrain from seeing what stood right before her. Both women were beyond elegant. They stood with poise and their clothing a high cut of material from the orient or of somewhere else just as sheik. The yellow and blue silk or satin had jewels stitched into the lace and was breathtaking.

"And you are..." Evelyn tried to sound unaffected by what these two women were trying to accomplish.

"Gina,"

"...and Sophie." Gina answered snidely, pointing as she

spoke each name as if Evelyn couldn't comprehend what was being said.

"Gina here is the latest but I have been in the picture for three years." Sophie replied stiffly.

"Oh, now I'm not the latest..." Gina argued softly. "That trophy belongs to Evelyn here." Gina smiled and Evelyn forced a dry smile to her lips in response. "You see, we are all in the same boat when it comes to Jackson. We are *all* the same," Sophie paused as both women eyed Evelyn and then simultaneously said "well, *almost* all of us are."

"I'm sorry," Evelyn shook her head. "I'm not following you."

"Well, let us help you to understand." Evelyn watched as the women turned around to face the crowded room. "Julia in the purple gown, Kelley, is wearing yellow, Bonnie is in baby blue, Jackson loves blue..." Sophie stated nonchalantly.

"Lisa is in pink, Tori is in green, although I have told her green looks hideous on her!" Gina gasped as she pointed out into the room. "This sweetheart, is Jackson's playground and *we* are his playmates."

Every one of the women who they so kindly pointed out was spitting images of the two standing right in front of her. Beauty from head to foot and... completely her opposite.

"Uh oh, I think we hurt her feelings." Sophie reached out to console Evelyn by taking her hand. "Don't let this bother you, it will soon pass. He will move on but he will come back..."

Gina laughed tenderly. "Yeah, Jack always returns to the good ones. And you got him to say 'I do' so you must be one of the good ones."

Let this bother her... Evelyn couldn't get Sophie's words to go away much less letting them bother her. How many women did Nicholas have in his bed waiting for him? Will he be back once they say their goodbyes, as Gina had stated he often did?

Evelyn tried to let it go but they dined several times with his friends a few nights later with her mind constantly asking if every woman she met had slept with her husband.

**

Jackson was to meet the lawyer one more time just before Christmas to have the wedding contract signed and then he had to work on getting his son. Once that happened, the Slade name continued and so did the inheritance. Things, he thought... were going well. They were no closer to intimacy then they had been, despite the interlude in his hospital room. Evelyn kept her distance and it seemed as if they were roommates rather than newlyweds. He had hoped that they had moved up a level once she knew how things could be if she released her inhibitions but alas... he was still sleeping on the sofa.

**

"Evelyn, do you have the runners ready?" Keli's uplifting voice filled the silence as it beckoned from the intercom. Evelyn had been deep in thought; she actually jumped from the sudden burst of noise. Her eyes shot to the large stack of Satin & Lace magazines.

Every year, she took all of the top selling items and pulled them from the magazine in which they sold the best and *that* photo went into the last magazines of the year. All magazines were edited and ready for print now, so the office could take the entire week after Christmas off, and enjoy some time with family or friends. It was her way of saying thank you for all they did. It was their third year together and the most profitable one yet.

Evelyn usually took the time and went home. The house was always waiting for her to decorate and if her father were up to it, he'd help out. Even though her mom wasn't there, it still felt warm and cozy for such a large place. She'd sleep in her old room and let the nostalgia overwhelm her.

This year though, she couldn't do that. It was her first year without any family members since leaving the church and when her father died in the spring, she has yet to go back. It didn't seem like home without him there. Somehow the place lost its appeal and the desire to return hasn't come back yet.

Therefore, she was going to be free for a week with nothing to do. Thoughts of spending every minute at the house she was temporarily residing in didn't have an appeal to it either. Her time was ending with her so called home, her fake marriage, and her fake husband.

His birthday was just a day away. He was married as to plan and once he signs those papers she was free to go, able to go back to her life as it once had been, which didn't seem very appealing either.

"I'll bring them out in just a minute." Evelyn replied through the phone and sat back once more looking at the magazine she'd been looking through: On the cover, was a pair of 'Holiday Cheer', which was also the caption in script at the bottom of the page, there to send a greeting and advertise the Santa suit that had been a 'Holiday Item' *only* and not part of the normal sales items. The suit was a bra and panty set in red satin with a lace ribbon attached to the leg holes of the bikini bottoms along with some white down stitched to the bra and panties outlining the edges, making them feel baby soft.

Evelyn ran a finger over the cottony edging in the picture and wondered if Nicholas would like to see her in such an outfit. She could almost see the way his eyes would sparkle with the same desire she'd seen in them every night before they went to bed.

Things haven't really been the same since returning from LA. They both had come to realize the relationship between them had shifted. He no longer could hide the lust and desire he felt for her. She has come to realize what that kind of tension can do to a person if left untouched. It has rendered her a nervous soul, twitching from anticipation of a soft caress that would send her over the edge. Did he go elsewhere for release since she wasn't giving in? Faces of all of his women suddenly came to mind. He had plenty of choices and by the sounds of it; the girls wouldn't turn him away despite his new marital status.

Her body was eager for him to repeat the hospital scene, so she remained as far from him as possible, yearning for a simple caress, but still keeping her distance. Again, her time was running out. She was not staying in this situation for much longer, and to allow the sweet pleasure of his love… to render her vows and her virtue for a few moments of complete and utter ecstasy was morally and spiritually condemning. No matter how often or how much her body begged for his touch, she refused to accept it.

The idea of wearing the skimpy outfit made her heart pound hard against her chest. He was the first to bring such ideals to mind. Wanting to wear soft lingerie, stand in front of a large window allowing him passage to her body. Knowing what his hot mouth felt like upon her aching breast, wanting the same sensations to touch her everywhere.

Indeed, she was certain he'd like the red suit and…*she'd*

like to wear it!

Would it be so bad to give in to temptation just this once? Maybe for his Christmas present she'd wear it and give herself the best gift of all, at the same time…

**

Jackson couldn't believe what he was looking at. He scratched his forehead as he skimmed over the papers and then looked up at Tom Nolan, the family lawyer. "Explain it to me again."

"You need her to sign away her company." He leaned forward laying his clasped hands on top of his desk. "Evelyn is gaining everything of yours and in return she must sign her assets over to you…In the event…"

"Yeah, yeah I get that, but I don't want her company." Jackson refused in anger. He watched as the lawyer shook his head. "Doesn't matter, Jack. You gotta get it signed. There can't be separate earnings in your inheritance. What is yours will become hers. It's not like she will lose it." He pointed out to him.

Jackson stood up and paced the floor. This had never been revealed to him before now; he didn't want her damn company! He told her that very thing not too long ago. What will she think if he asked her now to sign away Satin & Lace?

She already gave him her freedom, she just wasn't aware of that fact yet, and it brought much dismay to his heart to think of her reaction when she does find out.

"What if I don't?" He stopped by the long bookshelf and studied the old leather bound books and reference manuals that lined every shelf in front of him. Legal books that explained fine laws that were hidden in long words, laws bound centuries ago, hardly recognized in today's society, but laws nonetheless.

He can't ask her for her company, he won't. It was as simple as that.

"You've done all of this for nothing."

**

Now that things were slowing down at the office with the year ending, Evelyn had the time to explore more now when she got home with no pressing work to do. Every night, she slowly went from room to room to find every room in the place had its own special touch. She wondered who did the decorating. Did Nicholas have someone come in and specialize each room to his liking or just the way they saw fit?

Every time she entered a different room, she would say she liked it best, only to go to the next and discover *it* to be the best. That is until one night she made it into the parlor.

The rich mahogany floors and deep cherry walls spoke out to her the moment she stepped in. Ageless shelves with leather bound books that took her back to the days of old when the majestic socialite would gather in rooms such as these to speak of war and destruction of their time, boasting about their warriors and their strengths and… sometimes of their demise.

This room was all masculine and alluring in appearances. The walls changed colors as she moved, giving the room shadows that created an obscurity that not only made it gloomy, but restful, as peaceful and tranquil as a hot summer day laying on a raft gliding down a lazy river.

Evelyn spun around, taking in every knot in the walls,

and the bright-lit lamps beside them attached with twisted iron molded in elegant shapes. They were yellow hues glowing like beacons in a foggy haze, leaving murky splotches on the cherry woodwork.

Spying the deep brown leather chair in the corner, she rushed to it and settled herself into the large soft cushion, swept in the beauty, her eyes closed while the room seeped into her thoughts.

Hours were spent right there in that chair without a care in the world. The room welcomed her and she in return didn't see the need to leave. She'd made plans for that evening, so when the clock on the mantle chimed four times, she knew it was time to get things underway and reluctantly, she left with a solemn heart, wishing she could return another day and maybe slip into a good heartwarming novel and let the world slip away.

In search of help, she wandered in many of the other rooms and finally met up with Molly in the library hanging up the freshly cleaned drapes.

"Molly, I need some help." Evelyn instructed the house cleaner. "I wonder if you could tell me Mr. Slade's favorite meal."

"...Ma'am?" She questioned with dipped eyebrows.

"I wanted to share a special meal with him tonight. Being his birthday and all, I wanted to surprise him with a gift." Evelyn exclaimed. "Do you think he'll like a surprise dinner for two?"

"For, *his;* birthday," Molly stated.

Evelyn smiled and nodded. "Yeah, do you know what would be a good meal to ask Reilly to make?"

"I'm afraid I do not, ma'am. You'd better ask the cook... His birthday..." Molly inquired softly.

Evelyn nodded and then said, "Thank you so much."

Evelyn walked away in search of Reilly.

**

Evelyn had dressed in a lavender dress with a low front and skirt that lightly touched her knees. She colored her lips and cheeks a soft rosy red, and then slipped on a pair of black stiletto shoes to finish the look. Her pearl drop earrings matched her favorite necklace she'd worn plenty of times before.

As she placed the wrapped up box at Nicholas' seat at the table, Oliver came in the room. "You have a visitor Mrs. Slade. He is waiting in the sitting room." The butler held his place at the double doors and waited for her to proceed into the other part of the house. Evelyn wasn't sure who could be calling on her no one knew where Nicholas' home was.

Upon entering the sitting room, a tall rotund man stood up from the chaise lounge and smiled her way. Evelyn politely returned the smile even though she hadn't a clue about who he was.

"Mrs. Slade, I'm so glad to meet you." He held out a firm hand and gently shook hers the moment she extended her arm. "I'm Tom Nolan, I don't know if your husband has mentioned me in recent, but I am the family lawyer."

Immediately Evelyn knew to whom she was speaking. Her smile grew just on principal he was an acquaintance of the Slade's. "Yes, of course."

"I have been trying to reach Jack for several days now and he won't return my calls." He sighed with a short gasp following. "Thing is, I really need your signature to complete matters..." His eyebrows lifted in question whether or not she understood his meaning.

"Yes, I understand. I can sign it now." Evelyn claimed

feeling her chest heave with heaviness. She was a free agent once she signs those papers.

"Would you?" He asked with a soft smile. Evelyn nodded. "Great. Let me…" He opened his briefcase, "Get these out for you," and pulled out a file and laid it on top of the piano that stood next to them. He pulled the stack of papers opened in search of the pages needed.

"Here we are." He looked beseechingly into her eyes. "If you'll just sign right there at the bottom…"

"Sure."

Evelyn's hand shook while she reached out to take his pen. Her body trembled with the thought of what she was signing…What if she refused? Would it be so bad?

20

Jackson went to the family room and poured himself a drink before heading to the office. The day was finally over! He'd set up five auditions and six shoots for tomorrow and managed to dodge all of Nolan's calls. The last, was as he was heading out the door and told his secretary to take a message and he'd get back to him in the morning. He dragged in a deep sigh as he approached his desk to lay his briefcase down.

He paused offhandedly, with the case in the air as he spied a stack of papers lying on top of his desk, centered perfectly in the middle...Curious...

He wrinkled up his lips in wonder as he laid the briefcase on the floor at his feet, set his drink on the smooth desk and lifted the stack to examine it closer.

It didn't take long to recognize what it was in his hand. Question was...*how* did the damn thing get here?

"Your lawyer brought it by this afternoon."

Jackson's heart plummeted to the floor. His breath died out to mere gasps. The room began to spin. He closed his eyes, covered his face as it creased with deep dismay. *Shit!*

Evelyn waited for him to respond to what she said if he had a comment. She then stated, "He called several times, you didn't call him back."

Jackson pondered with what to say to her. At this point, he couldn't tell what she knew and how she was going to react to what he needed for this charade to be complete. He didn't want her to think the worst of this last detail. He did not want Satin & Lace, but he wasn't so sure she'd trust that.

Jackson slowly turned around to assess her mood. Searching for tell tale signs of anger or even mistrust in her eyes. Looking for a fight, to pounce the first chance she'd get but, none of those things were present. She showed no signs of being mislead. Maybe he was jumping to conclusions about why Nolan had stopped off. Surely, she didn't sign the papers in his hands without reading it.

"We were so busy right up to the end of the day. I had planned on calling him in the morning." He spoke softly while searching for details of what was going on inside her head. He scanned her frame starting at the top and slowly gliding down. He liked the flowing dress she wore. The light color made her dark eyes stand out more. The darkness in each socket was like looking into a cauldron of liquid chocolate.

"Did everything go alright?" Evelyn asked, trying to divert the conversation away from the papers, he was holding and what they actually meant. Which was what she'd been thinking about non- stop since the lawyer left. Was Nicholas going to request she leave right away? Will they have to wait just a little bit before they take that next step? She was going crazy with ideas of what he wanted. She even gave the idea of packing up her things a good once over, but couldn't get the nerve up to actually do it.

"Yeah, things are great." He answered lifting the papers up just a tad.

"Did Nolan say what he wanted?" He didn't dare ask her anything more than that, damn it… his heart was racing in his chest. Evelyn did not appear to be angry and that was confusing the matter. Why wasn't she upset?

Jackson lowered the papers when he noticed fear in her eyes. What, on earth was she afraid of? Maybe he misjudged her in an entirely different way. Fearing him taking what she'd worked hard for was more a realization than she wished to face.

"He lacked a few signatures." She found herself answering despite the fear that lodged within her throat. Was this it…she wondered. Once she told him she signed it, was he going to give Evelyn her walking papers? Oh, God…Her heart started to beat against her chest.

Something inside Jackson snapped the moment he heard her words and he spoke without thinking or retracting the sudden anger he was feeling.

"You didn't sign it." He demanded in short. "You did _not_ sign it!" Jackson couldn't believe how quick his anger rose. He couldn't control the way it took over his every thought. No…He didn't hear her say anything about signing the damn papers, but he'd bet his life on the feeling he was getting from the expression upon her face.

"Nicholas…"

"Tell me you didn't sign those papers!" He was suddenly yelling. Evelyn stepped back. "Evelyn damn it, tell me you didn't."

"Why are you so upset?" She asked him, trying to understand his anger. Had she done something wrong? Wasn't she supposed to sign them? His lawyer said he needed _her_ signature to complete the proceedings.

"You did, didn't you?" he asked stepping closer to her. "Why would you do such a _stupid_ thing?" He couldn't control his mouth from saying what his heart was thinking. She signed away her business without a single thought about what she was doing. She must be crazy to do that…he'd never ask her to do that! What was she thinking?

"Stupid…" She started then gasped in anger. "I was doing it for you."

"That's crazy!" he told her.

Evelyn stared dumbfounded at him as he fumed with rage, walking away from her to begin pacing the floor between them. He thought she was crazy for doing what she agreed to do. _He_ was the crazy one. She was doing what she said she would.

"Why would you do that?" he questioned.

"I told you, Nicholas. He said he needed it…I signed it for you." As hard as it was, she did what she said she would, despite the pain it caused her at that moment and the heartache that was sure to haunt her to the end of her days, because it was _not_ what she wanted.

"Did you read it Evelyn?"

"What?" She asked. "I haven't read anything we signed, Nicholas." Her words stabbed him in the heart. It was true. She signed his agreement without batting an eye, why was that? Why hadn't he asked her then? Because it suited his purpose, that's why.

If she'd read it, she'd have seen the clause in which made this marriage of theirs real with unbreakable ties that bound them together for life. If they were to separate or divorce, it canceled everything out even if a child was born, and had passed the inheritance down. Like his parents, despite their lack of love and devotion, they were as bound to each other as the day they married. The contract was 'til death do them part, as it also was in theirs.

Had Evelyn read that agreement, they wouldn't be here now arguing about this other part of the contract. He did _not_ want her business. All he wanted from her was a marriage and a child, a son to pass on the heritage of his name. That had been all until emotions got in the way. Now he didn't care about any of that.

Hurting Evelyn was the last thing he will do and he will

go to any length to prevent her from getting hurt, which was why he had been avoiding Nolan. Without that contract signed, it can't progress without him having to tell Evelyn everything and that was what he wanted to do. Because the other last thing he discovered he wanted, was a marriage like his parents. Evelyn deserved more than that and Nicholas intended to give it to her, if she will let him. He wanted to start this relationship over.

His anger rose at the notion that she signed something without reading it, for the second time. Angered, that she unconditionally trusted him. He didn't deserve that kind of loyalty. He deserved a swift kick in the ass that's what he deserved!

"You didn't even read the damn papers!" he snarled at her. "You have no idea what you signed, Evelyn."

"I signed *your* agreement, Nicholas!"

Damn! That hurt. Jackson felt the sting of the knife as she pushed it all the way into his chest. He struck back with a blow just as damaging.

"You signed away your company, Evelyn!" He growled, angry that she'd do something so foolish. Her look of confusion fell over her face without caution. She didn't understand so... he enlightened her.

"That's right. You signed over Satin & Lace to me. It was a part of the agreement." He didn't elaborate that he wasn't in accordance with said clause and he was going to fix it, if at all possible. Instead, he watched her compute what he'd said.

"I signed..."

Jackson nodded with a smirk on his face. "Yep, you no longer own your own company." Jackson swallowed his pride the moment Evie's eyes started to well up with tears as the sudden reality hit her like a two by four.

Determined not to comprehend what he was saying, she shook her head no. She didn't want to accept that as truth. Nicholas _couldn't_ own Satin & Lace. It just wasn't possible!

"That's not true. You're lying!" She demanded as the tears started to roll down her face. He had to be lying, she told herself. How could that be? She was just doing what they'd agreed to. How can that be? She didn't sign away her ownership...did she?

Moments passed, while she thought about what she wanted to believe, when a moment she shared in the hospital room cunningly slipped into her mind. The comment he made about buying shares in the company and how quick he was to assure her that it would be to help her. She'd refused his offer, and this was what he schemed to get what he wanted. Other conversations also came to mind, they could help each other out, be partners. His interest in her models, he had been trying to get information about her company on that tour he had pushed her into doing. It all was coming back and she did _not_ like what she was seeing.

How far back did this game go...the image of them having lunch, the day he brought up this game? Had it been before that...The cab ride? Did he somehow be in the same place as she by not coincidence but by clever representations? Had he planned to lure her into this charade by lying about his inheritance?

Jackson had been pacing, trying to figure out how to get this change. When a gasp filled the office he stopped, looking over to Evelyn, his heart stopped dead in his chest. Now...now the anger was coming. Her eyes snapped up his gaze and inside her beautiful brown eyes was a broken trust she'd instilled upon her heart. A conclusion to her disbelief was surfacing at a very quick rate, stymied for just a short second, and then suddenly she came to life. She spun on her heels, intending to leave.

"Evie…" He tried to stop her. She snapped her frame around and pierced his heart with her furious stare. Jackson froze where he stood.

"I need some time, Nicholas." She warned him and all he could do was nod his affirmation. What else could he do at this point? There was nothing to say to take that horrible expression from her sweet face.

Evelyn's eyes released so many tears; she didn't know her body held that much in her ducts, to cry as much as she did. It hurt, she couldn't deny the way her heart felt about his hurtful ways. Every word he spoke was a lie, ones that cut deep into her heart. Nothing he'd done or said had been the truth and *that* was the most painful part of this whole nightmare. Losing her company was *not* a part of that pain and she cried even more when she suddenly realized that. Her pride and joy had been Satin & Lace. Now it was gone, but all she seemed to care about was that Nicholas was also out of her life.

She ran from the house in terror of what she was learning about her husband and his lying ways. Truth be told, now, she wished she was back there. She'd found something wonderful and she would never be able to forget how it had felt and that loss was much bigger than any materialistic item, even Satin & Lace.

**

Upon the slamming of the front door, Jackson gripped the contract with both hands and ripped it in two and when that didn't take away the anger he ripped it again and again until it lay in shreds at his feet. This was a nightmare. He stood motionless and watched her walk out, unable to go after her.

The crushing heaviness that took over his chest made it hard to breathe much less go after her. He was afraid…

He didn't want to upset her more, didn't want her to leave. He didn't want a lot of things, but couldn't force himself to move from the spot he was riveted to. He wanted to hold her, tell her whatever it was that she was thinking, was wrong. Nothing was the way it appeared, not anymore. She changed everything about how he thought the way things should be. She changed his way of thinking…period!

"Dinner is ready to be served Mr. Slade. Will the lady be coming back?"

Jackson turned to look at Oliver. God, he hoped so, but wasn't holding his breath. He shook his head in reply. He wasn't sure about anything right about now. "What a shame…" the butler softly spoke. "All the trouble she went to…" Oliver was all the way down the hall before Jackson caught what the man was saying.

"Trouble, Oliver?"

The butler stopped and shook his head; he replied with, "Dinner will be in the dining room, sir. Just ring when you're ready."

Jackson remained by the office door for a few minutes before he strolled down to the dining room door and just looked at the elegant display before him. The lights were low, the fire in the hearth cast shadows over the crème embossed papered walls. The bouquet of white orchids in a crystal vase caught his eyes first, but then the rest of the table quickly came into play.

The elegant table setting, not the china they ate on every night, but the fancier tableware that was normally in the hutch. The ones that had a gold filigree pattern in its center and gold trim around the plates that matched the stemware's rims. In the plate at his chair, was a small box, wrapped in silver paper and a large red bow that overwhelmed the box completely.

A party was the first thing to come to mind. It didn't take him long to recall the date. He had told her his birthday was two days before Christmas, which was today. His eyes cascaded over the pretty table settings and then around the very elegant room. All that lacked of a romantic evening was low music to set the tone to perfection.

**

Her penthouse was silent and dark. She left all the lights off, wanting to remain in the dark to try to forget everything that she learned. Sitting in her soft pillow chair by the big double glass door by the balcony, she sat in silence until her cell phone rang. At first... she wasn't going to answer it, but old habits prevented her from letting the unanswered call continue.

"Hello?" She whispered through the line. She tried to hide the fact she was crying, still. Hours had passed and she was still in tears.

"Evie..."

Evelyn's soft gasp filled the room when she heard Nicholas on the other end of the phone. She couldn't hide how fantastic she felt hearing his voice. More... she didn't want to hide it. She was tired of hiding in fear of what her heart was feeling, she was so tired of holding back and not letting go. When she let go, things just seemed to fall into place and things felt so right.

"Sweetheart, don't cry." Jackson begged of her. It killed him to think she was still crying and he was the cause. "Come home." He begged her. "Please? So we can talk?"

"I can't." She cried softly through the line. Despite how

sad and lonely she felt, going back right now would be a wrong move on her part. She needed time and space, so much space between them right now. If she went home… she'll fall into his arms and not come out. God…She needed someone to hold her!

Her loud sniffle made Jackson sigh. All right then, if she wasn't coming home, he'll tell her over the damn phone, not exactly what he wanted, but it was better than not telling her at all.

"I don't want your company, Evie." He told her.

"No?"

"No. I'll figure something out, get it back to you, I don't want it. Never wanted it, so stop thinking that I did, okay?"

"Okay," She answered but the tears came again. She believed him. Sadness suddenly overwhelmed her. It seemed…he wanted _nothing_ from her. Just that stupid inheritance, the knowledge of that hurt deeply.

"Evie…" Nicholas called out. "Where are you?"

She looked around the quiet penthouse. "…Home." She answered, but felt it to be the worst lie she had ever told. Home doesn't feel like this. Home was supposed to be cozy and warm. It was supposed to make you feel safe and secure. She shivered, feeling none of that.

"_This_ is your home. Please come home, Evelyn." He asked her. She started to rock back and forth, gripping herself tightly as she did so. "I'm sorry." He whispered through the phone. "…Never been sorrier before. Please, come back so we can talk."

Jackson waited for an answer and, when she refused to reply he continued.

"Thank you for the gift, Evie." He paused then said. "I haven't opened it yet. Please come back so we can have the nice dinner you planned. Forget this damn marriage contract and come home. Please?"

...Why?

That one little question kept coming back and coming back to her. Why should she return to a fake relationship that was killing her from the inside? He hadn't a clue, and if she told him... he'd probably laugh at her.

No. She can't do that, even if her heart begged for her to tell him, she couldn't. He wanted nothing from her, only what she was good for, a short affair. Once things settled, he was going to move on with his life, leaving her to pick up the pieces of her shattered existence.

Her time was up, she played her roll and it was time for the curtain to come down. The show was over, there was no reason to stay, no reason at all.

He found her gift. Her heart quickened... will he like it? She sat forward in the chair, hoping that he indeed did like it. "Open it." She hoarsely told him.

"I was hoping to open it while we were together. Please won't you come home?" He asked her.

"I don't think so. I can't. What point is there?" She asked him.

Many points...he wanted to tell her. "Come home and we'll see if we can find one good one."

There it was again, an affair... All she can ever give him was something short and sweet. He didn't want anything else. She was in too much pain to go to the next level and expect to survive it. To give him what he wanted and then just walk away would be impossible and he wouldn't care how it was going to hurt her. He'd get what he wanted, he wouldn't care about anything else.

"I think I need to stay here, go ahead and open it though. I hope you like it. I had to order it special." She wiped her cheeks of all the tears that had stained them.

"Are you sure, I can wait until tomorrow night."

"No!" she spoke through the line missing his statement.

"Okay then."

The sound of ripping paper filled the airwaves while he opened her gift. Then, it was quiet on his end of the line. Evelyn held her breath, waiting and when he said nothing, she finally spoke. "You don't like them."

Jackson ran a finger over the cuff links made of white and yellow gold. The ends were small buds, almost like roses but with a closer look, they were kisses. Two sets, one of white gold and the other yellow, interchangeable to whichever would look better with the suit he chose to wear.

He swallowed hard as he forced back the tears that welled in his eyes. He can't recall the last time he cried. Her generous gift was more than jewelry, more than the precious gold. It was a link to their past.

They were symbolic of *that* day in the hospital where more than bids for hands had taken place and every time he'd look at those cufflinks, he'll be transported to that room and that sweet moment when she shuttered against him. A moment he really didn't need to have an aide to recall what it felt like to have her in his arms, her body clinging to him while he pleasured her was an image burned into his mind.

"You won't come back tonight, right?" He asked through the line. His mind was working in thought. He had to get her alone and talk to her. Had to be face to face with her while he told her how wrong he'd been in the past and how he changed his mind, tell her the truth about the way he felt about their union and what he wished to do about the sudden changes.

"No." She tried to hide her new tears, but he heard her voice tremble, his heart skipped a beat.

"You need time..." He claimed.

"Yes." She answered.

"I'll be by to pick you up around five. Will that be suitable enough time to get ready?"

"I don't..." she began but then his voice broke through.

"My parents will not allow us to skip another holiday. We must go." ...And endure the entire night, because what he really wished to do was eat and take his bride home to begin their long talk.

She'd forgotten the holiday dinner at his parent's home. They were supposed to exchange gifts and maybe even play a game of Hearts. A card game that Nicholas had told her they enjoyed playing.

"Will that be enough time, dinner will be at six."

"Yes." She found herself answering. Dear God...How was she going to sit through an entire meal with those folks? His mother will sense something is wrong. Trisha will be like a starving wolf smelling out a rabbit. She'll sniff out the pain and take charge of the tension that will certainly be present.

Determined to take this game all the way to the end, Evelyn went shopping the next morning. She needed _the_ perfect outfit to wear, needed the perfect attitude to go right along with it. Money was not an option for this last scene to play out. She needed something elegant because she was ready to show Mrs. Slade that she wasn't intimidated in any way by her aggressiveness. She was proud of who and what she was. She didn't need an old woman telling her how fat and incompetent, Mrs. Slade found her daughter-in-law to be.

Evelyn had all the confidence in the world that she, as a woman could please any man, if _she_ chose to do so. Nicholas didn't seem to have a problem with any part of her and he was more man than any man she'd had the pleasures in dating. Trisha was just an old bitter woman with nothing better to do then complain about what life had dealt her.

21

Evelyn flashed Nicholas a full smile when she opened her door to him, who was prompt. She quickly stepped out of her penthouse closing the door before Nicholas tried to get inside. He was too busy eyeing the long black formal gown with matching satin shoes and shawl. The low cut bodice was heart shaped and curved nicely around her firm chest and the waist hugged her tightly, leaving the skirt of the dress to flow elegantly down to just below her knees. Once again, she wore her pearls to give the perfect touch.

Jackson wrapped her up into the shawl she was holding, took her arm and led her down to the elevator without a single word. Did she notice he wore her gift? He smiled at the other couple that appeared magically as the doors opened up.

Evelyn allowed him to escort her all the way out to the front, down to the limo that waited, but when he tried to take the seat beside her, she did not move over. Instead, she looked into his bright eyes and shook her head.

"I'd prefer it please, if you sat in the other seat." Her tone was cold and slightly sharp. She hadn't meant to be so bitter towards him. She was on edge and was ready for that kind of reaction thrown or hissed toward his mother.

She watched his face lose some of its natural coloring, but he gave a solid nod and complied with her wishes. He reached across the seat to grab something off the seat next to her, a beautiful orchid corsage. Two things captured her eyes. First, the corsage, was it a bud off the bouquet from the table the night before? Her thoughts switched to the cuff link clipped to his shirt. He was wearing them!

He softly leaned forward. "Allow me to put this on." His fingers slipped into the low bodice, to make sure not poke her with the point of the pin. Evelyn and he shared a long look as he took his time attaching the corsage. He smelled spicy and very good she almost reached out for him but caught herself. Once the fragrant flower was secured to her left breast panel, he moved away with a quick slide back into his seat.

The ride completely in silence, there was so much he wished to say but didn't feel as if it was the right time. Since she quickly pulled the reins on him, not allowing him any closer then need be, he knew a much better place like the library in his parents' home or something close to it would be much better and more private.

Jackson took her arm in his hand, helped her out of the car which was Walter's job, but he didn't care. Jackson needed any excuse he could seize to touch her. The moment Evelyn stood beside him he smiled. Her black dress not only complimented his suit, it seemed to have paired with it. Her dress was satin and long flowing and was a perfect match to his attire. Her red mouth and nails matched his red shirt.

At the door Jackson's father welcomed them both, first his son with a firm handshake and then, he actually hugged Evelyn. Where, Mrs. Slade was less than inviting. Her smug look was observant, as she took in the sight before her.

"I didn't realize this was a black tie affair." Her tort was firm and solemn with a touch of snide interfacing. How dare they show her up! "I only invited family, Jackson. I hope they aren't put out by your vain performance tonight."

Evelyn was about to give a response, but didn't get the chance to.

"I think we look fine, mother." Jackson replied wrapping his arm around Evelyn's waist, his fingers enjoying the softness beneath the satin dress. He looked over at Evelyn with a handsome smile she had no choice, but to return.

"They look just fine. No one will notice anyway." Mr. Slade led the way into the house with his wife following not too far behind. "We have a little time before the gang all gets here, let's get a drink." He led the way to the family room.

Jackson took that opportunity to kidnap his wife without being too forward. "I need to speak to Evelyn first, we'll be in shortly." Jackson told his parents as he took Evelyn's hand and led her to the library.

"I really don't think…"

Jackson stopped short of the library door, spun to face her and shook his head. "You think way too much. Come on." He pulled her into the dim lit room, closed the door behind them before Evelyn could snatch her hand away from his.

"Nicholas…"

"Stop calling me that!" He snapped at her and then backed off. "Why can't you just call me Jack?" he questioned her. Evelyn only shrugged her shoulders, why did it matter anyway. They were almost through with the game, just a few more hours, and then all… will be, forgotten.

"I just want to thank you for the cuff links." He told her. She nodded as she headed for the door. "…and to talk a bit,"

Evelyn shook her head. "There is nothing to say."

"What about that amazing dinner you planned last night?" He asked stepping closer to her. Evelyn watched as he took her hand, gave it a soft caress as he smiled her way. "Come sit with me for a minute."

He moved deeper into the quiet soft-lit room. Tugging her with him until he was sitting on the sofa and she was sitting on his lap.

"What about it?" she questioned him.

"Yes, what about it," He questioned right back.

Evelyn's chest started to rise and fall in time with her deep breaths. "I don't..." she started to say, but when his finger gently caressed her lower lip, was cut off.

"You went to a lot of trouble Evie." He pointed out. "The good china, the crystal stemware, even my favorite meal was all waiting for me." His bright eyes parried with her stare as she tried to gather the strength inside to tell him. Could she tell him everything? She wasn't confident that she even wanted to voice her true intentions out loud.

"It was your birthday. I wanted..." She swallowed as his thumb followed his finger along her bottom lip, tracing it with firmness. Her heartbeat doubled in time.

"What did you want?" His husky voice tried to peel away the surface of her shell.

"What did I want?" she repeated after him.

"Maybe a little of this..." he enquired before pulling her down to meet her mouth with his.

The kiss was a light peck, but the moment their lips separated, they both lurched forward, unwilling to allow too much space to come between them.

"Mm," He groaned the moment their mouths locked together. Evelyn turned into him and opened her mouth the moment she felt his hot wet tongue graze her lip, allowing the heated tip inside.

"Mm, Evie." He spoke over her mouth in between wild kisses that were long and breathtaking. "I know I promised to leave you alone. I know I did..." he pulled her closer, twining his fingers around her neck, taking a stronger kiss with his fevered mouth.

Damn! He could sit here all night and never stop kissing her. The taste of her sweet mouth _infected_ his whole being. It was a taste that changed with every kiss, hard to depict what it was he tasted, all he knew was it wasn't enough, never enough.

"Were you hoping to maybe do this last night?" he asked over her mouth. Both of his hands held her face while they kissed, keeping her steady, his thumbs, now caressing her cheeks with tenderness.

Evelyn fought hard against all she had tried to believe was right. If she didn't stop this delicious encounter, if she allows her heart a smidgen of happiness, he will forever hold it in the palm of his hand.

It felt…so good! She argued with herself. The velvety caress of his mouth gave way to sudden fires that came out of nowhere and she couldn't deny them anymore. Evelyn needed just a little to take home with her, when this was over.

Struggling with herself, her throat clenched tightly when her body protested what she was trying to deny, and a low moan escaped and trickled down her neck. "Yes." She whispered gently over her parted lips.

Jackson felt the trembles within her throat before he heard them. His groin thickened at the sound. Her purr, created such an eagerness in his body to comply with her needs and right now, he knew she needed him to love her. He wanted to answer to those needs, throw her to the soft cushions of this sofa and quell every one of those needs that was begging for his attention. Damn! It was so hard not to do just that.

"I love it when you purr for me baby!" he mumbled over her mouth.

"Nich…" She whispered against his mouth, her breath catching as she tried to call out.

"I know sweetheart." Not able to control the desire any

longer, hunger taking charge, he passionately covered her mouth with his own. Opening and thrusting deep inside of her, her matching him stroke for pleasurable stroke.

Time no longer existed between them. Wrapping his arms around her, one hand groping her breast, the other holding her firm ass in a tight grasp he took what she offered and ran with it. Kiss after blissful kiss replayed, over, and over. Their moans of desire filling the room as the flames burned hotter than ever before.

"I want you so much." Jackson spoke into her ear. His fingers caressing her nipple once he snaked his hand inside her dress and beneath her bra. "Talk to me." He whispered. "Are you feeling as hot as I am?" he kissed her neck.

Unable to pretend and lie about what she was feeling, her heart spoke out before she had the chance to think about what she was saying.

"I feel it too." She moaned through parted lips.

"Take you home, now, so we can..."

"Are you sure they didn't go in there?"

His mother's voice cut off Jackson's whispers. They saw the shadow beneath the door before they actually saw the door move and neither of them moved from their positions. Evelyn remained in his lap, Jackson's hand down her dress, intimately caressing her breast, both looking flushed from the heated passion that had transpired between them.

The moment Jackson's mother stood in the door, staring at the image of her son, in the arms of passion, silence captured all of them. The look on Trisha's face made Evelyn smirk in an un-ladylike manner. Proud of what her mother-in-law had walked in on, and actually witnessed with her own eyes.

"Wha..." Mrs. Slade began to stammer and then closed her mouth, collecting her wits before she sputtered into gear.

"What is going on in here? How dare you bring smut into my home!"

Evelyn should have felt remorse for making the woman embarrassed, but she couldn't locate any kind of shame that belonged to this particular event. In fact, she was quite proud of the fact that Jackson didn't see the need to hide what they had been doing before they were rudely interrupted.

"That'll teach you to knock the next time." Jackson told her. Evelyn couldn't contain the sudden laughter that came out as she watched Trisha glare in her direction and still Evelyn did not care about being caught. She sided with Nicholas, if her mother-in-law had knocked instead of barging in on them...

"Dinner is being served in the dining room Jackson, if you can act like a gentleman, you may join us." His mother ignored the comment and snapped around, closing the door behind her in a quick departure. Both Jackson and Evelyn burst out with laughter for the second time.

Jackson eyed Evelyn as they laughed, his gaze moving around in search of something in her eyes. As his fingers smoothed over her breast, caressing her nipple, he continued to watch her trying to take in what she felt when he touched her like that.

"I'm, sorry we got interrupted and the last thing I want to do is go in there and eat." He pulled her down and grazed her mouth with a light kiss. He then searched her eyes, pinched her nipple softly. "Tell me you're going home with me so we can finish this." He searched the warmth in her stare and then kissed her again.

"Mm," She moaned.

Evelyn didn't know how to respond to him. She should be running away, not towards this man. She should be screaming in fear not coiling up inside his embrace and she shouldn't agree to go home with him, so he will be able to steal her heart indefinitely!

"Talk to me baby. Tell me you're coming home with me tonight, after we go out there and play Mother's little game." Jackson spoke over Evelyn's mouth. When she didn't give him the answer he was looking for, he then tugged her face up and looked into her eyes. "Come home with me, Evie."

It wasn't a request, it wasn't a demand. It was just like when they were in the club and he took her up to dance with him. He hadn't asked, nor did he demand her to dance anymore then he was doing so right now. It was the tone in which he used that made Evelyn's heart give in to what he had wanted and she readily agreed without question.

"Okay." She heard herself say and then smiled at him.

**

"Where did Jackson take you on your honeymoon?" Chloe asked Evelyn while sitting at the table. Chloe was married to Jackson's cousin Landon who was down on the other end of the table talking with Elliott and George, Jackson's other cousin that wasn't married yet. His fiancée Wendi was sitting across from him and right next to Trisha. Both George and Landon were also named Jackson, but because there were so many, at family gatherings, the first name was used to keep names straight.

Jackson looked up to Evelyn who sat right across from him and right next to Steven another cousin and his wife Daphne. "Hawaii." He answered for Evelyn.

"Oh, how nice…" Chloe sang amazingly sweet. "Steven took me on our third anniversary. It is so beautiful!"

Daphne then commented with, "What did you like the

best?"

"We really didn't..."

"Why don't you let *her* answer Nicholas?" His mother reprimanded sternly.

The whole table became silent as the tension began to build while they waited for Evelyn to answer Daphne's question.

Evelyn took a few moments before answering, and then looked at Jackson with a demure smile. He felt his chest heave with uncertainty of what she was going to answer. They hadn't spent much time exploring the islands.

"I think the best part for me..." She paused in thought and then said,

"...was when we were soaring like the birds." Jackson's heart double-timed its beat when he heard her statement and understood it to its fullest. He felt his mouth widen more as his smile took on a new look. His body sat straight up as a peacock would when he throws his feathers up to catch a female with his sex dance.

"Hang gliding," Chloe gasped in awe. "You went hang gliding! How wonderful was that?" Her green eyes grew the size of dimes as she looked at Evelyn in envy.

"Weren't you afraid?" Daphne asked her. "I wanted to try it but chickened out the last minute."

"I was at first," Evelyn revealed softly and then added, "I had never done it before. He held me tight so I wouldn't get scared."

"Awe, how sweet is that?" Both of the women cried out.

Jackson and Evelyn remained staring at each other, while the conversations around the table changed to something else. She really wasn't sure why she'd picked that particular thing to say, but it was the truth. She was tired of hiding... it was so tiresome. It was the truth. The best part of that trip was resting in Nicholas' arms while he took her flying into the heights of the clouds.

Talk then changed to work, and how things were progressing.

Steven looked over at Evelyn. "I hear you own Satin & Lace." Evelyn looked up at him, but quickly turned her eyes to Nicholas. He smiled softly.

"Things going all right for sales?" he asked her.

"Every year the sales have gone up."

"Impressive." Elliott remarked with a smirk.

"She sells underwear!" Trisha grimaced gruffly. "How *hard* can it be?" She asked with a snide snicker choking in the back of her throat. Her eyes then opened bigger as she glanced to Jackson. "Em, I am so glad Nolan finally got those signatures you needed for the contract."

"Mother," Jackson began but Evelyn kicked in with,

"Why wouldn't I sign it?"

Chloe butted in with, "See, I told you they were in love." She was speaking to Landon.

"...Love!" Trisha burst out in laughter. "Honey, you are terribly mistaken. The only thing Nicholas has ever loved in his life is his money and that isn't going to change."

"...Mother!" Jackson chastised her, but she wasn't listening to him.

The table hummed with gasps from the women and they looked from Trisha to Jackson, and then finally to Evelyn. Tension continued building like a thick fog.

"What?" Trisha asked curtly. "I'm just telling it like it is. They aren't in love, for heaven's sake," she laughed again. "...He *had* to marry *someone*, and now, they have to remain that way, until one of them dies. There is no love..."

"What?" Evelyn was silent while this was going on. Her heart raced in her chest as Trisha was telling everyone about

254

her son's ideals of what was important. Evelyn wasn't even sure she'd spoken out loud, but when every head turned her way, including her beloved husband's, she knew she had.

"Oh, he didn't tell you that part, did he, *sweet... heart*?" Trisha's mouth curved into a devilish grimace while she turned her eyes to Evelyn.

"...Mother!" Jackson snapped in anger once again.

"What Nicholas? Don't you want her to know the conditions of your *contract*?" she asked harshly. "Evelyn should know that everything you have done thus far is worth nothing if she doesn't produce a child." Trisha looked back to Evelyn with a snide smile.

Evelyn gasped inwardly as she looked at Jackson for confirmation of what she was hearing. He gave it without even looking her direction. His eyes held such contempt for the woman who had given birth to him, he needn't say a word.

Did she hear right, they will remain married until she or Nicholas dies?

"And how is that going my dear?" Trisha looked directly to Evelyn as she asked, "Are you even capable of having children?"

The world around her suddenly seemed tight and she felt confined. Claustrophobic, was how she was suddenly feeling and everyone was looking down at her, waiting for some kind of reaction...Was this true?

Her eyes darted around the table seeing a mixture of eyes looking back, shocked, terrified, and shame all of which Evelyn was feeling tenfold and it made her shiver.

"Enough!" Jackson yelled to his mother. How could she just blurt out everything like it was casual conversation?

"Did you tell her anything, Nicholas? Does she know she signed away her company and her freedom to you? Does she know she *must* give you an heir before your next birthday?" Trisha asked him and then turned her hard stare back to Evelyn.

"Well, now you know what is at stake here!" Mrs. Slade told her firmly.

"So, you see, it wasn't love that made him take you on as a bride. He will never love you, just like his father never loved me!"

"...Mother!" Jackson shouted, fuming with anger.

Evelyn shook her head in disbelief of what was going on. Anger made her jump up the same time Nicholas snapped at his mother for the fourth time.

Trying not to cry out her fear and frustration, Evelyn spun away from the table.

"Evelyn!" She heard Jackson call out for her but by that time Evelyn's feet were running out the front door. Fearing he will follow, she flew faster then what seemed humanly possible. The need to be free and alone was impeding her thoughts.

Jackson stood dumbfounded. He couldn't believe his mother, sudden anger hit him. Evelyn ran out of the house crying and scampering with her tail between her legs, again thinking wrongly about everything.

"How dare you!" He snarled at his mother, "You're a rotten bitter old woman!" Jackson could no longer hold back the words that were coming out of his mouth. Trisha's eyes widened in disbelief, he'd never had the gall to talk this way to her.

Jackson threw his napkin to his plate glaring a hole through the woman sitting with a smug demur expression. "How dare you talk for me in any way?" Jackson rounded the table in her direction. "I understand now why dad doesn't share his bed with you, you cantankerous old bitch!"

"Don't talk to your mother that way!" Elliott spoke up finally.

"And you," Jackson pointed to his father. "I know you had Nolan go to the house to get Evelyn to sign that damn contract. You are no better than she." Jackson nodded towards his mother. "You both sicken me! No better than the other, you're old, angry people who take their rotten choice out on others." Jackson slammed his fist to the table. "In fact, take that warped heart of yours and shove it down your blackened throat for all I care you rotten son-of a bitch!" Jackson started for the door.

"I am done playing this stupid game. I am _not_ taking that company from Evelyn and I am not repeating your mistake!"

Jackson paused at the door of the dining room and said, "In fact, I think I'll end this damn show by divorcing her, I'm sure after what you have done," He glared at his mother. "Evelyn will be pounding down my door asking for just the same."

It was a lie, a bold face lie spoken only to get a rise out of both of them and it worked, both Elliott and Trisha gasped at the thought of their hard work washing down the drain. "I trust that will do both of you some good."

With that said, he stalked out of the house with a heavy heart. It may have been a lie on his part, but he was afraid he might have been right on the mark as far as Evelyn was concerned. If she didn't think the worst of him, it would be a miracle and Jackson didn't believe in such fantasies. Life was what you make of it; his parents were perfect examples of that.

22

The huge clock in the entrance way chimed eleven times, droning inside his heart with each bong it made. Jackson sat at the front door, on the floor waiting, hoping that Evelyn would keep her promise. The night was almost over, another hour and it will technically be the next day, Christmas day. He called her cell over, and over but it kept going to voice mail. He left countless messages but she hadn't called him back, yet.

When it finally did ring, and it was she... he quickly picked it up.

"Evie?"

"Jackson," an unfamiliar woman called through the line. "Is this Jackson Slade?" she asked.

"Yes. Yes!" Jackson replied. "Who is this?" It wasn't Evie he could tell by the voice alone.

"This is Keli, you remember me from the club? I'm Evelyn's best friend her co-worker?"

"Yes." Jackson answered sharply. "I do, where is Evelyn?"

"I don't know." She replied.

"Have you seen her?" He asked sucking in his breath. If her best friend didn't know where she was, it wasn't a good sign.

"She just left my place about ten minutes ago. I'm really worried about her. What happened?"

"She didn't tell you?" He sighed trying to keep calm.

"She didn't say anything I could understand. She was hysterical. I thought she was on something. She was crying and mumbling to herself. I tried to quiet her down, but then she bolted from my house, saying something about going home."

Good! Jackson sighed deeper. She was coming home. She should be arriving any minute. "Thanks for calling Keli."

"Call me when you find her, she didn't look so well when she ran out. She left her phone behind. I don't think she was thinking straight."

"I'll call." He promised her and hung up.

Jackson got to his feet and started to pace the floor in waiting. He ran through everything he wished to say to her. If it were possible, he was going to get her to understand he is not the same person she met a few months ago. Some things were more important than money, he wanted to explain and seriously apologize for everything.

Another hour wisped by without her showing up. Jackson started to worry. Where was she? She was going home, but she wasn't here yet... Jackson stood rigid against the wall thinking of those words. This was _not_ her home... it was his...The penthouse...

Another hour was gone by the time he got to the penthouse, only to find it empty. He almost gave it up when her words filtered into his mind once more. She was going home. Home...could it be the same home she was trying to keep by marrying him? It was then he knew exactly where she went.

His flight landed in Montana and Jackson was standing out front of the large cobblestone two-story home as the sun started to rise above the horizon. The wintery scene he stood in was remarkable. Pristine white powder covered the entire landscape. The stables down back were red with stone foundations. The fences outlining the entire acreage, hidden almost by the snow, because they too were white, a bright white that would give the green grasses a splash of color during the summer. The sight around him was delicately perfect; much like the woman he hoped was inside.

The plowed driveway had a recent set of tire prints in the snow-encrusted dirt. Someone had been here recently and he hoped she was still there.

Using his key, he obtained from the bank. Jackson let himself in to the cold mansion.

"Evie?" he called out. "Are you here?" He called out again as he stepped into the long hallway that had a few doorways leading to some other rooms within the house. "Evelyn are you..." His words died out when she appeared in the first door on the right.

Wearing a long fluffy white robe with only a few buttons hooked up in the front. Jackson couldn't remove his gaze from her bare legs that peeked out from the slit in the front.

"Nicholas..." Her tone laced with shock. "What are you doing here?" She asked surprised.

"Might I ask you the same?" He inquired softly. At the sight of her, his heart hammered against his chest. All he needed was a few minutes, just to explain.

"This is my home. I'd like it if you left me alone." She told him turning away from him.

Jackson held in the gasp that came forth when he saw her hair for the first time. Down away from her head in long waves that settled right at the top of her hips. Each delicate wave was as brown as her beguiling eyes and satiny smooth. He hungered to run his fingers through the chocolate river before him.

"I waited for you, you promised to come home." He told her, following her into the sitting room where a raging fire was billowing in the hearth. A blanket was sprawled over the sofa in front of the fire, which was the only heat source in the cold house. Obviously, it had been her bed the night before.

Evelyn gasped harshly at his comment. She spun around, facing him just before she reached the makeshift bed. "You; waited for *me*?" She gasped a second time. "Well, I am so sorry about that. Come home…" Jackson watched the tear roll down her face. "I am home! This *is* my home!" She glared at him. "I want *you* to leave *my* home!" she turned away but then suddenly came back with, "You lied to me!" Her angry stare hit Jackson right in the chest.

"Not really." He replied but then added, "Technically, I just omitted a few things."

"Lied… It's called lying and I, trusted you!" Her tears flowed freely now. He watched her shutter, wrapping her arms about her frame as she tried to settle her nerves.

Jackson slowly nodded his guilty plea. "Yes, I lied to you." He didn't know… How could he have known? He wondered, would it even matter, now, that he did know?

He stepped forward when she turned around and shuttered to his words. "I'm sorry. I am so sorry about doing that. I should have…" he stepped up behind her and looked out the same window she was. The scene before them was serene. Majestic snow covered tree branches, hilly white slopes and evergreens with white down dresses that gently touched the ground. The blue skies above it all made the picture surreal.

"I should have been honest one hundred percent of the time and I'm sorry."

"I don't want your apologizes!" She snapped. "I just want to be free."

She spun around giving him an evil look. "Oh, I'm sorry, I forgot. I can't be free, thanks to you!"

"Evelyn…"

261

"No!" she pulled away from him when he tried to comfort her. "Get away from me! Leave me alone. I don't want you in my house."

"Technically..." Her horrified face stopped his impetuousness sharp tongue. Damn it...He didn't want to anger her any more then she was and by bringing that subject to life... he shook his head in disbelief, he was a damned fool!

Evelyn turned around, her whole body rocked with sobs. "Let me stay here today." She softly cried and then added, "I'll leave by morning." Her shaking frame sent unwanted pain into his chest. He didn't want her going anywhere! "You owe me that much." The last of her statement was a whispered plea. Indeed, he owed her plenty, and it ached him she didn't have a clue...not a single clue.

"Would you believe me if I said I didn't want your home?" He slowly stepped up behind her and put his hands on her shoulders.

"Don't..." She whispered.

Jackson was inches away from her long mane that smelled of fruit and sweet petals of lavender. He wanted to slip his fingers through the silky tresses. Instead, he clutched her shoulders tighter, refraining from touching her anywhere else.

"Don't what?" he whispered right back, leaning closer until his mouth was right against her ear. "Does this make your heart beat stronger?" He asked, moving his lips against her lobe. "Or does it stop altogether?"

"I..." she began.

"It makes mine beat stronger. Harder against my chest it hurts to breathe. Is it hard to breathe?" He smiled softly when she gasped and he felt her body shiver beneath his hands.

262

"Yes." She replied.

"Yes?" He asked her a little louder.

"…Yesss" She hissed seductively, in a demure prayer.

Jackson took her response as a request for more. Angry or not, she wanted what he could do for her. He wanted to give Evelyn everything her heart desired, and more.

His mouth took her ear in one swift bite and softly he nibbled at her flesh, but it wasn't enough. He tilted her head to the side, she complied in assisting him and he took her neck in a quick snatch and sucked the skin into his mouth. His eyes closed, relishing in the taste of her. He could eat her alive, she tasted so good!

Hunger for more riveted him to her shoulder. Nudging the fluffy robe aside, his mouth sought her flesh. His teeth bit attentively on her skin, licking the softness, dipping inside the hollow spot near her neck. She trembled when he remained there, kissing and sucking the strength right out of her.

The strength _he_ had been relying on suddenly fell away. His hands dropped down to her sides caressing her as he went. The fluffy robe hid very little of her feminine shape. He pulled her harder against him, as he clutched her. This time though, grasping at her frame, with one hand delving into the fluff of her robe, and the other actually hitting her firm breast.

Evelyn moaned the second she felt his hand on her breast, so he gave it a tender squeeze to test her. She arched, slightly moving against him, leaning into his hand. She wanted his touch. Jackson's hunger soared to strengths that were too hard to control. Nibbling on her sweet neck, he slipped his hand inside the robe and found her warm bare breast. Jackson's heart raced in his chest and his breath caught in mid intakes. She wore nothing beneath the robe!

He couldn't believe how quick his desire for this minx grew to a flame that ravaged throughout his system before he could slow it down. The need to have her consumed him completely.

"What's your heart doing now?" He whispered against her ear. "Is it fast and irregular?"

"Mm, yes," She spoke her reply before another moan escaped her parting lips. His forefinger and thumb twisted her nipple with delicate tweaks that was obviously rendering her into a willing participant of his lovemaking. She leaned against him, eager to accept his touches with a hungry need of her own.

She tried to keep the sound hidden but her throat betrayed her, and she purred. Jackson felt his groin jump to attention the moment he heard her.

"I want you." The crack in his voice only added to his rampant need. "Say you want me too."

The hand that was caressing her over the robe fell to her side and slowly made a path over her ribcage and down to her legs. Her knees buckled slightly when she felt his fingers glide over her soft skin.

"Yes." He heard her whisper.

Without hesitation, he slipped his hand between her legs and cupped her sensually.

"Mm," Her body jolted forward at the touch of his hand.

"Open up for me, baby." He begged lightly against her neck. His mouth nibbled at her tight throat, his hand kept vigilant upon her breast, squeezing and fondling her firm mound. Rolling the hard nipple between his fingers, rubbing his palm against it, bringing it to a hardness he hungered to taste. Just thinking about rolling his tongue over that hardened crest made his mouth water, his hips react with a thrust up against her backside and a throbbing erection with one thing in mind.

Evelyn responded to him with sweet moans of delight. Her legs did in fact open and her soft sensual moan filled his ears when he slipped his fingers into the silky dew.

She was the _most_ woman, he had ever met. Her hidden sensuality didn't compare with any other, hers was wild and carefree. It was all so new to her but she embraced it, nurturing it to a combustible stage, even she, couldn't douse and he was going to lose her…

Jackson gasped inwardly at the thought. She was unlike any woman and losing her just wasn't in the cards for him. He'd come this far, only to let her go…No way! She was his minx, and she was perfect.

Even the idea of another man looking at her, drove him over the edge. She was _his_!

"Oh, Evie…" his heart started to speak for him. It literally crushed at the thought of her in another man's arms. "…Make you mine…Right now."

Jackson pushed her forward and for support, she had no choice, but to reach out to the table in front of them. She clutched the wood, her fingers rolling around the edges as he leaned into her more forceful than before. His fingers left her breast and began to push the robe away from her body.

His mind was lost in a whirlwind of thoughts all jumbled up and nothing made any sense, until the moment his throbbing phallus was embedded inside her and all he could feel was a warmth so hot it was like dipping his wick into melted wax. Every pour tingled throughout his long shaft with sensation after sweet sensation.

"Jack…" Evelyn's voice choked out when her throat clenched tight.

Jackson grabbed her shoulders, pulling her backwards until she stood upright with her back against him. "Don't stop. Say it." He told her, thrusting his hips, surging into her for a second time. "Say my name." He begged her, taking her nipple between his fingers and gave it a tantalizing twist.

"Oh, Jackson…" She groaned, meeting his thrust with a powerful one of her own. Jackson brought his other hand up to her right breast, his fingers twisting that nipple as well, holding her against his tall frame while he savagely surged into her with his flesh over, and over again.

He'd wanted her for so long, his body was enjoying the taste of the splendid morsel in front of him, he held strong, not wanting it to end.

With aching pleasure, drawn out Jackson finally climaxed. Long pulsating surges came from deep within his scrotum and continued to flow long after the sensation had subsided.

Emotions flitted into his heart at alarming speeds in which he couldn't stop. The sweet scent of her long flowing mane called out to him, he wanted to wrap his fingers into the mass and caress it while he gently stroked her head. His mouth watered for a taste of her flesh. The throbbing of his hard erection, deep within her warm core, begged for a second round.

When the room came into focus, none of those things he hungered for took place. Realization of what he did came to him in a flood of images. The hunger that he couldn't refuse, the way he pushed her forward, the way he mounted her from behind. His mind raced through the events like a damn slide show and he couldn't believe it. *This* was not the way…His mind argued vehemently.

Mortification of how he'd let this take place filled him completely. How could he take her innocence, her virginity like a damn horse, pounding into her like a savage beast! *That* was *not* how he wanted her first time to be!

Sickened by his own actions, Jackson dropped his arms,

releasing her and pushed away.

Ignoring the cold air, he turned, righted his slacks and walked into the hall before he was completely out of control. Jackson was livid with himself for what he'd done. He couldn't fathom how he was going to explain, so he just removed himself away from Evelyn, before he did something else to make matters worse, although, he was beside himself with how he could manage that!

Jackson halted at the front door, his fingers grasping the brass door handle when his chest tightened right down and his heart painfully cried out. This was wrong. He knew it the moment he took his hands from Evelyn's body. It was so wrong of him to leave her like this. *This is not how you treated the one you loved*!

Jackson's heart jumped beneath his breastbone with more pain as it agreed fully with his thoughts …Love… He brought his head up, turned it toward the room he had just left, listened to the silence of the large empty house. Then his heart thudded with strong solid beats as he turned away from the door and walked back down the hall to the opened doorway of the sitting room.

The second he stepped to the threshold, he stopped dead in his tracks. His heart broke into thousands of pieces; painful shards went everywhere as he watched Evelyn burst out into tears, *drop* to her knees and began to pray.

**

The sun was down, had been for hours. The house was chilly despite the warm fire in front of her. The orange and red flames danced around the room giving it a picturesque atmosphere; small details that went unnoticed. Evelyn remained indifferent of her surroundings.

She sat on the sofa with her robe open on the lower half just below the last fastened button, her legs bare, pulled up to her chest with the cold air hitting her backside. She didn't bother to get dressed. She remained in her robe and nothing else.

Despite the late evening hour and the chill that had taken over the house, earlier events that continued to live within her soul kept her warm. Evelyn didn't give notice to anything, but her troubled heart and disturbed mind.

Points of thought hammered her mind over, and over again. She was married. That point came to mind more than any other did. She had a husband and the vows they'd spoken were binding, there had been *no* agreement, unbeknownst to herself, but the truth nevertheless. She was married, end of point. There was no way out of that.

Second point, her vows had been consummated. Despite the rather unconventional way, it was a done deal. In the eyes of the church, again, back to point number one... She was married.

The consummation... not the way she'd envisioned... Never in her wildest dreams had she given the idea that she'd be standing while a man took her for the first time. It should have horrified her. She should be weeping for the loss and the missing bedroom scene where her husband would hold her and kiss her into submission. None of that came to be.

She couldn't deny the true feelings she felt no matter how it came about. She was a married woman. Back to point one, she was married and her husband took what she willingly gave. She willingly... gave.

The picture in her mind of her in front of the window, bent over, holding the table while Jackson joined his body with hers, wasn't a pretty sight, but it was a bittersweet

268

moment that she would cherish forever. It represented their relationship. He dominated their union, taking what she finally gave willingly, wasting no time in formalities, making her his in the final stage of this relationship.

Her tears hadn't come until Jackson took her offer and ran, telling her, showing her, nothing had changed. He needed her for his money and he needed a child to fulfill his prophecy. Now that he got that underway...he was done. Will it always be that way? Jackson forgetting she existed until he could no longer fight what he *had* to do, until their hunger for intimacy came to life once more, their marriage would revert to the way it was.

Subconsciously Evelyn saw the picture of his parents hanging on the wall and immediately recalled the remorseful feeling she'd had while studying it...No love. No attraction. No kindness. Then she also recalled meeting the same people and it was then when her heart broke into millions of pieces. It was then, she realized the fate of her marriage and where she will be in the years to come.

Wishing that Jackson had embraced her, given her a small inkling of his affection, she fell to the floor in prayer for the things she knew were to come. She was doomed, trapped to a life just like his parents...Lifeless, and sad. It was then when her cherished consummated marriage fell apart and, there was no happiness in the result.

She'd spent Christmas day in her home, gave her innocence to her husband in her home and now sat alone...in her home but... it wasn't *hers* any longer. Jackson himself reminded her of that fact. She had no home; her home was with him in his fancy estate with empty walls. Despair hit her at that point. She lost her home, her company and her freedom. She was back to point number one!

All she had left was her marriage. A marriage she had

nothing to do with, except to give him an heir and then what? She didn't have to wonder for very long.

The image of Trisha Slade smacked her right in the face. The evil minded, crass woman, who had claimed to know for fact just how things were going to take place, Trisha had warned Evelyn early on and the image of her being a pale heartless being was what scared Evelyn all the way down to her soul.

Finally understanding Trisha, understanding her anger, because already Evelyn was getting bitter by what Jackson had taken, and they've just begun! Will she be in the very boat as her mother-in-law by the time she reaches that age?

23

Jackson looked up from the paper he was pretending to read to find the sound he'd heard was Evelyn taking the seat across from him at the breakfast table. He was more than shocked to see her.

Without trying, his eyes took in her appearances, noting the dark circles around both eyes, her demure expression and lastly the cold glance, as she looked straight at him. All motion and life around them at that moment went unnoticed. The servants placing their breakfast onto the table, ignored while Evelyn and he exchanged hard stares. Jackson couldn't believe she was actually there, understanding her anger but not the reasoning behind her presence.

He deserved her evil stare; he should be flogged repeatedly for what he's done to her. He wished it hadn't happened, not that way. Of course he was glad they had finally gotten that behind them, but not that way. He wanted it to be in a soft bed, with her lying beneath him. He couldn't be sorrier for the way things have happened and he opened his mouth to apologize for the pain he has caused her, but she spoke first...

"Molly is upstairs removing my things from your room." Her tone was evenly measured, Jackson wasn't sure if she was even speaking to him it was so calm. "I am moving down the hall, on the other side of the house," she informed him. "And...I don't care what anyone may think about it."

Jackson watched her lift her fork to eat a small bite and

then brought her eyes back up to him. "I'm sure you will be happy to have your bed back."

"With you in it," He replied sternly. She may be all calm and collective about things but he was not. He didn't want her down the hall for Christ sake!

"You, Nicholas have no say."

"To hell I don't..." Evelyn leaned forward and eyed him with dark impending gazes that stopped his mouth from speaking anything else he wanted to say.

"If you want me to stay your wife, I will do as I please!" She snapped evilly. Jackson gasped as he sat back in his chair staring at the woman who suddenly looked far too close to being his mother. Then her eyes grew much darker and her upper lip curled in distaste of what she was about to say she added, "If you want an heir, I will sleep where I please."

Jackson was speechless. What to say to the woman before him wouldn't go passed his lips even though there was plenty to say. For starters, he didn't like this version of Evie. She was cold and callous; much like his mother and that was not acceptable! He so wanted to word his truest feelings, but then her words filtered into his mind, past his stubbornness and struck paydirt into his heart.

If he wanted her to stay...YES! By God, he wanted that more than anything else. By giving her what she wanted, she will stay, and if he wanted an heir, he will like it! An heir...that meant... she was going to give him...without any other thought, he nodded his affirmation.

He folded the paper, not in its original grooves and then laid it to the table next to him. He then studied the food on his plate. He didn't touch any of it, he hadn't much appetite lately. He had been worrying about how to fix his doomed marriage, at least get her to listen to his explanations but, suddenly none of that was needed anymore. She was staying.

He wanted to be grateful about that one fantastic event, but darkness clouded his joy. This wasn't Evelyn, this was his mother talking and he was pondering if this was what he wanted after all. He could let her go, divorce her, even though he really did _not_ want to. He could though and try to get her to see he was mad with feelings he wasn't used to having. He hurt her when he really had no intentions and he was more than sorry.

He wanted her to remain his wife. That was a very important issue, but he wasn't sure if he wanted the change he was seeing in her. Was he wrong in wanting her? Would this new development erupt in his face? Trouble was he wasn't sure if these changes were reversible. That notion filled his heart with deep pain. Had he created his own mother?

"You don't look pleased." She noted the look of displeasure upon his face.

"This is what you wanted all along, isn't it?" Evelyn felt her heart stop in her chest. Had she done something wrong? It was obvious he wasn't happy about her decisions. It was the only demand she had. She'd given everything else to him. All she wanted now was a little space.

"Yeah," Jackson replied with nothing less than the truth.

"All right, then. It's settled. I'm so pleased to give you what you desired most." She got up from her chair.

"What was that?" He asked, his interest piqued, despite the warning voice in the back of his brain telling him he didn't want to know.

"...A barrenness union." She replied smugly and then walked out of the room.

Jackson sulked the rest of the day. Evelyn's words taunted

him. She'd been kinder than he deserved. She'd been wrong, in the end he didn't want that kind of marriage, that was what his parents had and no…he did not want that kind of union. For now though, he'll allow her to think that, until he can convince her otherwise and for starters, he knew exactly how he was going to change her thinking.

Mid way through the day, his mother called, he almost didn't answer it but did.

"I heard she returned." His mother's first words right out of the gate angered him.

"How do you know?"

His mother laughed softly. "That is not important, what is, is that she's back."

"Yeah, no thanks to you," He announced.

"I know and I called you Christmas day to apologize. I don't know what got into me."

Jackson smiled, devilishly. He knew exactly what had gotten into his mother. It was jealousy, pure and simple. He had something good, and she wanted to put a stop to it, quick. That was the best way to douse the fire that had gotten out of control. She couldn't stand to see him happy, not when she was so miserable in her own life.

"What did she say? Is she staying?"

"Why should I tell you? Ask your spy." He told her.

"Come on Jackson, tell me things are fine."

"Yeah, things are just fine. You can stop worrying."

"Thank goodness!" Her sigh filled the line as she spoke. "You're father has been impossible to deal with."

"Well you can tell him all is well with his money… it's, safe."

"Yes, now all we need is a grandson. Are you working on that as well?" She questioned him.

Jackson remained silent on his end of the line. He signed

some paperwork that was lying on his desk before he heard her call out.

"Jackson?"

"Yes."

"Yes as in, you're working on it." She paused before saying,

"Right,"

"Whatever you say," He replied continuing with work.

"Jackson!" She called out.

"What do you want me to tell you, mother? That I am filling her with my seed every chance I get?"

"You do not have to be crass about it!"

Jackson sighed, unfortunately he did otherwise they wouldn't be even discussing this at all.

"I'm just worried is all… You are sleeping with her, aren't you?" She had asked and then asked him, "Why did you pick her?"

"I don't want to discuss my private matters with my mother." He told her smartly.

She laughed through the line. "Private matters? Since when is any of this private? Seriously, though. You have a lot of women who would have made much better wives, younger, prettier ones, ones who will give you beautiful children, Jackson." She sighed the same time he did and neither were the same. "Evelyn is just a plain girl with nothing to offer you."

"It really doesn't matter, I guess she will do and you can always do as your father does…"

"What?" Jackson gasped through the line.

"Once your child arrives or even before then, you can find some pretty little thing and room her up in the best hotel in town and…"

"No!" Jackson yelled at her.

"Why are you yelling at me? It's what *he* did!"

That may have been so, but it wasn't what *he* was going to do! Jackson planned to be there for his child, he planned on fathering it and loving it. The kitchen help will not raise his child!

"Yeah, well." Jackson started, but his mother cut his words short when she spoke once again.

"Well, I have a lot of packing to do for our trip. I'll see you after the first of the year." Then, the line went silent. His parents were taking one of their 'special' trips, one that entailed his father to head in one direction, and his mother in the opposite.

Jackson tried to shake the thoughts that hammered his head the rest of the day. His mother's comments blended in with Evelyn's sharp tone at the breakfast table. It unsettled him to think Evelyn was beginning to think like his own mother. Did she also think he was going to cheat on her? Would he, if she refused to sleep with him once their child was born? Is that what had happened to his father? It was something he never really gave thought to, he automatically thought… would *he*… if Evelyn wouldn't sleep with him? He was back to that same question and he couldn't let it go. He wasn't so sure… would he? He loved the feel of a woman's hand upon his body, loved to touch women. There was nothing about the act of sex that turned him off, would he go elsewhere, if Evelyn refused him?

The question remained with him until he was home, sitting in the parlor drinking in the dark. He couldn't let the issue drop and finally when his mind spun with curiosity he picked up the phone and called his father.

"Hey, Jack. Your mother tells me you fixed things with Evelyn."

"Yeah,"

"Great son, Knew you would. I understand you feel trapped and I wish I could tell you it gets better but…"

"Can I ask you something personal?" Jackson asked softly.

"I have no secrets." Elliott stated nonchalantly. "Fire away."

"You didn't love mom, did you?" The line was silent for a few moments.

"Jack, your mother and I made an agreement long before you came along. We don't have what you do, son. It's hard for me to admit I envy you and what you have found in such little time. Wish I were so lucky and I hope you realize what you have. It's rare in our situation." Elliot gasped incredulously. "Hell, Jack… that's why I never told you in the first place."

"You should have told me." Jackson reprimanded in a stern voice. If Elliot had said something, none of this would be happening.

"I wanted you to have a choice about how you married. I hoped you'd find someone real and special to share your life with. I didn't want you to have what I was stuck with, you understand?"

"Yeah…" Jack replied and seriously meant it.

"You have affairs." Jackson was punching low and he knew if his father did not wish to talk about it, he'd say so.

"I have little choice. It was in our agreement."

"In your signed contract," Jackson asked shocked.

"Not that agreement, Jack." Elliott sighed. "My brother died when I was on a trip halfway around the world." Jackson knew that but didn't know the details about how his parents came about. They never talked about it.

"I was thirty three and was told I had no choice but to marry for my family or else we'd lose it all. I had no interest in ever marrying, kind of like you. You and I are alike in that respect. Which is why I never told you about the contract, son. I wanted you to have something better. I hoped that you'd find a woman you loved and wanted as a wife but you were too much like your old man."

"I didn't have a woman that called to me ever. I liked moving around, seeing what the world had to offer and sitting idle was not what I had envisioned at all, ever." Elliott sighed. "But I had to do what was right. I met your mother through a friend. She was in her third year of med school."

Jackson sat forward. "Mom was studying to be a nurse?"

"...Doctor." Elliott corrected him. "Yer mom is real smart. We met and I told her what I had to do. She was eager to help, wanted to continue her college and I wanted to travel, like I always did." Elliott sighed softly. "Thing was, it was harder than we thought it'd be. Getting pregnant, I mean. She wanted nothing to do with me, and well, if a woman isn't interested, then... let me just say... for the record, it's hard to conceive under those conditions. I got angry and she got spiteful. By the time she actually ended up pregnant, we couldn't stand each other."

"She never finished med school?" Jackson was sure he'd have known if she had.

"You were a hard pregnancy for her. I wasn't there, son and I should have been. She couldn't get out of bed the last part of it and she ended up having a C-section but again, I was on the road. She was sick most of your first year, and again, I was gone." His father cleared his throat and gave off a deep sigh.

"She became very resentful of both me and you. She gave me what I needed and somewhere I think she thought I'd be appreciative and wasn't. That broke her, Jack. It's been hard to look back on to what I have done, but I can't change it and

278

she won't give me the time of day to even try. I owe her a lot for what she gave me and I never once said thank you."

"Maybe you should tell her." Jackson stated.

"Maybe…" Elliott whispered. "Do me a favor, son."

"What?"

"Don't take what Evelyn does for granted. Let her know if nothing else, you appreciate her, what she is doing for our family. Can you do that for your old man?"

"I think I can do that."

After hanging up the phone, Jackson went into the office, pushed on the secret panel behind the door to reveal the safe set back into the wall. He opened the latch and withdrew an envelope and the stack of money lying beneath it. He slowly made his way to the dining room where he knew Evelyn would be hard at work.

She barely looked up when she heard him walk in. Her heart thumped wildly against her chest, which was why she refused to look up. The last thing she needed was for him to see how much his presence complicated things. She gave a beautiful performance that morning, one that even had herself believing it. She had to keep her head on straight or she will not succeed in the new persona she had come to be.

"How's it going?" He asked her taking a stance right beside her.

"Fine," She told him still trying hard to be indifferent. Her heart continued to race inside her chest. She took a deep breath, taking in his cologne.

"You know, Evie…" He took the seat beside her and paused as he waited for her to look up from her work. When she did not, he sighed deeply.

"Can you pause from that for one second?" His tone was sharp with impatience.

"Nicholas, I'm trying to work. What is it?" She snapped,

bringing her head up finally facing him, giving him a hard expression.

"We're back to that huh?" He asked her. Evelyn just shook her head puzzled. "Jackson. You didn't have any problems saying it at your…"

"I don't want to discuss that…ever." She told him as she glared at him. Jackson's heart stopped beating when he saw her eyes shift. The image of her kneeling on the floor, tears streaming from her eyes, and her mumbled prayers, all came to mind. It always seemed to find the right time to come alive, reminding him of the animal he truly was. Sometimes he would see it in his dreams and in those nightmares; she'd turn towards him with accusing eyes that seared him through and through.

"Can't you just call me Jackson?" He softly asked.

"I don't feel comfortable with that name. Never have been and you know it. Was there something you wanted?" She asked when he sat there just staring at her for some time without saying anything. She didn't seem to have any problems with his name while he made love to her.

He lifted the envelope and laid it to the surface of the table. He then laid the stack of money right next to it and slid both over to her.

"What's this?" she asked eyeing the money first.

"Something that belongs to you," He replied.

Evelyn eyed the money and then pushed it aside to look in the envelope. At first while looking inside, she wasn't sure she was reading the document correctly so she let it slide out and fall to the table. Face up was the deed to Habersham Farms.

Quickly her eyes snapped up to meet his blue gaze. Jackson tapped the deed. "I kept it in your name, it's yours fully. I paid it off."

"Thank you." She didn't know what else she should say.

"The money is for whatever you may need to bring it back to running order. Horses, gardeners, trainers, everything to bring it up and running as it should be." He shrugged softly. "Maybe we can use the place as a summer home, a place to sit back and relax."

"I can't take…" She started to argue, but Jackson shook his head.

"You will take it. I want you to have it." He then stood up. "It's a little something to show you… I am…a man of my word." He then strolled out. He needed a damn drink.

As he walked to the door, Evelyn's cell phone rang and she answered on the first ring.

"Hey, Steven…no I'm not busy…oh no."

Jackson was almost through the doorway when he heard her call that man's name out. Steven.

"I'm sorry to hear that. No that's fine. Tonight will be okay. Yeah, give me a few minutes and I'll meet you there."

Jackson tried to swallow his heart that had lodged in his throat making it hard to breathe. She was going to meet him tonight. He held in the sudden anger as he turned into the parlor and poured out a drink and downed it before he heard her walk out the front door. He figured after a few more drinks, he'd feel better and head to bed.

24

"Evelyn?" Angie called out as she entered her office. Evelyn glanced up from the numbers sheet just as Angie came through her door.

"Hey!" Angie smiled brightly. "I was wondering if you liked the robes for the 'Timeless' series."

"I loved them. I plan to have them in the next magazine." She replied leaning forward in her chair as her stomach churned in a funny way. She'd just eaten breakfast, it didn't seem as though the eggs and toast were agreeing with her.

"They will look great for the Valentine's..." She was saying when she felt her belly quiver beneath her blouse, then she suddenly felt flushed, about to pass out.

"Evelyn..." Angie called out. She went to the desk. "Are you okay?"

"I think," she was saying when her stomach lurched upwards and started to work its way up her throat. Quickly she rushed to the bathroom to get sick.

"You look real pale. Are you sure you're okay?" Angie asked her as they settled down by the door to her bathroom. Evelyn nodded her reply. She felt fine now. The nausea had passed. Evelyn stood up and took a few slow steps but found she was more than fine.

She shrugged to Angie. "Must have been the food." and with that said, she went back to work without another thought about it, until the next morning she did the same thing right after eating her breakfast. Breakfast, lunch and just the thought of dinner made her sick to her stomach.

Once the third day went by with the same symptoms, she went to her doctor to find out what the problem was.

Denial hit her first, pregnant… It seemed almost funny. Nicholas needed an heir and the one and only time he touches her, she becomes pregnant. What were the odds?

Once the initial numbness wore off, she began to feel a little   overwhelmed. A baby…she was having a baby. The thought of her chances of having a child were slim for her. At her age, marriage was almost a wishful thought she toyed with from time to time and without the aid of a man, the chances were nil.

Only recently did she have the pleasure of thinking about a child. Since discovering, Nicholas needed a son, a child to pass on his name. She loved children and the idea of being pregnant with Nicholas' child pleased her immensely.

Evelyn sat in the limo unsure where to head. Back to work or home. To the studio and tell Nicholas right away? She was confused, unsure what to do. She was feeling unsettled about the whole issue. She was pregnant, what happens now? She was almost afraid to ask.

It had been weeks since Nicholas had touched her. So many days had gone by without so much as a gentle kiss. How will things go from here? Now that she was actually pregnant, will he stop wanting her? Once this child is born, will that mean he won't come to her anymore?

As the long weeks passed, she laid awake in her bed, wondering if Nicholas slept well in his room, in the bed she had once occupied. Did he miss her at all? He didn't seem to. He had been gone this last week on a trip, had he gone alone?

She'd been so lost with what to do about the need and desire she carried like a torch waiting for his flame to ignite. Plenty of nights, she fell asleep recalling how it felt to be in his arms. How hot his touch could be and how sweet his kisses had been. Many a nights passed when she tossed and turned while her legs throbbed, hungry for the thickness of him.

She hadn't seen him in over a week. Hadn't even spoken to him and her decision was made by those facts alone. She wanted to see him, tell him about their child and maybe show him how happy she was about the whole mess.

**

Jackson wrapped his hand around his neck and gave a pull to the tight muscles that clenched and pulled at every nerve cell there. He was tired and sexually frustrated to put it mildly and the last thing he wanted to be doing was listening to Kyra's whining about her so called pathetic life. How agents didn't see things her way, they never got her the right jobs.

"If you are going to be my agent, what kind of jobs will I be looking at?"

Jackson eyed the tall twenty three year old with voluptuous breasts and pouting mouth. Her wavy red hair was not her real color but it looked good on her. Jackson stood behind the young girl and eyed her from that point of view and she patiently waited for him to answer her.

The girl in front of him was pretty without the frilly makeup and her big blue eyes were clear and bright. Her unblemished face held a few years of experience. She was a veteran behind the camera.

Jackson rounded her and took in the front view. Her long legs were thin, her waist narrow and her hands fine with long natural nails. Mentally he found her doing quite a lot of things.

"Have you acted before?" He asked her.

Kyra's eyes widened in surprise, "Really," She gasped in joy. "...An acting job?"

He thought only briefly before he nodded his answer. She had the girl next-door look that many producers wanted. He lifted her hair into a sexy pinned up style and eyed her closer. She could be a real looker in a serious roll as well.

"Do you prefer Soap Operas or TV?" He asked her.

"...Movies?" She inquisitively asked with a sweet smile. Jackson laughed shaking his head.

"How are you with love scenes?"

"You tell me..." She sprung from the chair she'd been sitting in and laid a full-fledged kiss upon him, expertly running her fingers through his hair while she did so. Her soft mouth took his in a sweet enticing embrace that felt like sandpaper against his lips. It was his first kiss that hadn't come from Evelyn and he just discovered a kiss from any other mouth wasn't a kiss at all. No one compared to the sweet kisses his wife gave. No mouth inflamed him the way Evie's did. There was no mouth out there he desired other than Evelyn's. That discovery saddened him more than it should have pleased him realizing, that an affair would probably be as lifeless, as this kiss had been. If Evelyn were to choose to cut him off, then he will most likely live a life of a monk.

"Mm..." Jackson pushed her away. He watched the young girl slip her bottom lip into her mouth and smile seductively. Apparently, she enjoyed their short heatless embrace.

"Did you like it?"

"You do that again, the only producer who will want you... will be making home movies in his damn basement, you got me?"

"I was just showing you," she told him.

"I don't run my agency that way. You get good jobs by earning them and…" He started up the stairs to the upper part of the studio. "That is not how you earn them around here." He warned her and left by the side door.

Jackson had been at the studio for less than an hour, and he was ready to go home. He wanted to see Evelyn, talk with her and he wanted that more now than ever. He missed her and the time they used to share. He'd flooded himself with work, hoping to kill the desire that simmered inside of him. It hadn't worked. Nothing works.

He wanted to talk with her, but what to say just wouldn't come. He was living as his parents do. In separate rooms with their separate lives and he was tired of it. He wanted her beside him not down the damn hall! He wanted to hold her against him. He wanted her. He loved her and he was losing her.

What could he say or do to keep her was lost to him. He was a time bomb ready to go off. He needed her more than anything but he was too afraid to speak his mind.

**

The tears ran down Evelyn's face like rivers as she grabbed bag after bag and piled her clothes into them. She was wasting her time here. Nicholas wanted nothing to do with her. He didn't want a life with her, was never going to want a life with her. She was ready to face that now.

She caught her reflection in the long mirror. Horror struck, she sat on her bed and cried out for the things she has known right from the start. The same things she will never get from the man who had claimed her as his wife, for nothing more than money and an heir.

She was willing to meet him halfway, trying to make this

endless marriage work despite his lack of effort, but she was fooling herself and today, she realized that when she saw him kissing another girl in his studio.

She had been a fool and she refuses to remain in a house with a man who was cheating on her. With a man who obviously didn't want anything to do with her... It was time to move on.

Jackson was just entering the house when Evelyn came down the stairs with a bag in her hand. Jackson watched her come all the way down not noticing the three other bags at the bottom of the stairs until she laid the one she was carrying right beside the others. Puzzled he looked at his wife.

"Nicholas." She addressed him sternly.

"Evelyn." He replied and then asked. "What's going on?"

"I have some news for you. Why don't we have a seat in the sitting room?" Without an answer, she automatically started to head in that direction.

Jackson eyed the bags once more and then followed her. He scanned her backside, gazing over her light blue suit as he walked behind her. The sway of her hips played a lovely song as she sashayed into the room.

"What are all the bags for?" He asked her once they were in the room. Evelyn spun on her high heels, watched him while he curiously eyed her. He wanted to get right to the nitty gritty, well... that was fine with her.

"Those are mine. Oliver is putting them into the car."

"Why?" He stepped closer to her, feeling his chest grow tight.

"I'm going to the farm, Nicholas." She informed him and then before he could even reply she started with another round of words that cut deep into his heart. "You don't want me here; anymore then I want to be here. I don't see why I have to be here." She casually looked away from him as she said the other part.

"I'm pregnant, Nicholas." She told him turning away. "Your job as far as a husband goes, is done. The rest will be up to me. I don't want to be here. I am taking our child to Montana where I will raise him or her by myself."

"Evelyn…" He gasped softly.

She spun around to look at him. Knowing exactly what he was about to say, Evelyn decided to address the issue right off the bat. There was no reason to dodge the inevitable. "You can keep it all. I want nothing from you. I don't want any of it."

"What about Satin & Lace?" He questioned. Was he nuts…Satin & Lace? He didn't give a damn about that rag of hers…but she did.

"I don't want it. Keep it, sell it, it's yours anyway."

She started to head for the front door. It was a lie… she did want it. What the hell was going on…Pregnant? How…Pregnant?

Jackson bolted from the sitting room to find her standing just outside the entrance door talking on her cell phone. He was about to interrupt her when that name came out of her mouth.

"Yes, Steven. I'm on my way. Do you think the red lace will be good this time? I really was hoping for the black, to start things off."

Jackson remained glued to the inside of the entranceway, while he listened to her whole conversation about sexy underwear, what she thought looked best.

Dumbfounded, he stood right there with images of her parading around in skimpy lingerie. Images of her in _her sexy_ lingerie and he was furious to know she was sharing such intimate details with another man.

He waited for her to finish her talk and then watched as she got in the limo and was gone. Everything happened in a matter of seconds, but seemed like slow motion as his mind took it all in. She was going to meet with him…With Steven!

"Oh no… you're not!"

Jackson felt his stomach clench tight as he got in one of his many cars and followed her back into the city. The further he followed the angrier he got. She was pregnant with his child, leaving him, thinking he'd be okay with her raising his child alone! Was Steven going to leave with her? Did she think Steven was better daddy material and was going to let him raise _their_ child?

Jackson followed Evelyn all the way back into the city, fuming all the way. By the time they arrived at her penthouse, he was raging mad. So mad he waited a while as he tried to control his anger. He didn't want to go in there like a lunatic. There was any number of reasons as to why they would meet at her penthouse. Hundreds of reasons and only one kept coming to mind.

He stormed up to her penthouse and pounded on the door. He barely waited a few seconds before he pounded again. He didn't announce who he was or call out he just pounded on the door, waiting for her to open up.

When the door did open, Jackson at first couldn't believe what he saw. A tall lean bronzed man that stood close to Jackson's height stood with his arm up, hand leisurely hanging off the edge of the doorframe. He had jet-black hair and thick wet looking eyelashes. His wide broad shoulders revealed power, as did his thick biceps that were bulging beneath the thin material of his shirt. He looked like a throwback from a beach movie.

His casual attire didn't say much about what was taking place between he and Evelyn but it did not clear them either.

Jackson held back his anger.

"Can I help you?" The man asked. His dark stare was bright, friendly and creased slightly while he smiled at Jackson.

"I'm looking for..." Jackson began to tell the man, but then stopped when a flash of woman came around the corner and stopped dead in the hall facing the door. Evelyn's brown gazes found Jackson's furious blue one's, saying nothing to him about what he'd walked into.

Jackson took in her stare briefly before seeing the rest of her in a lacy black bra and matching pair of panties. A sheer robe hung off her bare body, which covered absolutely nothing of her or the underwear she was wearing. Seeing her in such attire brought immediate uncontrollable rage to Jackson.

He'd caught them and what they were doing was quite apparent to Jackson. He felt his whole body rock with anger and without a second thought; he punched the man standing in front of him. The moment his fist hit the man square in the face, getting much pleasure in the man's out cries of pain, Jackson repeated it.

"Jackson!" Evelyn called out, running toward the door, but not before the man began to fight back. Grabbing Jackson by surprise he uppercut him with a left hit. Jackson responded with a jab to the face, cutting the man's upper lip.

"Stop it!" Evelyn cried out. "Steven!" She grabbed the other man and then shoved Jackson backwards. "Stop... it!" She yelled at them. Steven attempted to hit Jackson once more, but Evelyn held him tight. "He's my husband. It's Jackson!" She cried out for Steven to stop.

Jackson staggered, stepping away from the twosome that held each other. Evelyn was trying to steady the man, inspecting his injured jaw. Steven was eyeing Jackson skeptically and Jackson…his gazes were on the sweet little number his wife was wearing. God…she looked beautiful. Her hair was down, wavy locks of satiny brown flowing all over the place. The sheer robe hung loosely off her left shoulder due to her fighting Jackson and Steven off each other. Jackson couldn't believe his eyes as he watched her lick her finger and graze the other man's lip that was bleeding.

His heart cried out for the caring she was giving the other man, wishing, that she'd care for him in that same way. Graze his injured heart the same way, with her wet finger and loving care.

He watched as her legs moved when she walked to the sink to get Steven a towel, and on her return, he watched her ample breasts swaying to her steps. His eyes devoured every inch of her flesh. Despite what he discovered here tonight, he found he still loved her.

"What is your problem?" Evelyn's voice cut through his solemn thoughts and he looked away from her body to see her brown eyes searching his.

He was hurting, in the worse way, and she hadn't a clue. Evelyn didn't care about the way he felt and Jackson couldn't find the words to say what he was feeling at the moment. Would it matter if he told her he loved her and she was the world to him?

"Jackson?" She called out to him in anger. "Have you gone mad?"

"Yes." His voice caught in his throat and slipped out as a gasp, but the sound rejuvenated him. He lurched forward with a strong sense of need. "I don't want a marriage like my parents!" He suddenly spoke his heart. "I don't want you to move to Montana, and I don't want you sleeping around with this man… or any other man!"

"Sleeping..." She began as laughter filled the room. Steven was standing up now and laughing at the statement Jackson had made.

"No offense..." Steven slipped his arm around Evelyn's waist. "She ain't my type." Steven smiled, raising his eyebrows. "...If you get my meaning." He then laughed again. "I think this is when I take my leave." He kissed Evelyn's cheek. "I will talk to you later." He then turned to Jackson. "Man, ain't nuttin goin on here, but a little photo shoot." He then stalked out, leaving Jackson alone with Evelyn.

Photo shoot?

Jackson studied Evelyn with a soft expression. A photo shoot? It didn't take long for him to realize what he was looking at as he looked down at Evelyn with the lacy underwear on.

"You're the model." His voice insipid and soft, his heart began to thump loudly beating against his chest. His eyes cascaded down her entire frame, understanding what he was seeing. She was his dream model! The beautiful body that had triggered such desire in just a mere photo was standing right in front of him, better...she was his wife!

He looked at her face, her brown sexy eyes and those sweet lips of hers. "She's you..." and she was his wife...

Jackson couldn't hold back the strong desire to hold her. Taste her sweet full mouth and drown in her sensuous eyes. Softly he pulled her to him, wrapping his arm around her, pulling her towards him until their lips met in a heated embrace. He slowly stepped forward, walking her backwards up against the wall. Once he was there, his hands began to move up to the lacy cups of the bra.

The second he touched her a stronger desire to tell her everything came rushing out. "I can't stand being without you. I need you. I don't want to live like my parent's." He spoke right against her ear, moving his mouth to her neck.

Evelyn's heart, danced inside her chest with joy. He was holding her… could this be real? He was kissing her and looking at her with desire in his eyes, could it really be…

"Do you hear me?" He questioned her softly, running his fingers through her dark silky hair while his eyes danced around, searching her face. "I want you to stay here with me, in my house, and…" He planted his mouth over hers and then spoke in a whispered tone. "Not down the damn hall either, in my bed, with me right there beside you! Do you hear me?" He asked her pushing back away from her, his eyes searching hers once more.

"I love you. I don't care about this damn agreement. Not the inheritance, not even our baby," he smiled and pecked her nose. "…but I love the thought that we made a child. I don't care about anything else. A girl, I want a girl with your eyes and your long beautiful hair!" He cupped her face with both of his hands. "I love you. Do you hear me?" His eyes once more searched hers. "I'm so sorry that the one time I make love to you it wasn't in a bed. I wanted you so much and was so afraid I was losing you. I'm sorry I walked away after, I should have held you, but I was ashamed, oh, God how could I have been so ruthless to your feelings." He kissed her mouth with trembling lips. "Do you hear me, Evie? Are you hearing anything I am saying to you?"

"Jackson." Evelyn whispered his name.

"Evie…" He whispered right back while his mouth gently took hers in a long embrace. "I'm so sorry for everything…" He mouthed over her sweet lips. He couldn't stop kissing her but had to tell her what his heart was feeling. "Please don't leave me. I beg you…"

"Shut up… and make love to me."

Jackson stood still, his mouth stopped moving. Puzzled at first by her words but then he smiled softly. "Make love…"

She nodded. "Please …" She loved every statement he had been saying and was happy to hear it all, but the desire to have him love her was much stronger than anything else.

Evelyn sighed with relief when Jackson snagged his arm under her legs and pulled her up into his arms and started to carry her into the first doorway he saw opened.

"No, wait…" she stopped him. Their eyes met in a silent pause.

"That's the shoot room." She told him. Jackson smiled, lowered his head to kiss her mouth. Thoughts of that model and him making love in one of the photo beds she often laid on, wearing those thin pieces of sexy underwear overwhelmed him.

"Does it have a bed?" He asked over her sweet lips. "I envisioned making love to that sexy model, in one of those beds she was laying on." She nodded her answer not wanting to part from his sweet mouth.

In a matter of seconds, he whisked her into the photo room and laid her out on the bed covered with red satin sheets. His mouth moved away from hers only to caress her shoulder with blissful kisses and a hot tongue that he slid over her skin. His hand found her hard nipple through the lace bra and rolled it between his fingers.

"I gotta taste you." He murmured over her flesh. His fingers released the bra in the front and let it fall from her body. His eyes feasted momentarily until he couldn't stand it any longer. He lowered his head, flicked his tongue out and circled her nipple before popping the hardened bud into his mouth. His tongue smoothed it out and rolled around the peak while he suckled contentedly. "Oh God, you taste like honey. Milk… and honey, you're so sweet."

The flames that Jackson was creating deep within her core simmered to life, rocking her body, wreathing beneath him. She slipped her hand in his blond hair and caressed his head while his mouth remained on her breast, pulling at her nipple as if he were feeding on it. With every tug she felt, it triggered small twinges between her legs that only made her movements wilder, stronger with no end in sight.

It had been too long to feel this alive! Evelyn couldn't deny what this man did to her inside and out. She wanted him, needed him, hungered for him unlike she had ever before. It consumed her.

"Oh, Jackson," She moaned and then held back a groan that trembled inside her throat.

"That's it sweetheart, purr for me. I love it when you purr." He came away from her breast, slipping his hand into the skimpy panties, she raised her hips, meeting his thrust and gasped when his fingers sunk deep within her warmth.

Slowly Evelyn groaned as he slid his tongue over her flesh, trailing it down to her belly. Again, she raised her hips when he tugged on the panties. Once they were off, she choked back a loud gasp when she felt the heat of his mouth upon her.

"Jack," Her hips rotated and levered against his mouth. "...Oh, Jackson!" Evelyn about came off the bed when a shock wave of sensations rippled through her body. "Jackson..." she begged him. "Oh, God..." then her whole frame rocked beneath his taxing mouth.

"I need you." She moaned through her spasms. "...Mm." She hummed softly. "I want you inside me." She whispered into the air between them. "Please, Jack..." she groaned in desperation. It had been too long. Way, too much time has gone by, it seemed like only a dream; it had been so long and she needed him, wanted him.

Driven by hunger alone, she reached for his pants, yanked the buckle off and tugged the zipper open, then fished inside for the hard flesh that was so hot and ready.

Jackson's hips rocked forward when she touched his flesh. "You drive me crazy. I've been hard like this since Christmas, God…how I have wanted you!"

"I love you Jackson." She pulled him to her mouth, kissing him ardently.

Evelyn sighed when Jackson finally rose above her, joining his body to hers with a mutual groan between them as they met in sweet victory.

"Purr for me baby. Tell me this is what you want."

She swallowed hard and at the same time, she groaned. "Yes. Oh, yes! I want it just like that. Mm, Jack. That is so… good."

**

"Are you asleep?"

"No."

"…Why not?"

"Still on that cloud you put me on." Evelyn giggled at the tingles his fingertips created as he softly touched her inner thigh. "You keep doing that and I won't ever get to sleep."

"Ah, sleep's overrated anyway." He whispered against her nipple and then swirled his tongue around the peak.

"Aren't you tired?"

"And miss this?"

She giggled. "You can't be serious we just…mm…oh my."

"Have I ever told you, you taste like milk and honey?"

"I think so."

"What are you doing?"

"If you can…so can I."

"God…you're so good at that."

"First time's a charm."

"So I've heard. You want a girl or, boy? Oh, yeah… that's it, right there. Oh, God…Come here…"

Epilogue

Evelyn's screams filled the long corridor. "No!" she tried to halt the gurney as they wheeled her down to delivery. "I can't," she wailed as the pain shot right through her frame. A nurse dislodged her fingers from the doorframe Evelyn was holding on to and the gurney started to roll again.

"You are going to do this whether you want to or not." The nurse told her firmly. Evelyn shook her head, closed her eyes and cried out.

"Not without my husband... Jackson!"

"Evie,"

Evelyn turned, almost sitting up looking down the corridor. She could have sworn she heard Jackson.

"Lay back." The nurse tried to settle her back to the rolling bed.

"No!" Evelyn cried out again. He had to be here! It couldn't happen without him! "Wait, we must wait!" Evelyn turned to look down the hall and the gurney turned the corner and entered an empty room.

"I'm sorry, there is no more time..." the nurse told her and helped move Evelyn to the stable bed where the doctor waited.

The moment she was on the bed, her legs into the stirrups, a hard pain clamped on to her belly and she had no choice but to push.

"...NOOOOO!" Evelyn cried out in anguish. Jackson had to be here for this. He promised he would be...

"...Evie?"

Evelyn snapped her head to the side and smiled when she saw Jackson's blue eyes looking down at her over the green mask covering his face. His hand clamped onto hers and even though she couldn't see it, she could tell he was smiling down at her. "I love you." She told him. Jackson rested his head right on her forehead.

"Love you sweetheart."

"Let's have us a baby." The doctor announced.

**

She heard the baby's cries before she was completely awake. Evelyn felt her hard nipples react to her crying child and immediately awoke from a sound sleep. As she opened her eyes, she saw Jackson standing beside her, holding their sweet bundle.

"I think she's hungry." He told her, placing baby Leigh to the breast that was now leaking all over Evelyn's nightgown. Evelyn softly caressed Leigh's soft chin as the baby nestled against her breast and started to feed.

"She looks just like her momma." Jackson revealed with love and pride deep in his voice. "I have someone who has been waiting patiently for you to wake up." Jackson told her and turned to grasp the small boy up from the floor.

Evelyn smiled at her son, Eli. "Hi, sweet baby," Evelyn called out and watched as Eli laid his two year old head beside his baby sister and hugged her tight.

"I think he likes her." Evelyn smiled to Jackson. "He refused to stay at the house with Jack." Evelyn ran her finger over Eli's forehead.

"You didn't want to stay with your big brother?" Eli shook his head and smiled showing off his mouthful of teeth. Evelyn looked up when she felt soft lips against her own forehead.

"I almost missed this one." Jackson stated then softly kissed her mouth.

"I love you."

"Love you." He replied kissing her mouth again. "Have I told you, you taste like milk and honey?"

THE END